Contact Information

www.erinthorntonauthor.com

www.facebook.com/authorErinThornton

Follow my fan page:

https://www.facebook.com/groups/5078175395577875/

Follow me to be the first to know about future book releases or upcoming projects

Other books by Erin Thornton

Dangerous Series (Romantic Suspense)

Dangerous After Dark

Dangerous Calculations

Standalones

Disaster In Love (Romantic Comedy)

Dedication:

This book is dedicated to my husband. While it took a few…ok a lot of bad dates and relationships, I finally found him and am so happy to not have to endure another unpredictable date again.

Chapter 1:

"You really need to find a man, Samantha," her mother repeated her usual sentiment when Sam came over for their weekly dinner. There wasn't a better topic than her fading youth and shriveling eggs. Reality was her mother wanted grandchildren, while she was still young enough to keep up, and have fun with them. "At this rate, I'm going to be ancient before you have any kids for me to spoil." Right on time, her mother never missed a beat.

"Mom, I'll get married and have kids when I find the right guy." She defended herself so often with her mother, it was easier to avoid her mom throughout the week and save it up for these special dinner nights.

"You aren't dating enough. Why don't you let me fix you up? I know a great guy you are just going to love him. Christopher is a sweet guy. He's Jillian's son, you know she is from my book club." She certainly knew Jillian, she was the biggest gossip of their group. She is the one who convinced my mother that people were really streaking through the town square after midnight on the full moon.

"Mom, Jillian is like 75, how old does that makes her son?" Samantha knew he had to be older because she didn't go to school with him. He wasn't even an upper classman to her. So that meant he had to be at least 40.

"Oh dear, he's not that much older than you. Besides they say age is just a number these days. Mature only means they are more stable." Well, that meant she was definitely going on a date with a much older man.

In order to placate her mother, Samantha agreed to go on this date, but she knew she was going to regret it.

*****

Date night, Samantha's least favorite night of the week. Which is why she usually limited the days of the week with that title. She didn't date much, but being single was getting old.

Since this was essentially a blind date, she wanted to meet on neutral territory. She chose her favorite haunt, Joe's Bar. It wasn't exactly a hole-in-the-wall, but it wasn't a super classy joint either. It just made her feel comfortable.

She got there a bit early in hopes of calming her nerves a little. *Why did I agree to this? This was a stupid idea. I should have at least seen a picture of him before agreeing,* she thought as she sat alone at her table.

The waitress came over at that moment to take her order. "You read my mind, I need a beer. Miller Light, or whatever is cold and on tap is fine with me."

Leaving Sam to her thoughts again, the waitress quickly ran to put her drink order in. Just then a man walked in the door. He was sort of rough around the edges, but in a sexy kind of way. Just a touch of stubble, and rolled out of bed hair made him sexy all over. Dressed in jeans, and a black t-shirt, he made Sam feel overdressed. She went all out for the first date, with a traditional look, little black dress and matching three-inch heels.

Quietly getting her hopes up, they were quickly dashed when he passed her table without the slightest glance. He headed straight for the bar. *Well I should have known better. He looked only a couple years older than me anyway, that couldn't have possibly been Christopher. Wishful thinking got the better of me, yet again.*

While she was distracted with the mystery man, Christopher walked in and had made his way to her table, startled by his sudden appearance, Sam jumped

"Sam? Hi, it's so nice to meet you, I'm Christopher." He thrust his hand in her direction, and she quickly tried to regain her composure.

"It's nice to meet you too." Saving her from having to think of anything else on the spot, the waitress returned with her drink.

"Can I get you something, sir?" Sam stifled a laugh. He was definitely a "sir". Sam wasn't young by any definition of the word, she was long past her twenties. This year she would be 35 in May, but Christopher had to be close to 50, on a good day. Polite as her mother always taught her, she wouldn't ask, but her assumption was plenty close enough for her.

"Yes of course, I'll have two fingers of Scotch, on the rocks." He even ordered in a way that suggested his age. *What has my mother gotten me into? This is going to be a disaster.*

Attempting to push her negativity out of her head, she needed to make the most of this. "So, Christopher, my mom didn't tell me much about you. Why don't you tell me a little about yourself?"

"Oh, what kind of beer are you drinking?" Christopher flipped the conversation back to her. At first, she didn't find that odd, but her opinion would soon change.

"Oh, I just got a Miller Light. I'm not a fancy drinker." *Especially on first dates*, she added, but not out loud. He just smiled enthusiastically, and proceeded to keep control of the conversation.

"So, what is your favorite show on MTV?" That made Sam get a little concerned. How old was this guy, and how young did he think she was?

"I'm not sure, I guess I watch a video here or there, but not any particular show per se."

"Oh yeah, I love those music videos they are very...dope.

Sam fought a cringe, as she was slowly coming to terms with what was happening here. It felt like she was stuck in the Twilight Zone. What was her mother thinking? This guy is obviously trying too hard to prove that he is younger than he really is, but failing miserably. Without waiting for her to add to the conversation, not that she knew what to say anyway, he carried on.

"So, did you see Friends, last night? It was my favorite episode, where Ross gets his teeth over whitened and a horrible spray tan."

"No, I'm afraid I missed that. I had to work late," she added hopefully he would ask her about work, and forego this ridiculous line of outdated questioning.

"Oh, that's a shame it was a good one. Well, I was reading about Justin Timberlake and Britney Spears the other day. I sure wish they would get back together. Do you think that will ever happen?" Right then, the waitress brought his drink and Sam slipped her a piece of paper. This wasn't planned, but since she had no one else to turn to at this particular moment Sam hoped she got the hint.

"Justin and Britney? Uh, I guess I haven't given them much thought, recently. I guess they made a cute enough couple, but that might have been right before her crazy period, and probably was for the best that they split before things got too nuts." *This is officially the strangest date ever. Why did I agree to let my mom fix me up?*

Christopher lifted his drink to his mouth and sipped slowly. "Mmm, that drink is Chuck Norris approved." Sam didn't know what that meant, but decided it wasn't worth any clarification. Luckily, she was saved by her phone as it chose that moment to burst into Taylor Swift's, Shake It Off, at full volume. Glancing at the screen, she didn't recognize the number, but that wasn't going to stop her at this point.

"I'm so sorry, I should take this," Sam said to Christopher as she swiped her phone to answer.

"Hello?"

"Sorry it took me so long, I had wait til I could take a quick break. Sounds like a real winner you've got on your hands." Sam recognized the voice of the waitress.

"Oh no, it's fine. I understand," she replied vaguely not wanting to give too much away to her self-centered time-warped date.

"Want me to have someone walk you out? I'd hate for you to be stuck with him any longer than necessary."

"No, I'll be there right away. I'm glad you got ahold of me so soon. I would have hated to have missed it. Thanks for calling." With that Sam hung up the phone, and turned to her date who was lost in his own world, completely unaware of her conversation.

"Sorry about that, I don't usually leave my phone on during dates. I must have forgotten when I got here. That was my best friend's husband, and she is in labor."

"OH! Well you should head right over to the hospital. Do you need a ride? I could take you there myself."

Sam bit the inside of her cheek to hide the lie she was about to tell. "No, I drove so I'll make a run to the ladies room, and head out. I really enjoyed meeting you Christopher."

"Yes, this has been a great date. I'll call you soon, if that's ok? Maybe we can set up another date for dinner soon."

Avoiding that answer, Sam stood up abruptly and shook his hand awkwardly. Without another word, she made her way to the ladies room to hide. She waited ten minutes to give Christopher time to realize she wasn't coming back out to say anything to him. She opened the door slowly, praying not to be confronted by anyone outside the door. Pleasantly, the hallway was empty so she made her way to the bar to get another drink after that disaster. Then she would take a cab home and try and sleep off this mess.

As she approached the bar, she passed the waitress who saved her. Sam made her way up to her, "Thank you so much! I owe you one, that's for sure. What a mess tonight has been, I'm just glad it's over."

"You betcha! I'm just glad you slipped me your number when you did. I couldn't imagine sitting as long as you did before that with him. Was he like that the whole time?"

"It just kept getting worse. He was making out-of-date pop culture references, and expected me to have an actual response to them all. Not to mention, he was old enough to almost be a father to me, or an uncle at least. I should have known better than to let my mother fix me up."

"Wow, there are no words to express the level of insanity that you just spilled. I've got your back anytime."

They parted ways, and Sam continued on her way to the bar. She grabbed a stool, and wasn't surprised that the bar wasn't dead, but it had a few people here and there spread out. It took the bartender a couple minutes to make his way down to her, but when she looked up to place her order she was stunned into silence. The man that stood in front of her was none other than the mystery man from earlier, when she was waiting for her date.

"What can I get you?" a husky voice drew her out of her stupor.

"Vodka and Cranberry Juice, please," she said on a sigh. This night had done her in, and she was exhausted, but this new development was making her evening one for the memory books.

Chapter 2:

"Didn't I just see you over at the high top, in the bar?" the sexy bartender asked as he handed her drink over the counter. "Did you want that on a tab for the table?"

"No, my date is over, I just needed some liquid reinforcement before I head home."

"That sounds like there's a story, if I have ever heard one. I've been told I'm a pretty good listener." His offer was unexpected, but probably something he does often, given his line of work. He probably gets treated more as a therapist, than a bartender. Maybe that is why they call bartenders something different than servers. It is because their job entails a great deal more than just bringing food and pouring drinks. Her mind was wandering off-track.

"My life is more than a story, it's a reality show in real life. Trust me you don't want to know."

Laughing, he excused himself to help another customer and Sam was able to take her first drink, and it was pure heaven in a glass. It may have been a simple drink, but this guy knew how to mix. It was the perfect ratio, and when she watched him mix another drink she was in awe of how effortless he made it look. Sam knew that wasn't the actual case, because when she was in college she took a bartending class, and learned that lesson the hard way. She ended up breaking more glasses, and dropping more bottles, than not. Whenever she noticed a bartender who knew their stuff, and made it look this easy, she was dazzled by their skill.

She slowly nursed her drink, even though she knew she would be taking an Uber home. There was no reason to pace herself, but she wasn't in a hurry either. With the eye candy in front of her, who would force themselves to leave?

The bar wasn't exceptionally busy, the after-work crowd had dwindled, and all that was left were the regulars, and a few dates still lingering. It was only about eight thirty PM, it wasn't late by any means, but people had moved on to the clubs, and more exciting venues. That suited Sam just fine. She wasn't in the mood for dancing or wild parties, she just wanted to enjoy her drink quietly.

"Need another?" the sexy voice chimed in again forcing her attention to him then meeting his eyes. They were blue, but looked more like a stormy sea than a crystal-clear sky. They helped add to his air of mystery that she had given him when he first walked in.

"Sure, I'll take one more. I wish I could mix a drink as smooth as you do," she added as she watched him mix this round.

"Oh, with a little practice anyone could do this job." He was so modest, but he really had no idea.

"I'll be the one to break the news to you, not everyone is that coordinated. I'm one of the opposite breed." She left it at that and didn't elaborate, but he didn't let her stop there.

"You were right, your life is one big story worth telling, isn't it? You can't say something like that and then not elaborate."

"Let's just say, I have a serious case of the dropsies, and I've had that curse my entire life."

"Oh, you must be a real treat to take out. Is that why your date ended so quickly? I didn't hear anything hit the floor. I saw you when I got here, and your date didn't seem to have arrived yet. Now you are sitting at my bar, what only thirty minutes later?"

Sam glanced at the clock on her phone, "Actually that was twenty-two minutes of my life I'll never get back," she said dryly, with just a touch of sarcasm.

"Whoa! A whole twenty-two minutes, how did you ever survive? It couldn't have been that bad?

"Bad...no. Torture...much closer. The short version is my mother fixed me up with a guy almost old enough to be my dad. Though all she sees is someone 'stable'."

"Age is just a number, or so they say. Why was that such an issue?"

"It wasn't his age that was the deal breaker. It was the fact that he is stuck in an era trying to be someone he obviously isn't anymore. He kept making out of date pop culture references and seriously, who still adds 'Chuck Norris' to anything?" she added, actually using air quotes.

"Ok, I'll admit I'm not up-to-date on pop culture. Does that make me a horrible person?"

"No, but expecting me to answer questions as though it were current events would."

"Oh, that is awful. Your mother sure knows how to pick them." He said this in a way she didn't know if he was serious, or mocking her. "I think you need something a little stronger for your next drink, but don't worry it's on me." He proceeded to fix her drink as she watched him shot UV Cherry Vodka, two shots of Liquid Ice Energy Drink.

She took a sip of it and it coated her throat perfectly. It was so good she finished it in just a few gulps. "That was amazing, what was it?"

"The Chuck Norris," he winked and left her to attend a few customers that had approached the bar.

Rolling her eyes, she pulled up her Uber app, and requested a car. While she waited she finished her drink. Instead of sitting at the bar any longer she threw some cash on the bar, and headed for the door.

The wait for the Uber outside wasn't long. She climbed into the back, and confirmed her home address with the driver. As he drove, she thought back to the events of the evening. The only part that kept drawing her back were the last few minutes with the bartender. In that moment, she realized that she never caught his name. Then again, he didn't know hers either so now they were even.

*****

That night while Sam lay in bed, she couldn't fall asleep. Every time she closed her eyes she saw that strong stubble covered jaw, and those stormy blue eyes. All she could think to call him was the cliché "McDreamy" because she didn't know his name. What was she going to do now? She needed to get some rest, but at this rate she would be up all night. The last person she wanted to be dreaming about was the bartender. At first, she thought they had a decent rapport going, but as soon as he made the comment about Chuck Norris, she knew they weren't going to see eye to eye.

Instead of fretting about it, she decided to find another date. Obviously, her mother couldn't be trusted as a source to find the perfect guy. What else could she do? Her knee jerk reaction wasn't her favorite idea, but she didn't know what else to do. She got out her phone and searched Google "Hey Google, show me number one dating sites."

The list that popped up was terrifying. What was the world coming to, that there were over a dozen sites that just popped up image only? That didn't include the ones that she could just click on from the generated search options.

"How do I know what to pick? There are just too many." In the end, she decided to sign up for the first one on the list, because it had the most good reviews and positive interactions. She spent the next thirty minutes filling out login and profile information.

13

"Username? Oh great, so now I'm supposed to think of a kitschy name for myself to tell guys how witty and cute I am." She thought for a while, and opted for truthful. "*DisasterInLove,* what could be a more fitting name for me?"

As she worked through the profile information, she felt worse and worse. She was having to describe herself, which was unnecessarily hard. She didn't want to think of her height, and body image in terms of how others might see her, because that required her to analyze herself a little too closely.

Some questions were easy, like education levels and ethnicity, but who really needs to know her annual worth? That seemed a bit like a request for a loan, and not a date. "Why would anyone need to know that to decide if they wanted to date me?"

After all the life questions, she moved on to easier topics, her basic interests. "Now this part I can handle." She proceeded to click on all her interests; movies, dining out, music and concerts, cooking, coffee and conversation, nightclubs and dancing, museums and art, wine tasting, and performing arts. Looking over all her answers, she continued to the next section of the process. "Tell us about yourself," she read aloud. "Oh no, this is the last thing I want to do. I hate talking about myself, for any reason." After deliberating for a while she started typing, and at first, it started as just words thrown on the page. *I'm thirty-four years old and I love to travel. With my job, I get to see all the places I've ever wanted. I've been a flight attendant since I got out of college. I received my degree in communication, but figured this would be something fun to do while I am young and single. Now I've decided, it's time to settle down. When I'm on layovers I love to catch a show in NY or hit up a hot new club. That doesn't mean I don't know how to sit back, and enjoy the simple things in life.*

That was as far as she could go, and she ran out of positive things to say about herself. She clicked through and added a photo. She opted for a shot of her with her glasses on. It was a flattering pose, but her biggest concern was she wanted them to know who she was no matter what, and not just the face she put on in her contacts. She was a professional and looked the part at work, but in her personal life she just liked to be herself and not play a role.

Since she had gone this far she decided to peruse the site a bit, and see what her options were. First off, she was a bit worried, because her so called connections were not at all what she was looking for. They varied in age from at least fifty down to maybe early twenties. What had she gotten herself into?

After sifting for about an hour, she decided she must have made a mistake, and at least she had tried, but online dating just wasn't her cup of tea. She logged out and crawled back into bed.

The next morning, she got up bright and early. It was her day off, but after working four days on straight, she was at the beginning of her four days off. She loved this schedule, and wouldn't trade it for anything at this point in her life. It kept her busy, but left her with plenty of free time, and she was still able to spend lots of time with her friends and family. Although after last night's disaster, she was probably going to avoid her mother for more than a few days. Lifting her phone out of habit to check her emails, and other social media accounts, she saw an alert she didn't recognize. When she opened it her dating site pulled up, and she was shocked to see she had a message waiting. Shocked may have been too light of a term for what she felt. She actually threw her phone across her bed in disbelief.

"What in the world? This must be a joke," she said in disbelief. She had a message from someone off that ridiculous site. "Who would want to talk to me, or even date me after seeing all that nonsense?" She had spent an hour looking through it last night, and didn't find anyone remotely appealing, or that made her think it was any less than crazy for her to be on there.

She decided that she wasn't going to be able to see anything with any clarity until she had a cup of coffee. So, she left her phone where it fell, and made her way to the kitchen. A couple years ago she broke down, and splurged on the single cup coffee maker, she never regretted it even once. With her living alone, and rarely having company it wasn't worth wasting coffee to make a few cups only to drink a fraction of it. Sam was never a person who enjoyed day old coffee. Reheated coffee was likely a torture device used by the devil, in Hell. How anyone could drink it was beyond her.

With a cup of wonderful morning coffee in her grasp, she made her way back to her bedroom. She took a couple fortifying sips, and reached for her phone. Clicking on her dating app, she pulled up her messages. "His name is Marcus and he runs a fortune 500 company downtown," she read aloud. "He likes opera, hmm that is surprising. He is either very cultured, or trying to win points. Oh, he likes live theater. Well, he has that going for him I suppose. Loves to read, but doesn't get into a book, as often as he likes. Well at least I know he isn't just a pretty face." Observing his picture she noticed, he had nice features, something that wasn't a requirement, but definitely helped. He looked to be in his early thirties, but she didn't know exactly, because he didn't specify. His message was simple, and he asked her out for drinks. "Well, I don't know proper etiquette for online dating. I suppose I should send him a message back."

Marcus,

It was surprising to hear from you, so soon. I only just created my online profile. I think drinks would be nice. Could we meet at Joe's Bar? It is a place I know and it won't be too crowded and we can talk.

-*Sam*

Now that that was over with, he would probably just ignore it. So, she decided to get on with her usual day off activities. Nothing exciting for day one, but if she could get her chores knocked out early than she could go shopping this afternoon.

*****

By about one o'clock Sam was finishing up her basics, laundry, dishes, trash. This meant her apartment looked like a home, without the really lived-in smell and clutter. She reached for her phone to turn off her streaming music, that always helps her clean faster, and checked for missed calls. To her surprise she had another message from her dating app.

With less hesitation she opened it, and was pleased to read that he wanted to meet up, tonight. *Why not? I'm off for a few more days I might as well enjoy them.* Quickly typing her reply, Sam agreed to meet him at eight o'clock tonight, at Joe's Bar.

*****

Evening was approaching fast, and she needed to start getting ready. She went all out last night for her mom's friend, but that didn't get her anywhere. She threw open her closet and nothing in particular stuck out for her, or screamed "WEAR ME!" so she just opted for a simple sundress. Nothing too fancy, but still a bit nicer than her everyday street clothes. This one was a long maxi style in a pretty royal blue. Something that flowed when she walked, but had a deep V-neck to still draw some attention, but not too much so she looked slutty. She got enough attention at her job, since her uniform drew attention to her features, most of it unwanted. She wasn't too endowed on top, but she was definitely a plump average. With the right bra, she could give other girls a run for their money.

Especially since most of them had paid good money for theirs, and hers were all natural.

Arriving early was becoming a habit. It was her haunt, and she knew it better than any other bar. She recognized who the regulars were, even if she didn't know them by name. So, she placed herself at a table in the center of the room, that she could watch for new arrivals. The waitress from last night was working again, so she waved. Immediately, the waitress made her way to the table.

"Hey got another 'hot date' tonight?" she asked raising her eyebrow, with a touch of sarcasm.

"I hope so. Anything has to be an improvement to last night, right?"

"Ha! I hear you there. Not much could be worse than that. My name is Tania by the way. I'm here most nights these days. So, if you make a habit of this and have any other dead fish I'm here for you."

Sam scribbled her number out on the drink napkin, "You might want to hang on to this just in case."

"Right, I'll program it now. Do you want me to call at a particular time, or do you want to give me a signal?"

"No, let's just play it by ear. I imagine that if it is that bad, you'll be able to tell just like you did last night. Oh hey, is the same bartender working tonight?"

"Nick? I think he comes in later, so he can close tonight. He's new so he's picking up a lot of shifts and closing, because no one else wants to. The shifts throughout the week are slow, and no one wants them anyway."

Well that's a relief, one less thing to worry about. The last thing I want is for him to be here during my date, even if he was the one who interrupted my sleep last night. That wasn't my choice, and most certainly was because he was the person I saw who wasn't old enough to be a father figure.

"Ok, well if you would bring me a glass of chardonnay, I'd appreciate it."

"Sure, thing chica. I just hope this one is better than last night's poser." With that she turned on her heel, to go place Sam's order. Tania seemed like a sweet girl. Sam had a few girlfriends, but she was gone so much for work it had become limited to mostly the ones she worked with. So, when she was home she didn't have many people to hang out with. That was probably why she started this dating binge. If she could occupy her nights with dates, then she wouldn't feel so lonely when she wasn't working. She shook her head to clear the negative thoughts. She wasn't depressed, but sometimes she felt alone, and was becoming anxious to share her life with someone special.

A couple minutes later, Marcus walked in. He actually looked like his picture. Strong jaw and kind eyes gave him an approachable look. Like a businessman, who knew how to be firm as well as understanding. Perhaps that carried into other aspects of his life. Maybe he took a firm, yet understanding hand in his personal life as well.

No, she shouldn't be thinking about that, if she hadn't met him. Only the more she looked as he approached her, the more her mind wandered. His broad shoulders made his shirt stretch deliciously over his chest, leaving little to the imagination. She was pretty sure he was an athlete of some sort. Maybe he was a rower? Those guys always had some amazing upper body strength. *I bet he could lift me over his head, without any shaking muscles.* Smirking at her thought Sam let her mind wander, she didn't realize immediately that he had found her, and was approaching her table. Quickly regaining her composure, she took a sip of her wine.

As he arrived at her table she smiled, "Marcus?"

"Yeah, are you Sam?" His voice was a little higher pitched than she was expecting, but she shook that off, silently adding it to the small list of dislikes, since that list was vastly outweighed by the opposing list, for the moment.

"I am, it's so nice to meet you. Did you have any trouble finding the place?

"Not at all, it was one of the few places that the GPS could actually find without leading me on a wild goose chase first. I usually avoid hole-in-the-wall bars because of that, but I love the atmosphere that goes with them. So, I'm glad you picked this one," he said with a very sexy genuine smile. He took his seat across from Sam and Tania, the waitress, came around to take his order.

"What can I get you to drink?" Tania was direct, but Sam could tell she was only feeling him out. Apparently, she was taking her 'wing-girl' job to heart, even if her job was just to rescue.

"I'll have a tall wheat beer, whatever you have on tap is fine." Marcus ordered a fancier beer. Did that mean he had good taste or was a snob?

Tania, took another second to analyze the situation, and turned to place his order. Sam hadn't formulated a worrisome opinion yet, so she decided to continue talking to him, and see what happened.

"So, what is it that you do, Marcus? I know you said you own a Fortune 500 company, but I'm curious what your company does."

"We are an acquisition firm. I buy out businesses that are struggling, and on the verge of bankruptcy. Then I try to retain as many employees as possible, to avoid turnover. Also, most of them already know the systems, so the only retraining I have to do is in favor of profits."

"Wow, that sounds like quite the job. I can only imagine how stressful it must be."

"Yes, I suppose stressful is one way to consider it. I enjoy it though, they say if you love your job then you never work another day. Actually, I just feel like it is more time consuming. I don't get to date as much as I like but with a face like this who cares, right? I will say that there is a long line of women waiting to date me but they all end up rejecting me before it is all done." Moments later Tania came back with his beer, and quickly left to check on another table.

"Well, I guess that sounds like a horrible problem to have," she let a hint of sarcasm show in her voice, but was a bit hesitant, since she didn't know what turn the conversation had actually taken, or if he was joking.

"Oh yes, a problem is a good way to put it. So that is why I decided to look into online dating. Getting out of my existing dating pool and into a bigger pond. The current line is just women who want my money. Which for me isn't really an issue, because as long as they are interested in me in some way, then I'm ok with it. Unfortunately, I can't get them to go out with me after a few dates. I'm attractive, enough aren't I?"

"Oh...uh...well yes, I'd say you are plenty attractive." She didn't elaborate for fear of what that would get her into. As attractive as Marcus was, she was starting to figure out why most of the women he dated were running at the sight of him.

He ran a hand through his hair. It was already the perfect wavy look, every hair stayed in its place, even after he touched it. His hair screamed from the distance, about the money he had, and how his stylist must painstakingly take all the time in the world to give him the perfect cut. There wasn't a hair out of place, anywhere on his head.

"Yes, I can imagine you have taken in Every. Single. Inch. Of. Me." he punctuated every word, and didn't hide the fact that he was alluding to more.

"Oh well, I guess I noticed a little bit of you," stumbling again though her reply. What was it about these guys who reduced her to a few syllables, and not in a good way?

"Oh, there is nothing little about me I'm chiseled from my face to my…" He left the last part unsaid, but gestured to his groin area. What was it about this guy, and his appearance? He either had a lot to be proud of, or he was making up for his 'shortcomings'.

With that, she signaled for Tania to come back over. Noticing her signal, Tania nodded in her direction, acknowledging that she saw her. A moment later she came over to the table. "Can I get another glass of wine?"

"Of course, is there anything else I can get for you?"

"I'll take another beer, and Sam, do you think you might want to get some appetizers?"

"Actually, I'm only going to be able to stay for a little while longer. I have a busy day tomorrow." She fibbed, figuring it was easier for her to tell a white lie, than to hurt his feelings again. He seemed to have such a long list of hurt feelings, over girls not wanting to date him.

"Oh of course, I understand. Let's use our time to get to know each other better. What do you do again?"

"I'm a flight attendant. I have a set schedule of four days on four off and I love it, but it makes for a busy four days off when I have to use them to get everything done from while I've been gone. Being gone all the time isn't for everyone."

"I bet you make for a great flight attendant," he said with a seductive tone. "If you are ever looking for work, I could always put you on my private jet. You would make for some perfect eye candy on long business trips, or maybe another kind of candy too."

He really was very forward, Sam didn't know how to handle someone like him. He was a millionaire, or something, and she wasn't used to such obvious attention. Then again, for every piece of attention he showered on her he had previously given himself at least three compliments.

"Oh thanks, I'll keep that in mind, as for now I'm happy where I am. I've been working there since I got out of college. If I can keep it up, I'll have a generous package when I leave."

"Package? Oh, I could give you quite the package, whenever you want." He waggled his eyebrows in a very lewd gesture.

At that moment, Tania walked back up to the table with their drinks. As Marcus took a drink of his, she indicated a phone with her hand. Sam shook her head, she thought she had this under control this time. He wasn't forcing her to stay too much longer, and so she reached for her drink, and took a large sip. If she could finish her drink, then the date could be over sooner rather than later. She just needed to bear the conversation for a few more minutes.

"Oh yeah, I kinda walked into that one, didn't I?" she laughed a little to emphasize her point.

"Well with someone that looks like this," he gestured to himself, "you'll probably walk into a lot of things. There is probably so much a girl like you wants to do to a guy like me." It took every bit of restraint inside of her, for Sam not to freak out about the 'girl like you' comment. She didn't want to give him a reason to make the evening last longer. Although there was no statement that started a fight with her more than that one. Not to mention, she wanted to gag at the thought of what he might be picturing that she wanted to do him.

She slogged down the remainder of her wine in one last drink. "Well I guess that is it for me tonight. I'm a real socialite, these days," she added laughing slightly at herself. "I feel like I'm a slave to my work, but still haven't figured out how to regulate my social life."

"Oh, I understand, I've had to figure out how to function outside of a work setting, as well."

Ha, I think you need to keep trying, bucko!

"I'm business all the time, and when I'm not at work I've had to learn to focus on my social life and when I say that I really mean my sex life." As if he really needed to clarify his code, after a couple of drinks with him she pretty much had it all worked out.

"It was nice to get out this evening, thanks for inviting me." She held her hand out across the table to shake his hand. Awkward was like a second language to Sam. She was awkward in her everyday life, and her personal life. It was something she had to focus to work through, and not drown in her embarrassment.

"It was my pleasure, you were great company. I'm so glad I could grace you with my presence, as well. Not everyone gets that luxury. I'm a pretty picky guy, though I know that is hard to believe"

Wow how did he fit his head through the door? There were so many things Sam could say right now, but she held her tongue. Instead she stood up, bid him farewell, and headed straight for the door, not sparing him another glance. Before she made it through the door, she ducked right, and slipped into a booth. Online dating was still very scary to her, and this date didn't do anything to alleviate her fears. She wanted to deter him from trying to follow her home.

She waited for a few minutes while he finished his beer, and Tania nodded in her direction to let her know she was seen, but not outed. Soon Marcus got up, and threw some money on the table. He walked out the front door, and off to his chauffeur, she supposed. That is the thing you always see rich guys can't drive themselves. They are too pretentious for that.

Escaping her hiding space, she made her way to the bar. She told herself it wasn't because she wanted to see Nick, but because she wasn't yet ready to go home. Taking up residence on the far edge of the bar, not to draw attention to herself while she just observed. She didn't want him to think she was back for his company and poor sense of humor.

When had her life come down to bad date, and stalking bartenders? She was truly hopeless; her mother was right. She was going to be old and shriveled before she found anyone or she would be alone forever. No one wanted to be around someone as sad as her.

While lost in her reverie, Nick popped up in front of her, out of nowhere. Jumping slightly, she tried to minimize her reaction to him, hoping he wouldn't notice.

"What can I get you, Princess?" She realized he didn't know her name, like she hadn't known his last night.

"Sam, and I'll have a Mic Ultra bottle."

"Oh, you are really spicing things up tonight, aren't you?" he said in a tone of condescension. She knew this was a bad idea.

Setting the opened bottle on the bar in front of her, "So what brings you out alone tonight?"

She took a pull of her bottle, and delayed her answer. "I had a date," she mumbled softly hoping he would mishear her.

"What was that? It sounded like you said you had a date. What are you some kind of serial dater?"

"What is that? You act like it is a crime to go out on two dates in two nights. You've never had more than one date in a week?" She knew she was getting defensive, but he really was starting to bring out the worst in her.

"A serial dater is an indecisive person who can't help but date multiple people all the time. It's a lot like a player, but you shoot them all down rather than screw them down. We aren't talking about my dating life though, we are talking about yours."

"It's not my fault we don't click. I'm looking for a connection, and not just instant gratification." Sam took another long pull from her beer, needing the instant relief it provided. Nick really was infuriating. Why didn't he understand what she was trying to do?

"Alright, I'm going to go check on my customers, and then when I get back, you can tell me what was wrong with this one. Think that is enough time to come up with a good enough story?"

Sam just rolled her eyes, and drank her beer, ignoring his last question. Instead she just watched him walk away, and admired his butt in his tight jeans. She worked her way down his leg, and was thankful to find they weren't skinny jeans. *Something I don't understand, is the new fad that manly men should cram all their yummy parts into pants that restrict blood flow. Don't get me wrong, I love a good pair of jeans, that hug a butt so well it leaves little to the imagination, but skinny jeans just take that a step too far. Don't even start about that asinine so-called fashion about pants around their knees, held only by a belt, and a waddle.*

She had moved on from her inner monologue about men's fashion, and finished her beer before he made his way back over to her end of the bar. He seemed to flow behind the bar, as though everything were connected to him, like attachments to his arms. He showed little thought about the drinks he was making, as they came second nature to him. He was more than good at his job, it was a lifestyle as if he were born to do this. She wondered if he chose this job, or fell into it, and never left.

"Ok Princess, here's another round, it's a tall one and more than the bottle. That should get you through what I'm sure will be a titillating story of your serial nightmare date." Nick set a glass down filled to the rim, without spilling a drop. That is something she could never even think to accomplish.

"I told you my name is Sam. Why do you insist on calling me Princess? Do you suffer from short term memory loss?" She knew she was hedging, but it was the least she could do. She knew he was just vying for an opportunity to have another laugh at her expense.

"Nope, I just happen to think you're acting like a princess, so I've decided call you that, until I think you act otherwise. It will be easier to remember your name, when you choose to act like it, and not a princess."

"Well that is a very haughty attitude. You presume to think you know me well enough to tell me when I'm not acting like myself?" She was so used to her mother's little digs, that this shouldn't be affecting her, but she still reacted a little too quickly showing her frustration clearly.

"Easy killer! I just want to hear about this date, not pour salt on old wounds."

Taking a deep breath, she realized he was very perceptive. Sam released her anger, and made an effort to move past it. "It wasn't a horrible date, more like an odd one. Heaven knows a girl is supposed to be happy when she's on a date with a millionaire," she added that part in to gauge his reaction. He didn't let anything slip on his face, he just listened intently, so she continued. "It started out fine, he was quite handsome, and knew how to wear his clothes just right." Her eyes wandered over Nick's body as she said this, and he smirked at her, letting her know he just saw what she did. If she were a blusher it would have happened right then, but her complexion didn't lean to blushing, like a fairer person would.

She cleared her throat and continued, "He just seemed a bit self-absorbed, or maybe he was compensating for a serious lack of self-confidence, I have no idea. He spent the entire date talking about how good looking he was, but how many women have rejected him. Then wanted verbal affirmation from me, that I thought he was attractive. No matter how many women had told him he was attractive in the past, he either didn't believe them or just needed to hear it repeated, a lot."

"That doesn't sound so bad? You could have done worse for a first date that's for sure. Maybe he was nervous."

"Oh no, that was just the tip of the iceberg. I'm not a prude, but I am a bit subtler about my thoughts and try not to let them out, especially on a first date." He arched his eyebrow at her as though he was contradicting her statement about being subtle, she ignored him and carried on. "He was one innuendo away from embarrassing the waitress, as well as me. He made more penis references than a bunch of guys at a frat party. I'm not a blusher, but even those made me a bit uncomfortable." Just then her phone chimed with a notification. She slid it out of her purse, and groaned because it was a message on her dating app. She glanced up, and Nick was waiting expectantly for her to continue, but she just took a second and opened the message, to her surprise it was from, Marcus. Puzzled, she opened it, and immediately dropped her phone on the bar, and shrieked.

She saw a look of concern cross Nick's face, before he could conceal it. He scooped up her phone without permission, and immediately, all concern was gone and replaced with rumbling laughter. If Sam wasn't so pissed that he was laughing at this situation, she would've taken a moment to appreciate the rich timbre.

"Why are you laughing? This isn't even a little bit funny. Who does that? It hasn't even been thirty minutes since our date ended, and without promise of a second, to boot. Why would he send me a dick pic?" Sam was beyond flabbergasted, she was moving quickly to furious. Between Nick's reaction, and this new Marcus development she didn't know who to be madder at.

"Calm down, Princess, I'm just laughing because of your reaction, not because I think he should have sent this to you. Maybe you're right, he must have a complex of some kind." He handed her phone back and started working on a drink. So, she took the time to delete the message and block him. The last thing she needed on her phone coming up at random times, was a Creeper's rod. She glanced up as Nick slid the drink over to her.

"Oh no, I'm drinking beer tonight. I don't need anything else." She slid the glass back across the bar.

"Nope, this one won't kill you, and I think you need it."

Giving up her argument she took a sip, it was a little sweet, but had a tangy flavor deep down. It had an orange color which was deceptive, because she was expecting a more orange, or even a mango flavor. This was something she couldn't quite put her finger on.

"What is in this? I can't put my finger on it."

"Vodka, Triple Sec, Carrot Juice and Energy Soda," Nick said matter-of-factly.

"Carrot Juice, that was what I was tasting that was just a little sweet, but not quite. What made you think to put that in there?"

"Thought you needed a Cocky Carrot to top off your evening," with that he walked away just like the night before.

"Really? Could you be any more punny tonight?" She couldn't be upset it was kind of funny, and she was using all her energy not to laugh. He was quite clever, and he was becoming almost likable. She was trying so hard to not like him, that she opted to call it a night before she gained any more bedtime material.

Chapter 3:

Leaving the bar, Sam decided it was a nice enough night she would just walk. Making her way home she kept her pace slow and her gait steady. She wasn't in a hurry and this gave her plenty of time to think.

The past two dates were awful to say the least. *What am I doing? I'm a mess, but I thought the rest of my life was finally in a good place. If I didn't have to worry about me, then I could add someone else into the mix. Maybe I should have started with a puppy. On second thought, maybe a fern would be more my speed.* All she could envision was a tiny puppy corpse waiting for her after a long work shift. "I really am an accident waiting to happen," she mumbled to herself. She needed a new plan.

The next day was her refocus day. Sam decided it would be all about her. She started by making a trip to the gym. Getting ready she couldn't decide on yoga or spin class. "I'll just see how crowded they are when I get there." Throwing on a tank top over a cute sports bra, the colored crisscross straps exposed at her back. She paired them with a pair of black Capri spandex pants and laced up her sneakers. Opting to jog to the gym, Sam got her warmup in on the way. Slipping into a steady rhythm, she listened to music on her phone. To keep pace she used, RockMyRun. She first took up running out of college to clear her head while on long work trips. This was before she had many work friends and had little to do between flights. This app had been a lifesaver because she always got distracted by the things and people she passed. Before she found it hard to find her pace. Listening to random music was alright, but made her tempo inconsistent. Now she had a way to lose herself and the app did the thinking for her. The music changed according to her footfalls. Allowing her mind to drift, Sam made it to the gym feeling like she had been teleported there.

Walking inside, Sam wasn't winded and the cooler temps that morning lent to her not feeling too sweaty. They didn't seem too overcrowded today given that she didn't keep a membership at a super big gym. They still offered a wide array of classes throughout the day, which made it perfect for her. She's not the type to just go pick a piece of equipment and do her own routine. Being self-assured in her work life didn't translate to her workout regime in her personal life. She was always too concerned with how people perceived her. What if she did something wrong or didn't understand exactly how something worked? Would everyone peg her as the idiot and secretly laugh at her behind her back?

Instead of worrying about all those things she became a group participant. Since she already warmed up with her jog, Sam decided a spin class was just what she needed. Some mindless cycling to nowhere. Signing in at the desk she made her way to her locker. She always kept an empty water bottle here so she wouldn't have to carry one or possibly forget it. Grabbing the bottle and a complimentary towel, Sam made her way out to the water cooler. As she filled it, she heard a sexy deep masculine voice speaking to the girl at the smoothie counter. Trying to be inconspicuous she glanced at the reflection only slightly visible in the glass in front of her.

The man was leaning on the counter on his right hand, causing his muscles in his forearm to ripple. His veins were so tight under his sun kissed skin and rolled all the way up to his shoulders. Most men have bulging biceps here, but his ran through his entire arm in a way that meant he was a regular. Sam always had a thing for strong arms and hulking shoulders.

Tearing her eyes away from his delicious limbs, she made it to his face. He had a strong jaw that was squared off with a slight cleft in his chin. *Could he possibly have worked out his jaw muscles to achieve that perfect shaped mandible?* His nose was very aquiline, and made him look almost regal. As though he came from royalty, in a previous life. The distance and the light behind the glass made it impossible to see the color of his eyes, but he was obviously used to expressing a lot through them.

Something cold ran over her hand, and quickly brought her back to reality. Water poured over the mouth of her bottle and she gasped at her mishap rushing to stop the flow. Attempting to draw minimal attention to herself, Sam used her towel to sop up all of the mess. Keeping her head down she hoped no one noticed her.

As she stood up and sipped the excess water out so she could close her lid without creating another puddle, she casually glanced up at the unknown dream boat. Unexpectedly, he glanced at her and winked. His sandy blonde hair fell into his eye as he lightly shook his head to dislodge it. She made a break for her class as calmly as she could muster. *Man, I know I don't get in here that often, but damn, where did he come from?* She wondered as she chose an empty bike not too close to the front.

People were slowly tricking in as the instructor made her way to the front of the group. "Can I have your attention, please," the instructor called out over the group and the voices softened to allow her to speak. "We've had a private class overlap our regular sessions by mistake. Although our mix-up, is your gain. We were able to get a replacement instructor last minute from our other location. Let me introduce Kyle. He is the best in the business and you will get an amazing workout today." The class broke out in applause as Kyle made his way to the lead bike. Low and behold, Kyle was none other than the beach bronze god from the front desk.

Climbing onto her bike she got her water bottle and the towel situated and ready for the long haul to nowhere.

Purposely, Sam kept her head down and as quiet as possible. Drawing attention in anyway was the last thing she wanted to do. Sam ducked her head in hopes that he wouldn't notice her. She was already embarrassed from before, she didn't need him focusing on her throughout the class.

Class began without incident, Sam kept up with little difficulty. Kyle, was a driven instructor, but had a way of still making the grueling parts fun. There was no getting bored in this class, but everyone kept up. It was as though no one wanted to disappoint Kyle even a little bit.

He was so lost in the music it was more like a dance class. Sam was more interested in watching his arms flex with each up and down thrust on the handle bars. It was easy for them to match him pump for pump, everyone kept up.

Halfway through the song after repeating the rep pattern a couple of times, Kyle climbed off his bike and started to make rounds to correct form. He paused next to two or three people never letting his energy fizzle a fraction. Sam tried to stay focused on her rhythm and breathing. She did all she could to not need any help. She was attempting an impersonation of a chameleon. One time when magic would be a perfect skill to have right now.

Suddenly, from behind, a warm hand came to rest between her shoulder blades. Instead of playing it cool, Sam jumped out of her skin and promptly lost her footing and fell hard to the floor. The pedals spun out of control, smacking her shins painfully.

Strong arms quickly went around her, lifting her away from the torture device. She was carried out of the room and all the way into a lounge area that she hadn't seen before. It must be a break area for the employees to relax in between sessions.

Looking up at her rescuer, she saw a pair of grey eyes, so light they could have been two silver coins. "Let me get you some ice, and then I have to get back inside before the next song or they will be milling around lost until I get back. I'll come and check on you in a moment," Kyle winked at her and made his way to the ice machine.

This was an interesting turn of events. Sam was laying on a very comfortable sofa with her leg elevated being catered to by a swoon worthy man. Perhaps that meant things were turning around for her. Kyle brought back her ice and placed it on her legs where the peddles have left her skin red and scraped. "Stay here, I'll be right back."

Leaning her head back, Sam decided to relax and ignore her surroundings. Closing her eyes, she attempted to not think about the sexy instructor and failed miserably. She came in today with a plan in place to sort out her troubles in her life by working out and sweating through her thoughts. This isn't going to plan at all. Now her thoughts were fixating on the gorgeous creature who could crush her like a bug physically and probably emotionally. Having no more patience, Sam decided to just leave and walk home. She was supposed to wait until he came back, but chose instead to go home and wallow in misery.

As she started to get up the door swung open, and Kyle walked back in with a smirk on his face. "Where do you think you're going, Fumblelina?? I needed you to wait on me, so I could see how you were. Can't have you running off with major injuries, now can we?"

"I'm fine, just a couple scratches and a bump on my knee. Nothing to write home about, I'll survive." She made a move to get up again, and his hand came down on her shoulder to hold her in place. "What are you doing? I should be getting home. There is no way I can continue the class now."

"I'm just trying to ascertain if it is anything that needs more than ice. Don't worry, I'm not going to hurt you, anymore that is." He probed her leg in a gentle caress. She wondered if he was just doing that so he could touch her, or if there was any actual medical effectiveness to what he was doing.

After a minute, Kyle placed her leg on the ground, "It seems you will indeed live to see tomorrow. That being the case, you need to let me make it up to you. I would love to take you out to dinner tonight."

Sam froze, uncertain of how exactly she wanted to proceed. *Of course, someone like me would attract the next guy I see after making a decision to stop dating again.* She mulled her answer over for a minute and started to turn him down. "I just don't think that is a great idea."

"Oh, come on! I owe you something for scaring you and causing you so much pain."

"You don't owe me anything. I was distracted and you startled me. I'm not always the most coordinated, but I'm usually not that clumsy. I must have just been tired after my jog here." Making excuses wasn't her forte, and she was likely being very obvious.

"Ok, I'm not asking you on a date, we will just call it me checking on you to make sure I didn't cause you more pain than we think."

Running out of made up excuses, Sam conceded, "Ok, but just drinks, not anything else. I don't want people thinking this is more than it really is." She proceeded to tell him to meet her at Joe's Bar tonight at seven, opting for an early evening since she only had one more day off that week.

Sam got home from the day from hell, and felt all she could persuade her body to do was take a long, and extremely hot bath. Wanting to make the most of her current situation, she pulled out an aromatherapy candle, and a relaxing bath bomb. If she had them, she would have added bubbles just to add to the experience.

Why does my personal life seem so screwed up? She questioned meaningfully as she soaked. Taking up dating as if it were a sport was a plan to appease her mother. It was never intended to make everything feel so abstract. She was either going to weed out the herd, or just make mom happy, by putting herself out there. Now she was worse off than when she started.

She sighed, and just let the frustration and negativity flow out of her. Breathing in each and every relaxing smell put off by the lavender and chamomile bath bomb. Her sandalwood candle was nothing more than a hope dream to make her feel better. Not knowing what else to do, she got out of the tub and take a nap.

This was her last relaxing day before going back to work. Tomorrow would be spent preparing to leave again for her four-day shift cycle. In the meantime, she was going to relax and enjoy the rest of her day. Later she would need to get ready to go for drinks with Kyle.

Hours later, Sam was sitting in her usual spot at Joe's Bar. Unfortunately, it didn't seem that Tania was working. Now she wasn't going to have a safety net. This was going to be all on her, but this wasn't a real date and she had already met Kyle, so what could go wrong?

Right then, Kyle made his appearance and approached the table. He was hulking when she saw him earlier, but in jeans and a button-up shirt, he was a swoon-worthy dream. He really did clean up nice, as they say. Then he surpassed everything when he smiled at her. She now knew what it meant to melt. This was the moment she was waiting for, when she understood what all the romance books and movies were portraying. She was glassy-eyed and lost in his smile. He could say anything, and he would likely have her forever. *What spell does he have me under? Is he part vampire or witch? I shouldn't be this close to someone with so much power.*

Clearing her mind, she looked up and him and returned his smile with exuberance. "Hey, there you are."

"Looks like you have survived the day. So, I'm leaning toward you are in perfect health, but I'll let the evening tell all."

"Oh, I'm doing fine. I went home and took a bath to work out any tight muscles from my run and my bike ride from Hell. Then opted for a nap instead of any other major physical activity."

"That sounds like you made a great decision. I wish my afternoon had been that laid back. I had a full day of classes and personal training. This location may be small, but they are very busy all the time."

"You don't like what you do? I thought after being in your class, for even just a short time that you were doing what you loved."

"Don't mistake my complaining as anything other than love. I have slow days and busy days but if I'm going to be there all day anyway, I'd rather it be a full day. It makes it go by faster. Then there are less days, I feel the need to put in a workout of my own on my time."

"You're telling me you are one of those workout addicts?"

Just then, a waitress Sam didn't recognize approached the table. Her eyes lingered rudely on Kyle. If this were a real date, Sam would've had grounds to be upset, but the waitress didn't know that, so Sam decided to be bothered at the very least. They ordered simple drinks, and Kyle all but ignored the doe eyed waitress, though not for a lack of trying on her part. That made Sam feel better, Kyle seemed to have one focus and one focus only, Sam.

As the waitress made her way away from their table and Kyle smiled again. His eyes were practically sizzling with intent. She felt like prey, but in a way, she was perfectly calm, and welcomed whatever would become her.

"Where were we? Oh yes, I wouldn't say I'm an addict, but I feel the need to get in a certain amount of cardio and lifting in order to not let my muscles feel unused. I'm pretty open on my forms of exercise. I just need to feel like I've used most of my muscles every day."

So, let's say if you had a friend who needed to move, and you had to haul large furniture to a second story apartment, you would call that a good workout?"

"Exactly! Are you hinting at something, Sam dear?"

"Ha! No not at all. I'm happily placed in my apartment. I have lived there since I got out of college and it suits me just fine in my days off."

"Good, not that I wouldn't have been happy to help you. What did you say you did for a living?"

"I'm a flight attendant. Go ahead start the jokes. Everyone has at least one."

"What would I want to joke about? You are a beautiful woman and if you love your job, then that is all that matters."

The waitress chose that moment to bring their drinks. Taking a sip of hers, Sam waited for the waitress to move on. She was persistent, Sam could give her points for that. That didn't mean Sam had to like her.

Ignoring the hovering waitress Kyle continued, "You are probably really good at your job. Is it something you chose or fell into?"

"It was more something to do out of college. I didn't have a set job and they were hiring. It turned out I was good at it, and the bonus was I actually enjoyed the work."

"That is awesome. You know what they say, love your work, and you never work another day."

"Yeah, I go back to it in a couple days. Tomorrow is my last day off, but I'm not worried. I get to see the country and places some people never would get to go. I never have to pay for the flight or the hotel, and I have a meal allowance, since I'm on the clock technically, because I'm there for them."

"You seem committed to your work. They are lucky to have someone like you. Hey, I know you said drinks, but I'm starving, and I don't know about you, but this isn't exactly a chore to hang out with you. What do you say? Do you want to order some appetizers or something?"

Sam considered this before answering. If she ordered food that made this more like a date and less like a checkup to avoid a lawsuit. *Am I alright with this? Can I tolerate the rest of the evening with him?* Then he smiled at her again. That wonderful smile gradually broke across his face again. It was as if he knew something she hadn't figured out yet.

"You need to eat and this isn't a big deal. Food is food and that doesn't make this anything more than it started out as."

There wasn't any power that could keep her from agreeing to this man. He had a force about him that she was drawn to. "I suppose food won't kill me. What sounds good?"

The rest of the evening went smoothly and she actually had an amazing time. As they wrapped up he offered to drive her home to save her Uber fare. Surprisingly even to herself, she found herself accepting. They made their way through the parking lot and he offered her his arm as they walked to his car. The gentleman in him insisted on holding the door as she climbed in the passenger side.

As he started the engine a song played over the radio that she hadn't heard in forever. As he turned up the volume 'I'm Sexy and I Know It' played through the speakers loudly. "Do you want to see a cool trick?" Kyle asked looking at her with that smile.

"Sure," she replied without hesitation.

Before she knew what was happening Kyle was unfastening his pants and pulling out his member, just as the song approached the chorus. Then it started wiggling and dancing on its own to the music. Sam was frozen in shock. Not knowing what he was thinking by putting on this charade. He was twitching and flopping around on beat. It was like a car wreck, you know you shouldn't look, but you can't turn away.

As the chorus concluded Sam found her voice, "That was very unique." She glanced around as though she couldn't find something. "Actually, it looks like I forgot my keys, and I just remembered the regular waitress asked me to wait for her tonight. It's her night off, and we were going to grab drinks." With her fingers on the handle, she didn't give him a chance to respond, as she bolted from the car.

Speed walking, Sam made it back into the bar to cover for her lie. The night had been going so well, how did she miss his voyeuristic side? What made him decide, it was ok to do something like that? Had she said, or done something that convinced him it would be ok to let his guard down? Sam considered all this as she made her way to her usual spot at the bar.

Nick saw her immediately, "Did you have another date or did you just miss me?"

Rolling her eyes, she almost didn't answer him, "Neither or at least it didn't start out that way. I got hurt at the gym today and the offender invited me out for drinks to avoid a lawsuit."

His eyes flashed in worry just for a second she thought she was imagining it. "Well you look alright now. You said started out, did something change before the end?"

"Lots changed before the end. It was like a horror film. Starts out fine and ends in mass destruction. I need something strong."

Nick mixed up a quick Long Island Ice Tea for her and slid it across the bar. "Strong enough?"

She avoided her normal sip to test it and went straight for a gulp to get as much in her system at once. Taking a breath following her first drink, she sputtered a little, "Yeah, that will do."

"Ok, then tell me where this one went wrong. Maybe by the time you give up dating, we will be able to tell who your perfect match is by process of elimination." She could see the smirk he was trying to hide behind his snark.

"I'm not sure telling you is a good idea, because you always just end up making fun of me."

"You know it is all in fun, and I'm not actually making fun of you just giving you something to laugh about later. I'm honestly interested in hearing your stories. They are the best ones by far I ever have."

"You are just using me for my humiliating experiences then. You can't live your life while stuck behind the bar, so you just tell yourself, at least you aren't me."

"Exactly, I'm not laughing at you. I'm making myself feel better." Then he let a smile loose that would made her weak in the knees, if she were standing. This was by far better than Kyle's. What was she thinking getting lost in Kyle's smile? All she needed to do was see Nick's, and all other distractions washed away.

"How is it that you always get me to tell you everything?" Sam said with another eye roll.

"Because you think I'm charming."

"Ha! I can tell you that is NOT it, at all." With minimal hesitation, Sam continued, "Like I said it wasn't a date to start. We met for drinks so he could see I wasn't lying when I said I was fine."

"Wait, no you have to go back and tell me what happened as to why you needed to be checked in the first place." Begrudgingly, Sam recanted her morning escapades to Nick. "Seriously? Do you have bad date karma or are you a klutz?"

"Not at all I was just startled and distracted because my mind was on other things and not my immediate situation."

"Ok, I'll give you that for now, please continue." He made a flourish with his hands giving him the illusion of being courtlier than he actually was.

"Well, the night seemed to be going well perhaps because it wasn't a date. We had drinks and were just talking like normal human beings. Nothing awkward happened and we got along. Then he suggested we order appetizers and I was worried at first because food make dates more real than just drinks. In the end, I agreed and we had a great evening. I was even going to let him drive me home. That's when things got weird. Just before we headed out of the parking lot he made his penis dance. All while 'Wiggle wiggle wiggle, yeah' played on the radio." Nick's eyes were as big as saucers. "I can't make this stuff up. Why would I? It's not like I think it's funny to be known as the crazy chick who attracts the weirdos."

"Wow, I don't know what to say to that. It is beyond my wildest imagination. I agree these can't be made up. They have to be real, but why would anyone admit to that?"

Sam balled up her drink napkin and threw it at him, "Hey! You're the one who drug that out of me. It's not like I wanted to rehash my day with you. I think you secretly want to live vicariously through me and these guys are your test subjects. If something works, you are going to try it out."

"I guess I can check off dick dancing. That is obviously a turn-off."

"You are most certainly correct. There isn't a girl that I can think of that it would work on, unless you already had her in the bedroom. Even then though that is pushing your luck."

"So, you said this guy is a gym rat, right?"

"I wouldn't call him a gym rat, but he is a personal trainer."

Without anther word, Nick began mixing a cocktail. Sam had been down this road enough she knew what was a happening. So, she prepared herself for the worst.

He started pouring with his usual precision; gin, lemon juice, lime juice, lemonade and a splash of Blue Curacao Liqueur. None of these things were a no go for Sam so after he mixed it all up and poured it over ice, she took it and simply asked, "What is this one called."

"That, Princess, is a Blue Bruiser."

"I don't get it? The rest made sense. This one just sounds like I kicked him in the balls."

"Well in a way you probably did. This guy broke out a hard-pulsing cock and you shot the poor bastard down."

"What was I supposed to do, let him have his way with me and make him believe this was the best pickup line ever?"

"I didn't say you did anything wrong. This was just what I thought of when you finished your story."

As usual he left the drink on the bar and left her to take care of other customers. Sam decided not to be mad, because he was probably right. She didn't regret her choice at all. It was only another casualty of dating for her. She seemed to hurt guys left and right, but in her opinion, that was better than leading them on. She took a drink of her 'bruiser' and let herself think about her choices. If she had given into every guy who asked her out, because all they saw was a pretty face, or a trophy for their wall of previous dates, then everyone she dated would be miserable, and so would she. That wasn't who she was. She was true to herself and the decisions she made. It was her life, and she wouldn't let a bunch of crazies bog her down just because saying 'this isn't for me' might hurt their feelings. While they were pining for her, they might have missed who they were meant to be with after all.

Chapter 4:

A couple days later, Sam was on a plane giving her best for the passengers. She was helping them to their seats and putting on her best face. As the doors began to close Sam made her way to the phone to make the opening announcements.

"Ladies and gentlemen, my name is Sam, and I'm your chief flight attendant. On behalf of Captain Z and the entire crew, welcome aboard our non-stop service from Chicago to New York.
Our flight time will be of two hours and fifteen minutes. We will be flying at an altitude of thirty-three thousand feet, at ground speed six hundred miles per hour. Thank you." She milled around for a bit, helping passengers get settled.

She worked her way to the flight attendant station and picked up the main phone. "Now we request your full attention as the flight attendants demonstrate the safety features of this aircraft." The other crew strategically placed themselves around the aircraft in order to be seen by all the passengers.

"When the seatbelt sign illuminates, you must fasten your seat belt. Insert the metal fittings one into the other, and tighten by pulling on the loose end of the strap. To release your seat belt, lift the upper portion of the buckle. It works just like every other seat belt; if you don't know how to operate a seat belt you probably shouldn't be out in public unsupervised." The passenger audience chuckles lightly. She always enjoyed changing this speech in order to make it more enjoyable and perhaps help them to remember it, instead of ignore the entire thing. "Then, please remain seated whilst the fasten seatbelt sign is on, or we will be forced to re-seat you to the wing, and watch our own little version of 'Gone with the Wind'." A few more snickers follow. "We remind you that this is a non-smoking flight. No smoking is allowed, not even in the toilets. Don't be naughty in our potty," she wagged her finger as if she were a parent to all of them. "If you do, there is a two thousand dollar fine, and if you had that kind of money you'd be flying on a much more expensive airline.

There may be fifty ways to leave your lover, but there are only four ways out of this airplane. One located above the wings on each side of the plane. The others are located in each the front, and the back of the plane. Please take a few moments now to locate your nearest exit. In some cases, your nearest exit may be behind you. If we need to evacuate the aircraft, floor-level lighting will guide you towards the exit. Doors can be opened by moving the handle in the direction of the arrow. Each door is equipped with an inflatable slide which may also be detached and used as a life raft.

Oxygen and the air pressure are always being monitored. In the event of a decompression, an oxygen mask will automatically appear in front of you. To activate oxygen, simply insert seventy-five cents for the first minute," she shook her head to let them know she was only joking. "To start the flow of oxygen, pull the mask towards you. Place it firmly over your nose and mouth, secure the elastic band behind your head, and breathe normally. Although the bag does not inflate, oxygen is flowing to the mask. If you are traveling with small children, choose now the one you love the most," she tried to use her most mother sweet voice in order to convey that she understood this would be a difficult decision. "If you are traveling with a child or someone who requires assistance, secure your mask on first, and then assist the other person – unless it is my ex-boyfriend then don't bother." She had them all laughing loudly at this point and she was sure she had them all captivated. "Keep your mask on until a uniformed crew member advises you to remove it.

In the event of an emergency, please assume the bracing position. Lean forward with your hands on top of your head, and your elbows against your thighs. Ensure your feet are flat on the floor." The other members of the crew demonstrate this position for everyone.

"A life vest is located in a pouch under your seat or between the armrests. Folks this is a life vest, not a toilet seat cover," Sam said while holding one of the flimsy looking life vests, that would inflate when needed to support a large man with ease. "When instructed to do so, open the plastic pouch and remove the vest. Slip it over your head. Pass the straps around your waist and adjust at the front. To inflate the vest, pull firmly on the red cord, only when leaving the aircraft. If you need to refill the vest, blow into the mouthpieces. Use the whistle and light to attract attention. Also, your seat cushions can be used for flotation. In the event of an emergency water landing please take them with our compliments. Pull the cushion from the seat, slip your arms into the straps, and hug the cushion to your chest.

You will find this and all the other safety information in the card located in the seat pocket in front of you. We strongly suggest you read it before take-off. If you have any questions, please don't hesitate to ask one of our crew members. We wish you all an enjoyable flight." Sam hung up the phone signifying that she has finished her announcement.

The cabin fills with applause and Sam graciously takes a bow. Then she picks up the phone again, "We appreciate your applause, but frankly, we prefer cash," she says with a wink and replaces the receiver.

As the crew gets back to work one of the girls comes up to her after assisting a passenger, "Sam, I love it when you do the announcement. I almost have a hard time completing the demonstrations for fear I'm going to die laughing. I can't believe you come up with those on the fly. You never say the same things twice. I've never been that quick on my feet."

"I'm not that great, I was just raised on sarcasm, it comes to me before anything else. I can't imagine making anyone sit through that speech without attempting a little humor. It is a real snoozer."

Sam continued back to finish her preflight checks before take-off. After a few minutes, the Captain came over the speaker, "Cabin crew, please take your seats and prepare for take-off"

The team quickly made their way to their designated seats and buckles in. The take-off was painless and before they knew it the Captain had depressed the seatbelt sign allowing them to move around the cabin.

"Ladies and gentlemen, the Captain has turned off the Fasten Seat Belt sign, and you may now move around the cabin. However, we always recommend to keep your seat belt fastened while you're seated. The yellow button is your reading light. Please don't press the orange button unless you absolutely have to. The orange button is your ejector seat button. I'm sure I'm not the only one who would be sad to see you go.

In a few moments, the flight attendants will be passing around the cabin to offer you hot or cold drinks, as well as light snack. Alcoholic drinks are also available at a nominal charge. Please don't try and pretend to be old enough when you're not. We have young detectors now fully equipped on all our carts. Trust me you don't want to have to experience that, it hurts! Now, sit back, relax, and enjoy the flight. Thank you."

Making her way to the kitchen to help the rest of the crew with prepping drink and snack carts, in no time at all, they had everything ready and started making their rounds. Each one had their own area and were happy to help in any way. As Sam neared her first row she started passing out drinks as usual. As she approached the fourth row, she felt a hand touch her elbow. This wasn't anything abnormal, because people always needed something from them. As she turned she saw a strong jaw and a hint of a smile. Traveling up the obviously male face, she met the coolest blue eyes. They looked like the sky on a clear day, and they called her into them like the wardrobe, called

Lucy to Narnia. She would ever be lost in them. If that wasn't enough then he spoke. "I vould like to ask you more about zee detector on your cart. I imagine it vould be fun for me to experience new things, no?" His accent had a hint of French to it and made him all the more sexy. What was it about a good accent that could change the image of a person from bad to good or good to amazing?

"Ah, no I was just kidding about that device. Besides the humor in it, it deters any too young from trying, at least a little," Sam clarified. She was worried that with the language barrier she may have caused him to misunderstand a lot of her announcement.

"How you say, *tant pis*…I mean, that is too bad for me. I was quite intrigued by the zought of zat."

"Really? I can't imagine you'd want us to hurt you on purpose," she feigned naivety. He may very well be into that sort of thing.

"You cannot be sure of zat. I am fery intrigued by you, *valoir le coup*, it could be fery wors my time."

"What is your name?"

"My name is, Philippe. I am traveling for business een zee next few days. I will be back een Chicago een a few days."

"Why would you tell me that? Are you planning on being on my flight back to town?"

"Zat could fery well be a possibility. I may just buy a ticket on every return flight to Chicago, just to try my luck."

"What? You can't do that it would cost a small fortune."

"*Pas de problème*, that ees no problem for me. As I said, you are a creature who has piqued my eenterest. Why would I not want to see such a beautiful woman as yourself, eef given zee chance?"

Sam knew she should be alarmed by this man's behavior, she had surely been flirted with before, but this was different. There was just something about a man with an accent that made one want to believe there was minimal danger. "I could save you a lot of money and time by telling you which flight I will be on returning to Chicago." She really should be a more cautious person or at the very least get back to work and not continue this conversation. She still had a few rows to take care of with snacks and drinks. "Can I get you a drink or a snack?" she asked Philippe, so she was at least still working.

He shook his head to turn down the drink, "Zat would make sings easier for me, *si tu veux*, eef you would.

"I'll let you know if I decide it is worth it for me," Sam sashayed away without another word or backward glance.

She had stopped to talk too long, now she was in a hurry to pick up speed. Most of the other attendants were finished or close to it.

A couple hours later, the flight was coming to an end. The pilot was making his approach so Sam would need to make a final announcement before they could land.

"Ladies and gentlemen, we have just been cleared to land at the New York, John F. Kennedy Airport. Please make sure one last time your seat belt is securely fastened. The flight attendants are currently passing around the cabin to make a final compliance check and pick up any remaining cups and glasses. Thank you."

The passengers were all readying themselves to land and Sam still hadn't decided if she would pass along information to Philippe or just see if he follows through on his original plan. As the plane landed the Captain came over the speaker, "Thank you all for flying with us, we are currently recruiting people to clean the aircraft. If you wish to volunteer then please stand before we have come to a stop. The flight attendants will be happy to help you from that point on." The crowd laughs softly at the Captain's joke as the system clicked, the pilot went back to his regularly scheduled job of getting the passengers to their terminal safely.

"Ladies and gentlemen, again welcome to JFK Airport. Local time is eleven thirty-five am and the temperature is seventy degrees. For your safety and those you might fall on, please keep your seatbelt fastened until the Captain turns off the Fasten Seat Belt sign. This will indicate that we have parked at the gate and that it is safe for you to move about. Cellular phones may only be used once the Fasten Seat Belt sign has been turned off.

Please make sure you take all of your belongings with you. Anything left behind will be distributed evenly among the flight attendants. Please don't leave children or spouses. Please use caution when opening the overhead bins, as heavy articles may have shifted around during the flight.

If you require deplaning assistance, please remain in your seat until all other passengers have deplaned. One of our crew members will then be pleased to assist you.

On behalf of our airline and the entire crew, it has been great having you flying with us today. But just like my Dad said to me the day I turned eighteen, get out. Have a nice day!"

Making her way through the cabin, Sam and the other attendants helped the passengers clean up and gather their belongings. The Captain made it to the terminal and turned off the Fasten Seatbelt Sign. All the passengers patiently made their way to the door. Sam stood at the door with a smile bidding them all farewell and thanking them for flying with them.

As she made her way back through the cabin to check for lost items and clean up for the next flight. She was startled to see Philippe, sitting in his seat quietly. "Is there something wrong, Philippe?"

"*Au Contraire*, on the contrary, I was just waiting for you to assist me as your message conveyed. You did say eef one needed assistance we should remain een our seats, no?"

"I did say that, what assistance did you require?" she was worried where this was going, but was willing to play along.

"You were considering a possible way to make my next few days easier, were you not? I was merely waiting for your response."

"Oh, I see, well I hardly know you and it wouldn't be prudent to give all information to a stranger, but seeing as how you are going to do your research anyway. How about I save you a little money and time. I'll tell you I'm returning to Chicago O'Hare from JFK in a reverse flight plan of my schedule this week, Thursday. I'm running four days and then home for my time off." She didn't give everything away, but gave him enough information that someone who is determined and has the necessary means, will figure it out."

"Zat ees understandable, I appreciate zee eenformation you have given and I will put eet to good use. I will see you een four days." With that he got up and made his way to the door of the plane. He glanced back and winked at her and a knowing grin spread across his face. *Seriously? He can't mean that he is going to make every effort and spend mass amounts of money to make sure he is on that flight.*

The days passed with little excitement. She had normal passengers, no more strange men approaching her with magical accents, and eyes that could hypnotize with little effort. She gave minimal thought to Philippe, as the odds were not in his favor that he would be able to discern which flight she would be working, with the minimal information she gave him. On the other hand, she half hoped he would succeed. She'd never had a man work so hard to be near her. Usually they were out for instant gratification, and weren't willing to put in the effort for anything else.

As Sam boarded her flight a few days later, she found herself scanning the seats in hopes of seeing a particular Frenchman. When she didn't meet his eyes, her shoulders slumped in disappointment. *I knew he wouldn't be here, why am I so disappointed.*

A little bit later when she was giving her safety speech adding in new phrases such as, "If you are sitting next to a small child, or someone who is acting like a small child, please do us all a favor and put your own mask on first" and "Above your head are the control buttons for your reading light and the flight attendant call button. The reading light button will switch your light on and off. Yet no matter how many times you push the other one, it will not turn on your flight attendants," all in an effort to produce a laugh. Just then, she glanced around the cabin and her eyes met a familiar set of eyes. As if in a trance, she stumbled though the remaining portion of her presentation. Sam tried to wrap up quickly, so as not to look even more foolish, and made her way to the back of the plane to hide.

She kept her face away from the entrance in order to avoid attention. *I can't believe I acted like that. I'm more professional than this. I must have just made the biggest fool out of myself. Any chance I had is toast now.* Not really sure why she was thinking these things because he obviously liked her enough to go through the trouble of getting a flight back home on her plane. Whatever his motivation, could a simple slip make him run screaming?

When she was finished berating herself she straightened her clothes and smoothed her hair, in an attempt to put herself back together. She put her game face back on and was ready to face the crowd of people who had just witnessed her tongue-tied mess. As she turned around to face the entrance to the attendant station she gasped as she was startled to see Philippe.

"*Ma poupette*, ees everyzing alright?" Philippe said with a devilish smirk. Sam could only imagine what trouble a man like this would cause in her life. He seemed to be the kind of man who would get his way without a word. With just the curve of his mouth, he could have his way in any situation.

Feeling completely frazzled, she didn't know what to say at first. She hesitated and just took in his handsome face. He was wearing a dark blue button up shirt and charcoal slacks. He must be a businessman of some sort seeing as he is dressed up for a flight. He seems to play the part no matter what. This is obviously not a business trip for him, but he was willing to let others believe that.

"I'm fine," she faked a calm she didn't feel. "I just wanted to hurry back here and get my drink tray ready. It is a full flight and I didn't want to be behind from the start."

"I see. I was not sure eef you 'ad not seen me or eef you were merely 'iding from me."

"No not at all, I saw you. This is just the busiest part of the flight, and with it being so full, it will be even worse. I would have come up to speak with you as soon as everything settled down. Unfortunately, you aren't in my section today."

"Well zat will not do. I will make arrangements to rectify zat shortly." With that he disappeared from the room.

What does he mean by that? He can't make any arrangements midflight. Sam busied herself in an attempt to refocus her attention to prep her tray and make her rounds.

As Sam approached her coach class section she met faces with her usual smile. She offered each person a snack or a drink. It wasn't a long flight so no meals needed to be prepared or delivered. The occasional person requested a pillow due to being up for hours for this reason or that. She made her way through her section working methodically, but when she looked up and was startled to see Philippe sitting in the aisle seat along the center of the plane. He had chosen the most spacious area next to an emergency exit, but it still was nowhere near as comfortable as his previous first class seat. Why did he move to a lower-class seating? He was going to be cramped for the entire flight.

"What are you doing back here?" she uttered on a hiss of a whisper, trying to not to be heard by the passengers nearby.

"Deed I not say I was going to make zis arrangement? I zought I was perfectly clear. I wanted to be near you for zis flight so I offered my seat to a woman who looked like she could use some comfort een 'er life. She, I assure you, ees much 'appier een my seat, and I am much 'appier in 'ers, as well."

Feeling more than embarrassed that this has occurred purely because of her. She quickly offered refreshments to the couple occupying the inside seats of Philippe's row. Not ignoring him at this point, but definitely not paying attention to him. She needed to clear her head. He was putting a lot of effort into all of this, and she still didn't fully understand why. It was beginning to stress her out. She needed a moment to breathe.

The flight continued with little excitement. Sam kept up her routines and finished her tasks with ease. The guests were assisted to her level of care and her unexpected guest was keeping to himself. She expected him to be a tad bit needier, given the fact that he did cause some commotion at the beginning of the flight.

When the flight came in for a landing she wasn't surprised to see that he waited after all the passengers disembarked. She was making her rounds to clean up the plane for the next flight when he spoke, "Poupette, you are persuaded of my eententions, no?"

"What do you mean? I have figured out that you are persistent, I'll give you that."

"Does zat mean you will allow me to escort you to dinner?"

"Are you serious? I don't know you and you don't know me. Why would you want to take me to dinner?"

"Zat ees exactly why. I want to get to know you better."

"This is crazy. I don't date passengers, usually. It's not something that is very logical in my line of work."

"When 'as a passenger gone to zis much trouble to take you to dinner?"

Sam considered his question carefully. If she answered wrong she would back herself into a corner and not be able to work her way out. He was very attractive, but was it worth letting him into her life even for one night? Some of the girls dated from work, but Sam never thought it was the wisest thing to do. Did she really want crazies following her home or knowing the neighborhood she lived in? The more she thought about it the more she realized, her gut was right. Dating from the passenger list was a bad decision.

"Phillippe, I'm flattered, really I am, but this isn't the best decision for me. At least not right now."

"Well zan I suppose I will have to figure out where you will be after your vacation time."

"Do you realize how much that sounds like a stalker?" Sam decided she would need to worry a bit more about this guy. Then she remembered how much money he probably had and thought that he was just bored. Rich people liked to find things to spend money on for just entertainment purposes. That is probably all she was to him, his next plan for something to do. What if she decided to go out with him? He could get his fill and then move on to his next source of pleasure and spend more money on her. He seemed like the type who just didn't like to be told no. What could it hurt?

"If I agree to one date with you, will you let it be if no sparks fly?"

"But of course. Alzough I'd like to eenform you zat sparks always fly when I'm around. It's a bit hard to resist zee allure, zat ees me."

"Wow, nothing like a guy who doesn't need a compliment. You've got that covered by leaps and bounds. Ok, I'll only agree if you let me pick the location. I promise you it won't meet your standards, but I insist on this one thing." Sam wasn't going to give an inch on this. She had a new rule and safety was her top priority. She took all her dates in one place where she felt comfortable and knew if she needed an escape plan, someone was always there for her. She was so glad she met Tania; she had definitely been a lifesaver. Nick on the other hand, not so much. He would probably just laugh at her through a bad situation if he was asked for help. Worst case scenario she could hide in the bathroom until the coast was clear, but that was a coward's way out. She would only use that in a last resort situation.

"I will go anywhere you want to go. I am at your mercy. Just name the location and I will be zer with, how you say, bells on? I never understood that expression."

Sam sighed at his candor and wondered if this date was going to be lost in translation, but gave him the information for Joe's Bar, nonetheless. They made plans to meet tonight at seven thirty. She promised him dinner and that was more than she had granted most of her dates of late. She hoped she hadn't made a horrible mistake.

Evening came quicker than Sam had hoped, after she got off work she had a hard time finding a cab to take her home. There was an influx of vacationers making their way to Chicago this weekend for some reason or another. Flight attendants had a rule, they had to let the passengers have transportation first if they were on leave. If they were headed to another flight or getting to a hotel for the night they had a shuttle, but any personal time they were on their own. By the time she got home and unpacked she only had a couple hours before her date. It made for a long day. She was tired and not sure she had the patience for her date tonight. Unfortunately, Phillipe hadn't given her a phone number and she hadn't shared hers with him. It wasn't a priority since they were meeting at the bar.

Going through her closet felt like a chore. So she decided to take a shower first. Hoping that she would have more energy by the time she got out. If not, it wasn't going to be a good sign for their date tonight. The water was warm and inviting, just what she needed after a long day. She wondered, *why didn't I do this as soon as I got home? This is just what I needed after the day I had.* The water flowed over her, massaging her muscles and working out the kinks she didn't even know were there. It was perfect. By the time she got out, she was more than ready to take on this date. She remembered how handsome Phillippe was and couldn't wait to see him again.

She selected a cream-colored dress out of her closet. Since she had picked a less fancy establishment than she supposed he was used to, she was going to try to dress up the date in other ways. The way this dress draped her skin was as though it was a second skin. She could move with ease, but it gave the illusion of restriction. She loved how it hugged her body and gave her a sense of sensuality that she lacked at times. She paired it with a pair of flaming red heels. Just a pop of color to draw the attention from her curves to the length of her legs. She hated when an outfit caused the observer to linger too long in certain areas, she wanted them to take her in as a whole. That meant her whole body and not just the common places. To help with the story of her clothes, Sam opted to wear her hear down in soft waves. Nothing too dramatic, wanting them to make it to the dress and the rest of her ensemble.

After putting the finishing touches into her appearance, she felt like she was a model prepared for the runway, but when meeting up with someone like Phillippe, it felt like a necessity to dress the part. To be on his arm and underdressed seemed like blasphemy.

Under any other circumstance, Sam would feel uncomfortable. She knew she would be overdressed for the bar that she always chose, but that was her comfort zone and she wouldn't stray from it.

As always, she arrived a few minutes early. She never wanted to be the last one to arrive and miss out on the possible chance to run if need be. Tania was working and that made Sam feel that much more at ease. She had a good relationship with the waitress and Sam enjoyed the nights Tania worked all the more. Not to mention, Tania was a great 'wing-girl', in that she has been known to save Sam from her awful dates.

"Back for more punishment?" Tania knew what was happening. Sam might make a trip in here this week just for her and to throw everyone else off her scent. They all seemed to know what was happening if she came in.

"Won't know what you can't handle if you don't put yourself through it."

"You are all dolled up for this one. Is he drop-dead gorgeous or just trying to make a certain kind of impression? Tania winked at her and made a curvy gesture with her hands over her own hips.

"Gorgeous and then some, this one is French."

"Ooh La La!" she wagged her eyebrows at Sam and laughed. "Well then, I can't wait to see this one."

"Trust me, it is worth it. Can I get a cranberry and vodka? I'm feeling sophisticated tonight. I feel like I have to play this part right."

"If he doesn't like you for you and all your drinking habits, then he doesn't deserve you, girl." Truer words were never spoken and one day Sam would believe them through and through. Unfortunately, today wasn't that day. Tania left to get her drink and Sam was left to wait.

She didn't have to wait long, Phillippe came in looking like an Armani model. He was absolutely dreamy, even a little dangerous at the same time. Sam wondered if this date was a good idea or if she bit off more than she could chew.

"*Ma poupette*, eet ees wonderful to zee you. You look amazing zis evening." Phillippe had a wonderful flourish even in the way he carried himself.

"You don't look so bad yourself. I didn't know you could make a suit look this good even when that is all I've ever seen you wear." Sam was glad she wasn't a blusher because she could say mostly whatever she thought without obvious embarrassment.

Phillippe took his seat at the bar top table, "Zis establishment ees fery shabby chic, no?" Tania made her way over and her eyes got bigger the closer she got to their table.

"Hey there handsome, what can I get you to drink this evening?" Tania was in her element and didn't seem to be concerned with what others thought of her.

"Could I please 'ave a Weeskey Sour?"

"Doll, you could ask me for anything and I'd figure out how to get it for you. I'll get that right out for you.

Phillippe turned back to Sam and smiled. "Words cannot express 'ow beauteeful you are zis evening."

Sam smiled sweetly, but decided to pursue other topics of conversation. "Thank you. So, what is it you do for a living?"

"I do not want to talk aboot work tonight. What do you do for fun, *Mon petit poil de cul*."

"I don't have a lot of free time, but when I do get some I love to walk along the riverfront. What does that term mean? I don't believe I've ever heard it before."

"Oh, zat? It means my little buttér."

Sam was confused, perhaps this meant he had a strange attachment to food condiments. She didn't know exactly how to respond to she smiled and volleyed the conversation back to him.

"Do you get to travel back home to France frequently or do you keep too busy here in the states?"

"I traval to Marseille, every ozer weekend. Eet ees a commitment I made to my family at a fery early age. When I started my company, I wanted to make sure my family was never neglected."

"That is very responsible of you. How old were you when you started your company?"

"Even zo I said I deed not want to speak of work, I will answer your question. I was twenty-two when I left 'ome and started my business."

"To make that commitment to your family at such a young age speaks volumes about your character. I have just seen you through new eyes."

"*Ma crotte*, you do not need too zee me through new eyes, your old ones are magnifique."

Sam was starting to become rather concerned about how he was acting. He couldn't carry on a serious conversation to save his life. Every time they got remotely involved in a subject he would change it and call her a pet name. Should she be concerned about these names? Did they mean he was more interested than she thought?

Tania came by to ask about a second round, "So I hope all is going well, you two look absolutely adorable together. You are getting quite cozy over here." Contrary to popular belief, she wasn't actually looking at the two of them. She was looking straight at Sam to get any visual cues that she might need rescue. Sam shook her head subtly indicating she had this under control. Phillippe might be acting strange, but it all could just be lost in translation.

As the evening progressed they had a few too many drinks and Phillippe started getting a bit handsy. Sam didn't know exactly how to handle this situation because she was afraid with his native language she might be misunderstood. She let it go for a few more minutes, but finally she had enough.

"Phillippe, I'm afraid you are getting the wrong idea about this date. I'm not a rush to the bedroom kind of girl."

Phillippe's face took on a strange distortion. Sam got extremely nervous. What had she done? All she wanted was for him to back off a little without hurting his feelings or a chance at a second date. What was she going to do now? She had already brushed Tania off and sent her away with confidence that she had this under control. Now she was in a situation she didn't know how to get out of. Phillippe was ultimately a stranger before tonight and she didn't know what his temperament was. Did he usually get his way? Had he never heard the word "NO" before?

Phillippe stood abruptly and threw a wad of cash on the table. He looked at her as though she had grown horns. Sam prepared for the worst.

"My meestake, I zought you were a *putain!*" With that he stormed out of the bar without another word. Sam was stunned to silence. Did he really just walk out on her? No explanation or anything to help her understand.

Tania made her way back over to the table. She took in Sam's stunned face, "What happened?"

"I'm not exactly sure. It all went well up until he started getting really hands on. I chalked it up to a few to many whiskey sours, but then it was getting to be too much. So, I just laid it out there and told him I wasn't going to sleep with him."

"You said it flat out like that?"

"No, I was tactful about it and told him I wasn't that kind of girl. Then he got very hot in the face and I got a little worried."

"Did you think he was going to hit you?"

"No, but I couldn't rule it out since I don't really know him that well. What if he's never been turned down before?"

"There's a first time for everything, hun." Tania laughed and started gathering up the extra drink glasses so she wouldn't look like she was just standing there.

"Anyway, on that note, basically he left and called me something in French and stormed out."

"What did he call you?"

"I don't know. I don't speak French. In fact, he called me a lot of names tonight that were kind of lost on me."

"You do know that Google can translate all of those for you, don't you?"

"I was so caught up in the moment and the thought that it sounded so pretty to hear him speak in his native language, that I didn't really think that far."

"Well, get your butt out of my table and head up to the bar. You can use this time to reflect and Google away." Tania wasn't one to sugar coat things and that was one things Sam really loved about her.

Sam drug herself up from the table. As good as her evening had started it ended in utter failure. Now she felt like she was out of place in the bar now. Quietly trying to sit down unnoticed, she broke out her phone and started listing out the names he called her. *Ma poupette, mon petit poil de cul, ma crotte, putain* were all things he said to her. She was almost nervous to look up the translations. Was she ready to know what these beautiful sounding words meant?

Before she could lose her nerve, she typed in the first one. Well this wasn't so bad, "my dolly" ironically, Tania had called him "doll" earlier this evening. Sam thought that maybe she had overheard him and knew that term. She would have to remember to ask her later.

With a false sense of bravery, she typed in the second one, immediately she regretted that decision. "WHAT! He said this meant butter!" She distinctly remembered asking him about that one. Instead of "butter" this meant "my little butt hair" and Sam was beyond disgusted with his term of…endearment? Is that what people in relationships do? Do they call each other strange pet names just because it's quirky? If that was the case, Sam might be rethinking her decision to settle down.

Nick made his way over, "Hey, Princess. Are you dressing the part now?" he asked glancing up and down her upper half that he could see. She glanced down out of habit and forced herself not to cover her cleavage, not that it wasn't tasteful. If he was going to look she would let him get an eyeful.

"I suppose I am," she was inadvertently short with him and regretted it instantly.

"Wow, this one must have been a doozy. You are in rare form tonight, Princess."

"I really wish you wouldn't call me that. Can I have a beer, please?"

She ignored him and proceeded to torture herself further and looked up the third one. She rolled her eyes and tried not to let herself get any angrier. "My little turd! Seriously, what is wrong with this guy. Are all Frenchmen this insane?"

Nick returned with her drink and placed it in front of her. "Did I just hear you say Frenchmen?"

"Yes, my date this evening was an insane Frenchman, who had a strange sense of humor. At least I hope he was trying to be funny."

"Do I really want to know about this one?"

"Well, to give you an idea, he went from calling me a doll to calling me a turd. He also made me believe he was calling me butter, but that was lost on me between his accent because he actually called me his little butt hair! Who does that?"

Nick couldn't help but burst out laughing loudly. His laugh was rich and full. It vibrated the space around her and it gave her tingles in places she should be tamping down. "You must be setting a record."

"What do you mean?"

"A record for the most insane date stories ever."

"Yes, of course I am. That was my goal all along. I planned this to the most minute detail. I sent out a survey for all the men in the area to fill out. I only chose the top players and I'm planning on writing a book of memoirs." This was dripping with as much sarcasm as she could get in there.

"With all this material, you should."

"Well, I have one more to translate care to stick around? Perhaps you could even add a drumroll. I'm sure it will be worthy."

Sam typed putain into the translator and waited the few seconds for it to appear. Without saying a word, she laid the phone down in front of her facing Nick. He glanced down and read it aloud, "Whore? Seriously? This guy is a real winner. You sure know how to pick them."

Sam put her head on the bar and didn't answer him. She couldn't believe Phillippe thought she was a whore. What gave him that impression? Were all the other flight attendants on his other trips very easy to get into bed?

Not waiting for her to make eye contact again, Nick started mixing a drink. She chose not to look up to watch him mix it. He was either making it for her or for someone else and at this point she didn't care. All she wanted to do was wallow in her misery. When she looked up to guzzle her beer her eyes met Nick's perfect blue pools. He wasn't pitying her or even being mean. He just had a look of calm. How could he be so calm after all I've gone through? He just read what I had been called tonight and he has no emotion over it? At that moment, she blinked breaking the spell. He reached over and set a glass in front of her.

"Do I dare ask what that is?"

"If you don't, it takes away my pleasure in making it."

"OK, fine tell me."

"It is a 'Bitter Frenchman' it's made with gin, Campari, simple syrup and dry champagne. This one is so simple even you could make it. Just please, promise you will use plastic to avoid broken glass."

"Well where is the fun in that?" she didn't usually banter with him, but for some reason she was feeling better after doing it. Did she derive some sick pleasure from this? What was happening to her?

"Ok, then make it with a friend. That way you can avoid bleeding out on the floor with no one to find you."

"What makes you think I live alone?"

"You're right I don't know for sure, but seeing as you never have a person call or pick you up after your tragic dates, I'm going to assume you have a short list of people most of whom you wouldn't call unless you were dying and maybe not even then."

"Wow, when you put like that, I sound like I'm borderline the crazy cat lady, minus the cats. That just makes me crazy and I'm not sure I like your tone."

"I think you like being told how it is. Maybe that is what is wrong with your dates. That you just can't handle the guys who are too big of a pussy to hold their ground with you."

"What are you saying now? You seem like you can't figure out if you want to tell me how it is or just make fun of me. Is this your way of making fun of me now? Are you going to insult my date choices rather than defend the guys who's hearts I'm obviously breaking?

"No, I just think you need to screen them better. You seem to date guys who are either compensating for something or aren't man enough to hold their own."

"So, you're saying you know this from experience of someone on the outside looking in. These guys are what you aren't so you can objectively judge?"

"I wouldn't say objectively, but I can obviously see what they are lacking. You seem to need a man who is confident enough to talk to you and still be down to earth. Not someone who puts on a show or hides behind what they think you want."

"For a guy who doesn't seem to be in a relationship, you seem to act like quite the know-it-all about them."

"I might not be in a relationship currently, but that doesn't mean I haven't ever been in one or know how to make a relationship flourish."

Sam sipped her drink, it wasn't something she would have ordered for herself, but it was definitely good in a dry sort of way. Her eyebrows raised and she nodded her approval. Nick walked away to check on other customers allowing her to have time with her thoughts and her drinks.

Why do I keep getting myself in the situations? First, I thought it was just my taste in men, but I went for a completely different type and he wasn't an online find. I still ended up regretting it and this time I feel so stupid about it.

She spent the next few minutes drinking her Bitter Frenchman and mulling over life itself. This dating side of her life was becoming a hassle. Finishing off her special drink and moving back to her beer, Sam realized that she wasn't a quitter. She needed to push through the bad to get through the good. Just like in other aspects of her life. The good didn't just fall in her lap she needed to work through whatever came her way, eventually she would find what she was looking for. Then she would get to live her happily ever after. She refused to believe they didn't exist after everything one goes through in life, everyone deserves happiness.

Chapter 5

Sam awoke the next morning with a splitting headache. Gripping her head, she thought, *why did I let myself drink so much? Mental note, don't drink more than two or three drinks on a date, before or after.* With every motion, she felt a slicing through her brain. She decided she was going to need coffee before she could move on to anything else that day. Making her way to the kitchen she was thankful for Captain John Smith, who brought the first coffee to America in 1607. That has made for a much improved four hundred plus years. Sam rolled her eyes, "Thank you to my high school history teacher for the random factoids that I don't need with a hangover. The extra brain power that I had to use while in pain to spew that was a bit much."

Trying her best not to exert any extra brain power, Sam went about making herself a cup of coffee. As she sat at her kitchen table, she took her first blissful sip of coffee. Sam closed her eyes taking in all the elements of her sip. The steam on her face billowing from her cup. The bitter aroma relaxed her muscles instantly. There was just something about the smell of a good cup of brew that could take a day from bad to good.

After she had consumed enough to function, Sam decided to check her dating app. She remembered enough about last night that she had promised herself to not give up. To her surprise she had a lot of hearts on her profile page. She never would have expected to have garnered so much attention. She started scrolling through who had hearted her picture and realized that not all of them were bad looking or outside of her comfort zone, but she wasn't going to fall for pretty faces again. She planned to do some research first.

Systematically, she worked through the list and moved on to messages. She had five messages. Most were one liners, *Hey you're hot! Wanna meet up?* Then some a few more eloquent, *I thought your picture was the best thing I've seen all day. I'd love to take you out for drinks and see what develops.* Unfortunately, she wasn't swayed by a pretty face and promise of a good time. She was determined to dig deeper. She found one guy who had a handsome face which is a good starting point, but it looked like he almost had an old soul. She had been told a time or two that she had an 'old soul', but she never really knew what that meant, until now. He had kind eyes that showed his compassion, but his strong jaw gave the illusion of power. Could this guy actually be worth the struggle? He hadn't sent her a message, but had hearted her profile. She had yet to make the first move online, but was it really the first move if he clicked on her first?

Rather than overthink the situation, Sam clicked to open a new message screen. She was hesitant to type because she didn't want it to sound professional, like a work email, but she didn't want to come across like the people she immediately wrote off. Nerves started to kick in and her palms got sweaty. What was wrong with her? She didn't get this nervous on a first date. Snapping herself out of it, she began to type. *I'm not sure how to start this, I'm new to online dating. I saw your picture and was in awe. Your face gives me the feeling that you and I share a bond. You and I possess what they say are old souls. I'm not sure if anyone has ever told you that, but it really spoke to me. I would love the opportunity to learn more about you, to see if your personality speaks to me the same way your face does.*

Sam worried that she sounded like a creepy stalker, but instead of lingering on it, she clicked send and hoped for the best.

The day moved slowly since Sam spent most of the morning in hangover fog. If nothing else she had a constant reminder as to why over-drinking because of a bad date is a bad idea. Of course, she remembered this happening a time or two before and she had yet to learn from her mistakes. In the moment, she forgot the smartest advice she had ever given herself then always paid the price afterward.

As the afternoon progressed, she forced herself out of bed and into the kitchen to eat food. It never failed that greasy and salty foods would be her cure-all when she was sick from the brown bottle flu. Logically, one would think it would make you worse, but it actually did the opposite and settled her stomach. Here favorite were McDonald's French fries, but unfortunately, she wasn't in any shape to be going outside. She hadn't showered and she still looked like death warmed over. There was no telling who she might bump into on that outing and so she settled for making herself a cheeseburger from the frozen patties she kept in her freezer just for these situations. One bite of the burger made her moan, as she realized this was the first thing she had eaten since yesterday at lunch. Second mental note, *eat before dates to avoid possible over-drinking due to no food consumption.*

As Sam finished up with her burger quicker than she would have liked, her phone chimed an alert. She wiped her hands on the napkin to avoid getting any of the beloved grease on her screen. Picking up her phone, she was pleased and surprised at the same time. It was a message from her online suitor. He must not have taken her message as creepy after all. His message was sweet and she decided she made a decent choice. Only time would tell if it was fate, destiny or any of that mumbo jumbo that people always speak of when they find their 'the one'.

As usual she liked to get her dates planned on her days off and sooner rather than later. So, they decided to meet up tonight at Joe's Bar. He was a local and knew the place well. Maybe she would recognize him when she gets there. Pictures could be deceptive as much as they speak a thousand words some of those words could be photoshopped these days. One couldn't be too careful when it came to online dating. Sam was considering if she needed to invest in some pepper spray in order to ward off unwanted followers.

After Sam started to feel better the day went by faster. She was excited about her date and anxious at the same time. She didn't know which emotion was better or if she was setting herself up for failure by allowing either to penetrate her senses.

Opting for something less formal since the previous night she felt way over dressed for the bar, Sam chose a pair of jeans that hugged her every curve like a glove. These pants left little to the imagination, but they made her feel pretty. Since they were so snug she picked out a peek-a-boo tunic that exposed her shoulders. Not wanting to draw too much attention, she went with muted colors, more greyscale. After putting on minimal makeup, Sam decided to opt out of her contacts tonight. She didn't wear her glasses very often, but after feeling like crud all day she couldn't get her eyes to cooperate. So instead of fighting her itchy, dry eyes, glasses were the next best things.

Sitting in her regular spot at Joe's, it was as though they had started saving this table just for her. *I'll have to ask Tania about that. A different waitress approached her table to take her drink order.*

"What can I get you to drink dearie?

"Can I have a coke to start? I think I over did it last night I'm planning to start slower tonight. Is Tania off tonight?"

"Yeah, she picks one night a week to have off, but she never takes the same night consistently. She has regulars and doesn't want to miss them, but management makes her take one day off a week no questions asked. Most days she doesn't even give anyone any real notice. She just flips out days with another girl at the last minute, like tonight. She's been with Joe so long he pretty much lets her have free reign, but he figured out a long time ago that she is so addicted to this place she would live here if it were allowed."

"Wow that is work dedication. Sounds like she needs to work on having a life outside of work. I might have to make that a pet project."

"Definitely, well I'll go grab your drink."

With that the waitress turned and walked away from her table. Sam fiddled with her coaster as she waited for her date, Richard, to arrive. Moments later her drink was placed on the coaster, taking away her fidget device. She always though those spinners were stupid, but right now she wished she had one or something similar. Anything at this point to keep her nervous fingers busy.

A little while later, an older gentleman approached her table. "Sam?"

"Uh, yes," she hesitated unsure who this man was. He looked familiar, but she couldn't put her finger on where from. Perhaps he was a passenger or one of her mom's friends.

"I'm Richard, it's a pleasure to meet you."

Sam didn't answer right away, she blindly shook his hand unsure of what to say or how to act. This was not the handsome young man with an old soul she saw pictured on her online app. In her head, she wished she had left the page open on her phone so she could discretely glance at it to be sure, but it was a little difficult to miss. This guy was not in his twenties at all. It looked more like she was having dinner with her father than a potential suitor.

"Obviously, I'm not what you were expecting, but let me explain before you freak out, I guess more than you already are." Sam still didn't speak she just stared at him. He had released her hand and she just let it settle onto the table, but she didn't really pull it back or move it much at all. She just sat stunned waiting for him to explain whatever it was he thought was going to help this situation.

"The picture I have on my profile is me, but it's one I had taken in my youth. I used it because it speaks more about who I am rather than who people see me to be. I work with younger people and I've figured out I'm a twenty-five-year-old stuck in my fifty-year-old body. I've made a choice to only surround myself with people my emotional age. Some may not understand, but after talking to you online, I had a good feeling about you."

Sam was at a loss for words, he essentially lied about his age. *Who does that?* Sam became more and more infuriated by the second. There was nothing left to contain her rage. All that was left was to enlighten him.

"What made you think it was ok to lie to people? Your picture is the first thing people see and whether any one wants to admit it, is the first deciding factor to know if we are going to talk to you. So, to post a picture that isn't actually you now, is worse than just lying about your age. Now, I'm here thinking I'm on a date and everyone else thinks you are a creeper or I'm having dinner with my dad. How in your mind, was that even remotely ok?"

Richard was a bit startled by her reaction, to say the least. "I'm not sure what to say. I thought we had a connection online and that this wouldn't matter to you."

"Wouldn't matter to me? Did you give me a chance prior to now that I could have been warned and then in turn given you the impression it wouldn't matter to me?"

"I just neglected to mention my biological age and show you a picture of me now. I still showed you a picture of me at the age I feel. You are still getting what I offered, the twenty-five-year-old is who I am. Portraying myself in a way that I feel, isn't lying."

Sam had to actively keep her voice down because she was getting more and more angry. She didn't want to share this conversation with the tables around her. "You aren't lying to yourself I suppose, but by taking away my chance to decide if I was ok with it, you lied to me by default."

"I think you are overreacting. If you would just take a chance to get to know me then you would see it's a non-issue."

Sam couldn't handle it anymore, more than anything she hated when people told her when she was overreacting. She was an adult and had every right to be feeling the way she was no matter what anyone else believed.

"I think this date has gone on long enough." With that she stood from the table and didn't spare him another glance. She stormed off and headed straight to the bar away from him, hoping beyond hope that he wouldn't follow her. She didn't care if he left or stayed.

Laying her head on the bar, Sam didn't care if there were any spilled drinks or any other sticky substances, that may now be sticking to her face and hair. She had promised herself she wouldn't give up, but she never made any commitments about not wallowing in self-pity. Amidst everything she didn't hear Nick approach her end of the bar.

"You look like you need something strong tonight. Care to tell me what happened?"

Sam didn't even pick her head up to acknowledge him. She wasn't ready to come out of her head yet. No one could say anything that would change the way she felt at that moment. All that mattered to her was staying locked inside herself where no one could hurt her, at least for a while longer. Nick got quiet, so she assumed he got the hint and walked back to the other side to help other customers. A moment later she felt something cold on her arm. Startled she jumped and flailed her arm back, only to knock a full glass of beer onto the bar top, pouring its contents all over herself.

Immediately she jumped off her stool trying to wipe off all the liquid, glancing up she saw Nick convulsing with laughter he fought to contain. Glaring at him, she finally spoke, "What the HELL! Why are you laughing at me? Can't you see I'm having one of the worst days in history?"

Nick in his infinite wisdom replied while shaking his head, "Now, don't you think that you're being a bit of a drama queen?"

"Don't you dare be that guy."

"What do you mean 'that guy'?" Sam couldn't blame him for being confused. She had spent the entire time at the bar in silence. He truly didn't know what she had been through that night.

"The guy that assumes that all girls overreact to bad situations."

"Ok, seeing as you are obviously having a rough night, I'll give you a little room. I don't believe it's all as bad as you're making it out to be, but I'm willing to listen." He threw his clean bar towel at her and proceeded to wipe up the spilled beer off the bar top.

"Well, seeing as you're being so generous I'll sit down and tell you why I'm being rational." She quickly wiped herself down as best she could, not caring that she was now going to smell like beer the rest of the night. It was the least of her concerns tonight.

When they had finished cleaning up, Sam took her seat again. Nick looked at her expectantly, "Can I get a new drink first? All I've had today is a soda and I probably need to add that to my tab over here. I'm not sure that bill has been settled up yet." He nodded his understanding and brought her a shot of Jack.

"Your other bill has been taken care of, I guess the poor sap you had tonight was nice enough to cover the bill."

Sam resigned herself to the fact that there was no way to make him understand without telling him the story, so she let her anger fizzle to a small glow under the surface. If he didn't understand after she told him the entire story, then she would give it a chance to smolder and take over at that time.

"Your reaction is understandable, but now are you willing to hear my side of the story?"

He nodded and she quickly threw back the shot, but with her sizzling anger she didn't even feel the burn as it slid down her throat. He raised an eyebrow at her, in question to how she didn't react to the drink. She didn't acknowledge his unspoken question.

"Tonight, was going to be a new start, it was supposed to be me proving to myself I had the ability to make good life choices. All of the rest of the dates, came to me and I was just more flattered that someone had actually asked me out, rather than deciding if I really liked them. Honestly, I think I need to go back further for you to understand why I'm truly upset." As Sam started to tell the tale, she found herself lost in her memories.

After a long talk with her best friend from college about her lack of a man in her life, Sam was feeling distraught. The evening had taken a turn down a more depressing road, then again that was why she was talking to Gabby anyway. Gabby always knew how to make her feel better. "You know my friend, Scott, is available?"

"Who is Scott, how have I not heard of him before?" Sam was getting a little excited at the prospect of a guy from their circle she hadn't met.

"Scott, he's a guy I used to work with. He's a bit shy, but super hot. Trust me you will like him. He's had every girl wrapped around his finger, for as long as I've known him. His height alone isn't something to shake a finger at. He is at least six-foot six and is always up for a pickup game of basketball. I used to love watching those guys on lunch break work up a sweat." She could tell Gabby was picturing glistening muscles and shirtless men. It was her favorite pasttime.

"Well, if he's single, what is wrong with him?" A guy that attractive shouldn't be on the market.

"He's playing the field a bit, but mostly just hasn't found the right girl yet. There is nothing wrong with that man. I'll give him your number if you want and you guys can see if you hit if off"

Days had passed and Sam was sure Scott wasn't interested, because he never called and Gabby didn't even call to let her down gently after finding out he wasn't into her. So, she moved on as usual, but then one evening her phone rang to an unknown number. On a whim, she went ahead and answered the call.

"Sam?" a husky male voice asked.

"This is she." Sam didn't know who this was and didn't know if it was a personal call or not.

"Uh, hey. This is Scott. I got your number from Gabby. I hope it's ok that I called."

"Oh of course, I thought Gabby had forgotten to give you my number. It's so nice to hear from you."

"Yeah, I'm sorry it took me so long to call. I hate phone calls, but I thought it would be rude to text a complete stranger. Not to mention I wanted to know the voice associated to the words on the screen."

"That makes sense, I have to confess I have a bad habit of texting more than calling now days. You are probably right, it would be best to hear the right voice in my head rather than make one up."

The conversation went on awkwardly for a few minutes before they couldn't take it and disconnected. Sam was worried, that she didn't make a good impression. There just wasn't a flow to the chat and it was easier to end the call rather than both of them suffer any longer.

A few days past, and she received a text alert. Much to her surprise, it was Scott.

What are you up to today?

That was actually, a pretty normal question and conversation starter. This became a norm for them. Small chats about nothing in particular. Then after a few months Sam was ready for more. They had gotten to know each other pretty well and flirted off and on. She was pretty sure he was into her on some level at least. It was time to move forward.

If you aren't busy tonight, do you want to come over and watch a movie?

She assumed it was an innocuous request and she wasn't pushing too hard.

I don't know.

He was always good for a one-liner response when he was likely to refuse. This wasn't the first time she had hinted at meeting, but this time she was doing more than hinting.

She was flat out asking, this was the furthest she had gone so far.

After much convincing, he got into his car and was on his way. She scrambled to get changed into something worthy of a first date, even though she wasn't sure that was what this was. He said he may not stay very long which would be discouraging for Sam, but she would count it as a victory just to see him for the first time.

They had exchanged pictures, but nothing was like the first time you laid eyes on a person. You could tell a lot about how you felt in that moment. As your eyes, locked and the brush of their hand to your own or the feel of their arms embracing you in a hug. So many emotions could travel through the body in one instant. That is something a picture couldn't do.

That night would be a night, Sam would never forget. Her text alert rang out again and she quickly retrieved her phone.

I can't do this. It's too much. I don't want to ruin what we have going for us. What if this changes everything?

Sam panicked, she couldn't believe he was really going to back out.

Where are you? You are probably almost here already. Let's just say hi face to face. Then you can decide from there.

Scott waited for what felt like an eternity to respond. She was sure she lost him to the black hole of over-thinking. Then when she was about to give up hope, her phone chimed.

I'm in the parking lot.

A simple response for having taken so long to answer. She didn't waste any time. She had seen a picture of his car once from when he was walking out from work, and he wanted to show off his 'baby'. Granted a dark colored car might be challenging to find in the complex parking lot, but she wasn't going to let that discourage her. This was the closest she had come to meeting Scott in person, she wasn't going to leave that to fate any longer.

She burst through the front door of her apartment and onto the sidewalk leading to the lot. Scanning back and forth, Sam tried to remember what cars belonged to tenants. The harder she looked the more worried she got. Surely, he wouldn't leave after telling her he was there, would he?

Sam ran to the end of the building and saw a man leaning against a dark car. He was tall, but not your average tall, more of a basketball player lean and legs that stretched on for miles. His light-colored hair was blowing slightly in the evening breeze. He didn't move right away, as though he didn't want her to notice him, but that he just wanted to watch and take her in one breath at a time.

Sam stopped, somehow even though she couldn't see his face she knew it was him. Everything about him that she knew was radiating from him. She started in his direction at a slow walk. That didn't last because just knowing he was there meant more to her than anything and it was as though a magnetic force was bringing them together.

When she got about half way to him she increased her speed. He immediately pushed off the car and headed toward her. When they stood mere inches apart no words were spoken. He swept her up into his embrace into the air. His lips came crashing down over hers and she was lost in the most passionate kiss she had ever received. It felt like they were long lost lovers and they were reconnecting after years away. When they were together nothing else could penetrate their existence.

All too soon, Scott ended the kiss and placed her back onto her feet. Instantly, she missed his warmth and strong *arms around her. She was frozen in time, and without a word Scott turned and returned to his car and left.*

Days past before Sam heard from Scott again. Her phone chirped a text alert and she grabbed her phone without urgency. Since they hadn't spoken since the kiss, she assumed things had changed. That is what they both feared the most. Opening the text, she was surprised by what she saw.

I'm sorry. I didn't know what to do after I kissed you. I should have said something first, but I couldn't help myself. Then I was worried you were upset so I just left.

Sam burst into a fit of laughter, how could he think she wasn't into that kiss. She did kiss him back and gave as good as she got. If he hadn't ended it, she would have probably drug him back inside her apartment.

You have nothing to be sorry for, except maybe avoiding me all week. I thought I must have been an exceptionally bad kisser or something.

After hitting send, Sam immediately regretted the last part. She didn't want to know if she was that bad and this opened a door for him to be honest with her. They were always honest even if it was brutally so. It was their thing and it was something she loved was their ability to be so candid. With reluctance, she read his next message.

It wasn't your inabilities that kept me away. It was how amazing it was and how it made me feel. I was afraid you didn't feel the same way. I got nervous and since I'd already left abruptly it gave me a way out for a while.

Sam, was pleasantly surprised by this turn of events. He seemed to genuinely like her, but this was quickly becoming a very strange relationship. So instead of digging further, they fell into a sense of normalcy. She didn't want to scare him away, but she also wasn't sure how to pursue anything more involved with him right now.

The rest of the year passed, and they talked every day. Flirting became a communication, but never a physical thing. They talked about dates they were set up on and became strong friends, who never saw each other. Her feelings for him never changed, but she was resolved to let him make the next move. A move that never came.

One night in a moment of weakness and a need for physical companionship, she sent Scott a text.

I need to see you. Is there anyway I could convince you to come over for that movie we never watched?

It was a long shot, but she hoped he wouldn't turn her down. It took him almost an hour to respond and she had already resolved that it would be another 'no'.

Are you sure you can handle it?

What was that supposed to mean? I've never lead him to believe being around him was anything more than pleasant. We didn't talk about our one-time meeting and kiss, not since the week after it happened, but it was always thought about and subtext was sent around it. Instead of questioning him she opted for flirty.

There is nothing about you I can't handle. Get your butt over here before I come and find you.

That was the most forward she had ever been. She knew where he lived, but she had never ventured over there as they weren't at that point in their relationship, but that night she was in a different place. She needed someone and he was the only one who would fit the bill.

Since you are being so demanding, I suppose I have no choice. One movie, but no chick flicks. I'm not going to suffer though any of that for you.

Sam laughed, because she had an extensive movie collection and such versatile taste he could pick anything he wanted as long as he was with her that is all that mattered.

An hour later, a knock sounded on her door. She panicked because this was the closest to her space he had ever gotten with the exception of pictures she had sent him of her in her domain. She worried that it wasn't clean enough or was too small. What would he think? He knocked again and she realized she was taking too long so she hurried to the door.

He was dressed in jeans and a plain t-shirt, but to her it was the sexiest thing in the world. She was in trouble because her hormones were thrumming out of control. What was happening to her? Before she could stop herself, the magnet drew her to him and she threw her arms around his neck.

He smelled all male that was just him. He didn't need cologne or aftershave to draw people to him. His own scent did that without any effort on his part. She reluctantly let go of him and stepped back and waved her hand to welcome him inside.

As he walked in he took everything in, standing awkwardly across the room by the front windows. Sam grabbed her DVD cases and handed them to him. Without thinking, she headed out of the room, glancing back at him.

"I'm going to go change into something more comfortable for the movie."

Tucked safely inside of her bedroom she couldn't get herself under control. He was under her skin and his scent still in her nose. She couldn't escape him. Without thinking she reached into her lingerie drawer and pulled out a nightgown that was more see-through than not. Her breasts were pressed into the fabric leaving little to the imagination. The silky fabric brushed against her skin right above her knees. She always liked the color black. It made her feel sexy.

Making her way out of her bedroom, the hallway was too short to give her a chance to second guess herself. She arrived in the living room quickly and watched his eyes roam her barely clothed body. She stepped closer and his eyes darkened, she could feel his attraction radiate through the room. He slowly lowered the case of movies to the sofa and stood. It was as though they were in slow motion as he moved across the room to stand in front of her.

"Are you sure this is what you want?" he asked, his voice dropped down and was deliciously husky, as he brushed his fingers over her shoulders across the thin straps.

"I'm sure," she leaned into his touch that was like electricity across her skin. His hand moved to her jaw and he kissed her as he backed her back down the hallway and into her bedroom. She held on to him tightly so as not to fall walking backwards. His steps were sure and driven. He knew what he wanted and there was going to be no taking it away.

Sam was lost in his kiss and barely registered making it to the bedroom until the backs of her knees brushed against the bed. She quickly divested him of his shirt and took in every sculpted inch of his massive chest. Her eyes roamed over him and took in his flexed arms as they lifted her off the floor and placed her onto the center of the bed. Sam always had a thing for a good set of arms, she was lost in the way each muscle rippled and tightened under her weight as he shifted above her.

He was like a wild cat stalking his prey and she was the prey. She shivered in anticipation when he slipped his hand under her nightie and pulled it from her body, leaving her naked to his hungry eyes. Now more than anything she needed to be touched. Any type of connection would rid her of this fever coursing through her body. His lips quickly covered her bare breast and she moaned in ecstasy. It was the best feeling she'd ever experienced and she never wanted it to end.

Grasping sloppily at the button on his pants, Sam attempted to get them open quickly, but fumbled and couldn't get them lose. He brushed her hand away and tore apart the button. She tried to push back to work her way into his pants, but he held her back to keep her from getting to the goods.

She laughed at his attempt, but let him be in charge. He freed himself from the entrapment of his pants. She realized that he was indeed freed from a prison, she was enthralled by the size of his member. It was easily the largest one she had ever seen and was admittingly a bit intimidated considering she wasn't sure how he was going to get that inside her, but she wanted it more than anything at this point. Nothing was going to stop her from feeling him moving inside her.

Sam lifted her body and reached for his shaft, wanting to know if it was as velvety to the touch as it looked. She gripped it tightly, and stroked easily finding a rhythm. He moaned his pleasure and began to thrust into her hand. Before long he couldn't take it anymore and he flipped her to her back. In one fluid motion, he impaled her. She screamed at the intrusion, but her body adjusted to his size as though they were made for each other.

Sam woke the next morning in post coital bliss. Scott left in the night, saying he had to be at work the next day. She didn't complain, seeing as he had left her completely sated. She didn't think there was anything that could top that night.

Unfortunately, that was the last time she ever saw him. They still chatted via text and the occasional email, but it never fell into place for them to see each other again.

A few years down the road, she got a text saying he had gotten married. She was at a loss for words. He didn't tell her directly that he had been seeing anyone, let alone proposed. They hadn't been as close as the years passed, but she hadn't been seeing anyone at the time and she was devastated by the news.

Sam's hands started to shake as she finished that portion of the story. She hadn't told anyone the entire backstory that lead to her dating disaster montage. The past few weeks had just been on steroids. She continued to explain tonight's disaster to Nick.

"Tonight, was just an addition to my bad luck and continued proof of my inability to make the right decisions."

Nick interrupted at this point, "I'm sorry I have to stop you. First of all, the guy from your story obviously didn't deserve you, but how could he have anything to do with tonight's date?"

"If you wouldn't have cut in, you would know by now. About Scott, I could have tried harder, he wouldn't have been the one who got away, I'd already be living my happily ever after. I let him go without a fight."

"I'm going to agree to disagree on that one. In the meantime, continue about tonight's date because I am dying to know what happened and after that lengthy interlude it had better be good."

Rolling her eyes at him, she continued and told him about how she met Richard and their date this evening.

"So, you are saying he posted a picture of himself from twenty years ago and passed it off as current? How did you not notice the difference in the picture that it wasn't modern?"

"I thought it was a filter. I feel stupid about it now that I've seen him. I can't believe he was over fifty and I fell for it hook, line and sinker."

"It doesn't sound like the old guy was trying to pull one over on you, but more like just be heard above the crowd. He probably has a hard time getting people to take him seriously when he shows them his true identity before explaining to them the background or his true nature."

"You're probably right, but I don't care if he was magically imprisoned by a genie in his aged body. I'm not interested in dating my father in any description of the word." Sam had finished and she was drained. Hopefully, Nick was better aware of her situation. He had to know she wasn't just a serial dater and truly was just looking for Mr. Right.

"Princess, you really are high maintenance. Whoever you end up with better be worthy." With that he turned to mix a drink. She watched him closely as she considered his words. She didn't think being with her would be such a chore, but perhaps she wasn't made to have a steady guy.

Nick mixed with his usual precision, he premeasured his vodka and poured it into the shaker. Then he picked up a bottle she didn't recognize and poured that in as well. Mixing in some lemon juice and fresh mint leaves, he added a couple ounces of wine. *What kind of a drink was he mixing?* She thought absently, but as he began to shake she got lost in the rhythm and the motion. Without preamble, he placed the glass in front of Sam.

"What is this one?" she asked not having realized he was mixing her drink.

Smiling as usual he leaned in really closely and drew out his response. "This one is perfect to top off this evening. It is one that is very rare and made with obscure mixers and flavors that you haven't ever heard of. This drink stands the test of time far above any other."

"Ok, so with that introduction I hope you tell me there is gold in here somewhere. What is it called?"

Nick was grinning now like a Cheshire Cat, she almost regretted asking, but it was also becoming an entertaining game, "This magnificent drink that knows no age, is called 'The Fountain of Youth'. Do you like it?" His smile never faltered once.

Sam started giggling as she took a tentative sip. There were things in this drink she either didn't recognize or understand his inclusion. "What was that second bottle you poured, it looked very elegant? It looked like you pulled it straight out of nineteen fifty."

"That is St. Germain, it has a bright and fragrant flavor, it's made with elderflower. It's a flower that can only be found in the Swiss Alps and harvested only for four to six weeks in the spring. I love finding recipes to use this in because it has such a unique taste."

"What made you think that the wine would make a good mixer? You seem to have found a very special combination and I thought it was random when you were pouring."

"Mionetto Prosecco, is a fruit flavored wine with a strong apple flavor. It offsets the floral flavor of the St. Germain in such a beautiful way. It just creates a sense of balance. I didn't create this one, but when I found it, I fell in lust," he finished that statement with his eyes closed as though he were tasting it.

Sam reached across the bar and took a small stir straw. She dipped the end into her drink and before he could open his eyes, she touched the straw to his lips and slipped it inside. She released the sealed end, all done in one fluid motion. Nick's eyes flew open and connected with hers. She was startled by the intensity she found within their depths.

"Why did you do that?" Nick questioned as he licked the remaining drops off his lips.

"You looked to be reliving the flavor, I just thought I would help the memory along. We all have flavor memories, but why not take an opportunity to savor it all over again? I didn't give you enough to worry about drinking on the job. Most bartenders will taste their mixes to be sure they are getting them correct. Are you upset with me?" Sam didn't know why she did that, she just had an overwhelming urge to allow him to taste a bit of lost time.

"No, I'm not upset with you. You just caught me off guard. In all my years of bartending, I've never had anyone do that. I tell people the history of drinks all the time, it's kind of my thing. You and I never get there, being that you are too angry with me before I can give you any added tidbits to go with your drinking experience."

"I don't know what came over me. I'm sorry I surprised you. I'm not sure what I was thinking." Sam felt her face heat, but was thankful that her complexion wasn't giving her away. She was embarrassed by the fact that she had gone so far as to intimately feed him a sip of her drink like a longstanding couple. That couldn't be further from the truth. With that, she finished her drink and paid her tab.

Chapter 6

Sam awoke in the middle of the night. She groaned because she was having yet another mind-numbing dream about her friendly neighborhood bartender. Rubbing her eyes to wake up further she reached for her phone.

"I have to get Nick out of my head. He doesn't even like me half the time and when he is nice to me I screw it up by doing stupid stuff like giving him tastes of my drink. What is wrong with me?"

She realized that it was only just after two in the morning and if she fell asleep now she would just have another intimate dream with her latest leading man. *Why can't it be an actor or one of the attractive men I've dated recently that didn't end in flames.* Yes, they all ended, but some were horrifically worse than others. Sam stopped that instant and realized what she was saying. Did she really think there was a scale of bad, really bad or maybe, plane crash bad? Ok no, maybe not that bad. Thoughts like that brought bad karma to flight crews. Instead of letting her thoughts wander further she opened her dating app while still lying in bed. Then if she dozed off perhaps she would have handsome profile pictures to lull her into sweet dreamland.

Sam decided as she scrolled flippantly through each page, things would be a little different than last time. Still grabbing her destiny by the proverbial balls, she opened Evernote and decided to make a checklist. Nothing cleared one's head like being able to mark things off a list. This wasn't a list like what she wanted in a man. One, because she didn't want anyone to come across it and make fun of her - her thoughts drifted to Nick again when she realized he would likely be that person. Two, because she still didn't know what she wanted in a man in order to make a list. Instead this list would be of questions she needed to ask to select a date. Then perhaps she wouldn't be surprised by any older suitors at the least.

Several weeks passed, Sam has had multiple dates, never slowing down her original timeline. Nothing has gone according to plan. Only date after date of disaster after catastrophe. Each one it was little things, but all along it was enough to end the date.

First there was Benjamin, he was perfectly normal and met all her list criteria. The list that has grown beyond age now after this short string of wrong guys. So she decided to meet him. Usually, she arrived early to get a table, but was running behind for that date. As a result, they arrived at the same time. Since she had seen his picture previously, Sam instantly recognized him. Walking inside together he pulled out her chair and held it for her as she sat down. She thought he was the perfect gentleman. Then the date took a strange turn. Usually one would start the conversation off with interests or at worst case, how was your day. Not Benny, he leaned across the table just as Tania had left to go put in their drink orders, and said "I shave my balls!" Somehow, he just leaned back as though he had just revealed why the sky was blue.

What was Sam, to do? Who starts out a date by announcing that? Sam decided the only thing she could do, "Well Ben," she purposely shortened his name because he had given her his full one, "I guess that makes you well trained. Do you want a treat?"

At first his eyes got large in disbelief and Sam wondered if she offended him and in some sick place in her brain she was thrilled. Then his face took on a darker look and she got worried for a split second. "Why yes, Sam I'd love a treat from someone like you."

Sam's favorite, not so favorite, phrase came out of his mouth and she lost it. Tania chose that moment to bring their drinks. Sam's didn't have a chance to hit the table.

She instantly flipped it from Tania's hand into Benjamin's lap. He lept up from his seat wiping and patting his lap.

"Oh, I'm so sorry." Sam feigned sympathy and got up from her seat. "At least you won't have hair stuck in your crotch when that dries." With that, she stormed away from the table. Now that was a tame version, they got worse.

Then there was Gregory, now he was a real winner. Sam agreed to go out with him and he met her at the door as well, a practice that didn't upset Sam as much as she thought it would. As always, the date started off normal. As normal as can be expected when two people are sitting in a situation and they don't know each other. Once their drinks were served and they each had drank over half, tensions settled to a low hum. Gregory was actually quite the talker. Although, his topic was a bit alarming. He spent the first thirty minutes of the date talking non-stop about his ex-wife. Not to worry too much, he wasn't hung up on her as some guys are. Apparently, she was a horrible wife and he decided that she didn't deserve anything he had. Since they didn't have kids, he thought he didn't owe her anything. His stories continued, telling of her infidelity and how he caught her with multiple men. Until he finally had enough and chose to write her off. She begged him and pleaded for him to take her back as her lifestyle had left her with nothing to show for herself.

"That sounds like a lot for you to have gone through," Sam tried to sound like she cared, but didn't know how well she pulled it off.

"Not to worry. She got what was coming to her." Gregory reassured her so that meant her acting skills were improving.

"Really? Did she find another man or get cheated on herself?"

"No, a few months ago they found her dead in her shoddy little apartment. I guess she couldn't take anymore and slit her wrists." Gregory sounded so nonchalant about the entire situation. Not ignoring the fact that he had just stated she got what was coming to her. Sam was worried what kind of man this was and found herself backing away from the table her mouth hanging open in shock.

"Wow, that must have been a hard pill to swallow."

"Nope, I was happy to have her off my back and I could move on without her calling me multiple times every day." That had sealed the deal for Sam. She excused herself and didn't come back. There was nothing else she wanted to say to a man who could disregard a human life no matter his mixed relationship with that person. A life was a life and not to be thrown away because you didn't like them.

Cooper was the icing on the cake, but still not the worst one, though it was hard to believe even looking back. Cooper, she met online and had wonderful chat conversations with him lasted late into the night. They had so much in common it was uncanny. She couldn't believe she could relate to someone she had never met as much as she did him.

Their date came around and he was charming as expected to the point they decided to order food. This was a big step for Sam because most of her dates didn't progress this far. As they sat and ate they shared stories and dreams and fantasies. Sam was blown away by his aspirations. Then she didn't know if it was that he felt comfortable with her or just had had too much to drink, but he started asking about sexual fantasies.

"Do you have one thing you would love to try in the bedroom, but have been to leery to ask." Sam had never had a man ask her this let alone someone she didn't really know, but she let it slide and thought about it for a moment.

"I'm not sure. I guess I haven't given it much thought." She thought for a moment then gave him an answer. "I guess I would like to be a little adventurous and maybe attempt to be sneaky and have sex in a public place. Not where anyone could see me, but the thrill that someone might walk in at any moment." This line of conversation was embarrassing her and she couldn't meet his eyes.

"That sounds very exciting indeed." Cooper confirmed, but when he continued she got nervous. He placed his hand over hers in a gesture more intimate and far beyond where they should be at that point in the date. "Mine is a little darker. Do you mind if I share?" In hindsight, Sam wished she had said no, but unfortunately that is twenty-twenty.

"Of course, be my guest." Also, regretting her choice of words and realizing that Disney catch phrases were going to have to be burned from her vocabulary from that moment on.

He leaned in very close to her and she had flashback to Benjamin, but he kept a straight face looked her right in the eye, "I want to roleplay a rape fantasy ending with my lover taking a crap on my chest."

Sam couldn't make this up, it was the most insane thing she had ever heard. There were no words to handle that situation. After a long silence Sam took a sip of her drink, "Well, Cooper I'll have to say that is probably the craziest fantasy I've ever heard vocalized and I'm not sure I can be with someone who thinks like that." With that she exited to the bar to wait for her next drink from Nick.

Eli was a character and a half. She wasn't sure what to think about him at first. He made her laugh in all of her messages with him. He said some of the craziest things that she just laughed infectiously. She even shared a few of his messages with Tania one evening and she thought he was hilarious. With Tania's approval, she accepted and planned a date with Eli.

The night of her date though she was worried that Eli had lost his spark. He was very mundane and didn't hardly smile. He almost seemed dark or emo in nature. This wasn't the person she chatted with for days prior to her date. Not only that, but he was talking about how much he didn't like his boss and that he wanted to poison her.

"That's hilarious, I can think of a few coworkers I didn't get along with and remember picturing bad things happening to them just to get even." Eli's mouth didn't even twitch with smile he merely pulled out his phone and googled ways to kill and not be caught as he turned the phone in her direction.

"I can forward this page to you via our chat window. It could come in handy, you never know." He was so serious and Sam wondered if he was just one of those people who could pull a straight face no matter what the situation.

The evening progressed and he kept mentioning poisoning his boss. Sam patiently waited for him to end with a 'just kidding' and a smile, but neither came. The longer this went on the more nervous she got. The final straw hit when he pulled a vial out of his pocket.

"A couple more days and a few more doses of this and I won't have to worry about the "Fire Breathing Dragon" anymore. That was what he started referring to as his evil boss.

Trying not to sound as freaked out as she was Sam answered, "What is that?"

Without batting an eye, he looked at the vial, "Wolfsbane." Eli said this in a way that sounded like it was everyday normal conversation. "It's completely untraceable and given in small doses can take time to work versus instantly killing her and making it seem obvious.

No additional words were spoken, Sam stuffed her napkin in her drink to absorb the remaining liquid. Thankful she hadn't needed to use the restroom at any point during their evening. Then she got up and walked away. She didn't know what to say to a psychotic killer, but Sam knew she didn't want to be in his company any longer.

Then there was Kevin, oh dear Kevin. He was studying to be an undertaker and was in his final year of Mortuary Science at Waterman University. He was a bit dry, but after Eli it was a breath of fresh air. No more talk of murder, just the science of death. In most cases, people would think this was comparable, but when you've experienced a situation where you didn't know if you needed to call the police about a simple conversation or just hide under your bed for fear of them finding you, it's an improvement. On a side note, Sam did call the police from the bar under Nick and Tania's orders, but she left it anonymously and only gave the important details as to why she knew the facts.

Kevin was a science nerd at heart and wanted Sam to love his work as much as he did, unfortunately perfect was only relative. As always, things were going well if not, a little boring when they took a strange turn and Kevin asked off-the-cuff, "How do you feel about taking a cold bath before sex and then staying very still throughout?"

Sam didn't see that coming and at first didn't know how to respond, but then decided on honesty.

"Are you asking how I feel role-playing a corpse during sex?"

"Essentially, yes, but only because I have been wanting to experiment on something and seeing if there is a way to get necrophilia patients an outlet for their disease. I would like to write a paper to be published in a circular that could be a breakthrough in their recovery."

"So, are you asking me to do this for you or a patient with a disease?" Sam didn't want to shut him down right away if this was a theoretical question for research purposes. She always enjoyed filling out online surveys just to see their results.

"I don't suffer from necrophilia, Sam. I wouldn't need you to perform like that for me. I prefer my women hot blooded and breathing." Sam breathed a sigh of relief, but that was too soon. "I do ask all my dates the same question because at some point I hope to find one that isn't repulsed by the idea and I can bring her into the sessions at some point."

Sam faltered as to whether or not to respond, but her curiosity won out. "So, you are saying you would be willing to share your girlfriend with people who have slept with actual dead people and have been hospitalized for it?"

"I would do anything in the name of science and I hope to find a woman who would do the same." Kevin was starting to be so normal and then he had to go and say something like that.

"Well, Kevin I thought we were doing ok, but after that I'm not sure I'm the girl for you. I think you live in a gray area that I'm not ready for." Sam stood and leaned to give him a hug and left him stunned at the table. She was proud of herself for getting better at explaining why she was walking away, but it still felt awful doing it so frequently.

Her date the previous night was, by far, the weirdest one yet. There was no one in this world who could have prepared her for Shelton. He was the most attractive man she had ever met, it was too good to be true. That was a truer statement than she knew. They met online, as usual, but he didn't set off any of her red flags and met all of her checklist criteria. After a shorter chatting period, for fear she would run out of things to talk about, she set up a date.

Sam arrived earlier than usual since her nerves were out of control. It was difficult to describe him in words but he put the underwear models to shame. He would give the most attractive actor a run for the title 'World's Sexiest Man Alive' and Sam would be first in line to vote. How this man hadn't been scooped up yet was beyond her.

Sam hadn't been this nervous since she was asked to give a speech in high school about 'Sexual Education and the Pros versus Cons of teaching it in schools'. That was a different kind of nerves though resulting in the same fears. *What if I make a fool of myself? What if I say something stupid? What if I puke?* Yes, at that moment all of those fears were rolling on a loop in her mind. At that moment, Shelton walked through the door and every eye in the room turned to face him. Sam heard a collective sigh roll through the room of every woman married and single combined. At that moment, she knew her perception of Shelton was accurate.

Waving her hand in his direction, he smiled in a way that once again the room swooned. Too bad for them this man was headed straight for her. She felt like she was on cloud nine or else she was about to realize she was a part of the world's worst prank.

"Good evening beauty, I have been awaiting this meeting for millennia." Shelton certainly had a way with words. "You are even more ravishing in person than in your online image."

"You are even more than eye catching than I expected." Sam said gesturing to all the women in the room, but her smile never left her face.

Shelton glanced around the room and Sam watched him meet eyes with every woman in the room. "That happens all the time. I just don't exactly know why."

"I have an idea or two." Sam replied coolly even though she felt anything but.

The two ordered and began talking and it seemed Shelton had a vocabulary right out of a Jane Austin novel. It was refreshing to speak to someone who was so proper and such a gentleman.

The date was going so smoothly and she was really starting to like Shelton. *I really think he might be worth a second date. I haven't had one of those in a long time.*

They ordered food and made it all the way to dessert when he asked, "Can I tell you a secret? I haven't told anyone this ever."

By this point Sam was lulled into a sense of security. She was a bit doe eyed and he could say anything, as long as she was under his spell, it would sound like poetry.

"Please, you can tell me anything." She leaned forward and placed her head on her hand that was supported by her elbow on the table. Batting her eyes slightly, she waited for his next words.

"I am an alien who has come to Earth to find a mate. I think you would be a fine wife and would produce many fine children for me."

That snapped her out of the trance. *What did he just say?* Sam blinked a few times trying to clear the fog that she was enveloped in.

"Um…I guess that makes you quite the foreigner. How long have you been in town?" She was trying to play it cool, they say you shouldn't agitate the mentally insane. At that moment, Nick walked by for some unknown reason.

He glanced over at her and she went for it and sent him a pleading look. Not knowing if he would read her panic correctly, she just hoped he would come to her rescue. The last thing she wanted was a person psychologically challenged to react poorly.

"I've been here just over six months and I've been very pleased with my overall impression of the women here on Earth. Most are very pleasing to the eye, but you are exceptional. It was beyond my wildest dreams to find a specimen like you who could please me and bear my young. I can't wait to show you the rituals of my kind to consummate our marriage."

Sam had no words to express her level of shock. They had just met and he was talking about consummating their nonexistent marriage and having alien offspring. Luckily, she didn't have to think too long because a silent observer came to her rescue.

"Well, as wonderful as marrying my Princess sounds I'd say you should probably look for another host for your little green babies." Nick grasped her hand and gently pulled her up from the table. Slowly he pressed her behind him, putting himself between her and her unwanted alien lover.

"I didn't say I was looking for a host and I had no idea she was royalty. That is an entirely different matter." Shelton leaned to look at Sam over Nick's shoulder and then turned and scowled at the Nick himself. "I said I wanted a wife. Children of any race should be raised by dual parent households."

"Oh, an *alien* with morals, that might be a new one for me." Nick was playing along, but said the word alien with more disdain than anything. With slight movements, he started moving backwards with Sam in tow, but it was almost imperceptible to Shelton.

"I'm very moral and I would never ask her anything I wasn't willing to follow through with."

"I think you've asked my Princess enough. We will be going now. You can find a new wife." Without another word Nick took her hand and marched her back to the kitchen. He bypassed everyone and everything, never letting go of her hand. He walked straight out the back door.

"Are you ok? What was that back there? Are you picking up your dates in the asylum now?" His hands were braced on her shoulders and he had her backed up against the alley wall. She could feel him pressed up against her every curve as he leaned into her.

"I'm fine," she said breathlessly. Realizing what she sounded like, Sam cleared her throat and attempted to wriggle out of his embrace. "He was another online date. I had no idea how insane he was."

"Well, it's a good thing I happened to be getting to work late today and walked past that disaster." Nick winked at her and slowly separated them. His hands ran down her arms, lighting them on fire in their wake.

Sam looked him in the eye. Feeling him everywhere had wreaked havoc on her senses and her emotions. "You called me *your* princess." Sam whispered barely audible. She wasn't trying to make him hear her, it was more of a passing thought, but they were still so close he heard every word.

"What did you expect me to call you? You are MY Princess. I'm the only one who calls you that." He said in a deep rumble again spoken so only they could hear. This was a conversation that no one needed to hear besides themselves, even if they were spending it in an alley. Without another word he sealed his lips over hers and even though Sam was startled by his visceral reaction she responded with a fervor that she didn't know was in her.

She could feel her hear her heart racing and her blood rushed in her ears. It was overwhelming and she didn't know what else to do, Sam reacted by instinct. She pressed against his chest to separate them. "I believe you are my knight for the evening. What can I do to repay you?" She wasn't sure what she was offering, but at this point she didn't care what he asked for.

Nick cleared his throat and smiled roguishly, "I don't need anything. It was the least I could do. Anyone else would have done the same." He backed away and headed for the door. "Do you think we've given him enough time to clear out?"

Sam realized the moment had passed and he was obviously just doing the right thing by helping her and it didn't mean anything. So, she headed back to the door alongside him. "It never takes them long to bail after I get finished with them. You should know that, you make me a drink every night in their wake."

"Well then I guess I owe you a drink." He ushered her back inside and into her spot at the bar. Upon arriving back at the bar, Sam noticed that someone was covering for Nick behind the bar. So the customers hadn't been neglected during the time he was away coming to Sam's rescue. She was much more at ease now. Nick didn't miss a beat, he immediately started mixing a shot. Not his norm for drink choices when presenting her with an end-of-date joke, but under the circumstances it was probably the best choice.

Nick mixed in butterscotch schnapps. *Yummy this is going to be a good one.* Sam thought as he poured everything into the glass. Bailey's went in next and Sam knew instantly she was going to love this one. The last ingredient was new to Sam, but that had never stopped her before. She only drew the line at Jäger, but that was because she couldn't do the black licorice flavor, period. This time thankfully it wasn't Jäger, but a melon liqueur. *That sounds like it could be sweet or tart, which way will it go?*

Something was different tonight. She had never paid close enough attention to the mixing of the drinks that she actually ran an inner dialogue about the individual drinks mixed into them.

Nick placed the shot in front of her and leaned his arms against the bar top and placed his chin on them. He was anxiously awaiting her first taste. She knew better though, what he was doing was waiting for the right opportunity to tell her the incredibly clever name.

Without a word she raised the glass to her lip, closed her eyes and threw back the liquid in the glass in one gulp. It went down smooth and had the sweet creamy flavor she expected, but followed with a hint of tart from the melon. It gave it just the right amount of kick, it couldn't be described as a girly drink.

Slowly she opened her eyes and met Nick's exhilarated ones. *Why is he so excited, by someone else drinking something?* She didn't ask him aloud though, she preferred to wonder in silence. Instead she matched his look and waited. Sam knew he would divulge the mystery name in his own time. Nick seemed to be a man who loved to make things happen in their own time. Sam was beginning to see the beauty in it.

Raising up off his hands Nick smiled like a fool. He must have a doozy on his hands to be acting like this.

"Are you ready?" Sam didn't have to ask for clarification. This was all old hat for her by this time. She merely nodded her accession and allowed him to continue.

"Alien Nipple." Nick stated succinctly and waited for her response.

Sam didn't want to disappoint him, but that name just felt anticlimactic to sum up the date from Mars, or was it

Venus? She was never good with remembering those things.

"Really? That's all you've got? I was sure this one was going to be a good one, but I think it was a letdown. Honestly, you had better luck with the Blue Bruiser and the Bitter Frenchman if you really want to know. Now that I've had time to cool down from those horrific experiences I can tell you that from the bottom of my heart. I expected 'Take Me To Your Leader' or 'The Mothership' to be in there somewhere, not 'Alien Nipple'. I feel shortchanged. You need to up your game, Bucko." For whatever reason, Sam was feeling a new sense of kinship to Nick and she could give him a little grief, as though she would a friend or a brother. Who knew the moment they shared in the alley would lead to this.

"Oh well, I must be off my game. Perhaps you should stick around and test all my signature drinks tonight and rename them at will." Nick was in good humor so she knew he didn't take her ribbing to heart.

"Will? I don't know a Will, but I could rename them all if I weren't such a hot commodity. I have an early morning, but thank you again for rescuing me, good sir." She fell into damsel who was in distress mode quickly and he didn't let her down.

With a flourish of his hand and a deep bow, "It was an honor m'lady. I only wish I could have saved you sooner so as to procure you from the grief in which you were forced to bear." He played the knight role all too well and she wondered if he made a habit of it.

"Thank you for my drink, good knight, and I will take my leave of you. You are now free to watch for any other damsels in need of your assistance." With a curtesy to Nick, she sashayed out of the bar.

Chapter 7

Another date another disaster, Sam was over it. Nick rescuing her was the best thing she could have ever imagined.

Getting up early the next morning, Sam had decided she wanted to spend the day outside. She grabbed a market tote and headed for the Farmer's Market and hoped for a wonderful day. If nothing else, making it home with fresh produce so she could cook a meal or just have a healthy snack would make her happy.

Sam walked aimlessly, taking in all the booths. Some had fresh corn on the cob, advertised as the sweetest right off the stalk. Others had fresh tomatoes saying they would make the best salsa one had ever tasted. Sam wouldn't know the first place to start to make salsa, but imagined if she put her mind to it anything was possible. She saw cucumbers and fresh romaine lettuce and got an idea for lunch. Sam started making her way around tables in an attempt to make the best and freshest salad she'd had in ages.

Making her way to the last table to get fresh mushrooms, Sam looked up to find a tall man with wavy black hair. He was absolutely dreamy. "Hi there, sugar. What can I gettcha?" He had just enough of a southern twang she was helpless to his accent. She didn't know how far South he was from, but it didn't matter. A country boy could set her blood to boil faster than a house on fire.

"I saw your mushrooms from three booths away and my mouth was watering before I could get over here. I was so excited I just knew they would make my salad perfection." Sam laid it on a little thick and she knew it, but hoped he didn't notice.

"Well, little darlin," Little indeed, Sam felt like a child standing next to this man, tall, dark and handsome had nothing on this cowboy. "I'd be happy to get you fixed up. I only bring in my best crop so I'm sure you will be satisfied with whichever bunch you want. How much do you need?"

Sam hesitated, she was never good at face to face flirting. It always came out awkward and stunted. She was bound to look like a complete idiot.

"Well it's just me so the smallest bunch you have will suit me fine."

"You can have this one then, but only if you tell me your name. You are the prettiest creature I've seen all day." Now it seemed he was laying it on thick and she wondered if it was a direct result of her previous ministrations.

"Samantha, but everyone calls me Sam."

"Well Sam, it's a pleasure to meet you. Now if you don't mind me sayin' so, you are too beautiful to be eating alone. My name is Gavin and I'd love to take you out for drinks tonight and hopefully a little dinner, but that is up to you."

Sam hesitated for a moment, but since she didn't have anything else to do tonight she stopped herself from declining. Her goal was to get her love life sorted out and there was only one way to really do that.

"Well since I always start out my dates with drinks first, I think that sounds like a great idea. I'll just make my salad for lunch this afternoon. What time do you finish up here?" Sam trying to not sound too eager, but she worried she was failing miserably.

"I usually finish up here about one o'clock and am home after cleaning up by midafternoon. Do you want to meet for drinks at about six o'clock and that will give us time to decide if we want to upgrade this to a dinner date?" He winked at her and she was hard pressed to find anything wrong with his suggestion.

After giving him directions to the bar, she paid for her mushrooms and he sent her a panty dropping smile and she knew she was in trouble. His charisma was almost too much to combat with but she hoped that wouldn't bite her in the ass.

The rest of her day went on with little excitement to which she was grateful. Her love life was all the excitement she needed. Although right now it was stirring a different kind of excitement than what she was hoping for. Thankfully, she was able to keep those thoughts at bay throughout her dates so she isn't so desperate that she can't keep up the pretense of her dating life.

Sitting in the bar waiting for Gavin to arrive, Sam was thankful she had already seen Nick behind the bar. So she knew that she had backup if it was needed, but she hoped it wouldn't be necessary. Taking a sip from her wine glass she tried to calm her nerves. With so many bad dates recently, a girl could get a complex. Facing the door, she patiently waited and prayed this one would be at least a little better than her previous disasters.

The time came and went that Gavin was supposed to arrive. She couldn't believe he stood her up. This was his idea and she hadn't even been flirting that much before he asked her out. He had a personality that drew a girl in and took away rational thought. "I should have stayed home." Sam grumbled to herself and she finished off her third glass of wine. Glancing over her shoulder she cursed herself for being so weak as to check and see if Nick was looking. Unfortunately, she saw him glance her way before she quickly looked back at her table. "Great, now he feels sorry for me." Quickly she threw some cash on the table to cover her drinks and gathered her purse to leave.

Suddenly Gavin burst through the door looking winded and disheveled. Rolling her eyes, she was torn between being concerned by his appearance and frustrated with him being almost an hour late. He glanced around quickly scanning the room when his eyes caught hers, he made his way to her without hesitation.

"I'm so sorry I'm late. I had to take an emergency phone call as I was leaving the house and it took longer than I expected. Please tell me you'll stay and talk for a bit to let me redeem myself." Gavin's eyes were pleading and she was a sucker for his accent. At least this time, the accent wasn't foreign and she was sure she would understand every word. With a sigh, Sam relented, knowing she couldn't stay mad at him forever.

"Fine, I'll stay but you are buying every other drink from now on." *He better be as wonderful as I imagined because I can't take another let down right now.* The last part she didn't say out loud but failed at not letting her face change into a wistful gaze. He didn't hesitate getting the waitress's attention. Tania was working tonight and although it was a busier night she took a second to let Sam know how hot she thought Gavin looked. Sam smothered a laugh as Tania took off to get their drinks.

"You said you had an emergency phone call. I hope it wasn't anything too serious." Sam was going for sympathetic, but since he had nearly stood her up, she felt like an explanation was in order. His face didn't change though Sam was sure she saw something pass across his eyes. Not knowing him well enough she wasn't sure, but it looked an awful lot like guilt.

"Oh no, nothing serious." The words rolled out of his mouth smoothly leaving Sam the impression it was the truth, but that look in his eye still worried her. "I've been trying to get a job the past few months and it's been a struggle. You see I'm an Elvis impersonator and since I left Vegas, work has been a bit light. That is why I started working at the

Farmer's Market. I have the stamina and skill to be a farm hand, but am just not feeling it. My passion is acting and when one has any skill at all at something, nothing else will do." Sam sat stunned into silence. Thoughts bounced through her brain, but she couldn't get the right things to come to her mouth. *Elvis? Seriously? I guess his accent probably comes in handy for that. Is his accent real or is that an act too? He did say that he was from Vegas not Texas. Now that I think about it his hair is a bit long in the front. I just thought he hadn't had a chance to cut it with the market being most every weekend.* Shaking her head, she dislodged the thought process and forced a smile. "That is quite interesting. What was your best gig in Vegas?" Sam hoped she sounded interested and not weirded out. Everyone was entitled to have a job they loved, this one was just a little out there.

"I worked in the Elvis chapel. I loved watching happy couples say 'I do' and head off to live happily ever after." Shocked yet, again, Sam didn't think it was possible to surprise her further.

"So how long did you live in Vegas?" Hoping to move onto safer topics and perhaps something more normal she pressed him.

"I was there for a couple years before that I lived in Utah." He took a drink and Sam took a moment to figure out what that meant. It sounded like he was a bit of a drifter and couldn't stay in one place long.

"Wow, Utah! That is pretty country, what made you decide to leave there?" Mentally patting herself on the back for keeping the conversation going and onto less strange topics.

"My old lady and I split up after a big fight. I stormed off and just took a drive. When I was finally cooled down I was in Vegas. Realized the lifestyle there was more my speed and never looked back." Gavin spoke as if this was a totally normal way to act and that she might not see anything wrong with it. His good ol' boy act never dropped and his accent carried him through every word.

"Never looked back, goodness. How long have you been divorced?" Sam was starting to get uncomfortable, but didn't want to conversation to bounce back to her yet, so she pressed on.

"Nah, when I said never looked back I meant it. She was a constant nag and wouldn't let up for anything. Instead of worrying about who got what and who paid who I just decided to let her live and let live. The kids and her can stay there and be better off for it. Then I don't have to listen to her whine about me never being enough for her anymore." Draining his glass, he motioned for Tania to bring him another. Sam mentally counted his drinks now realizing how quickly he was drinking them. If it were just a beer she wouldn't worry but Gavin seemed to like his whiskey like he liked his life, wild and free.

"Kids? How many kids do you have?" Sam took a tentative sip of her drink and waited for him to answer.

"Three." Gavin didn't elaborate and Sam took that as a bad sign. She didn't push her luck, but moved on to another safe topic, hopefully.

"What do you do for fun, Gavin?" She suppressed a sigh carrying the conversation topics was becoming exhausting.

"I like to draw." Gavin was already halfway through his second drink that Tania had dropped off on her way to drop an order at the next table and take an order a few more over.

"That's awesome. What do you like to draw?"

"I have a comic strip that I do just for fun. You should check it out." He started tapping away at his phone and pulled up an image, turning his phone so she could see.

Sam wasn't sure what she was looking at so she decided to read instead. "Does that say 'Puking Cats'?" The image depicted a couple cats chatting over a can of tuna and one proceeded to start hacking up a hairball. The other, it seemed, was sympathetic and began heaving himself. The ending was just a splatter inside the comic strip box.

"Yeah, it has become a fun project over the past few months since my girlfriend left me. I caught her with another man in the back seat of her car. There were two cats nearby that had puked on the sidewalk outside their car. It just resonated with me. I started releasing them online a few weeks later." Gavin was very proud and Sam wasn't going to say he wasn't a good artist because she could tell what everything was without question.

"Have you gained much of a following?" She didn't know if that was the right question to ask, but she went for it anyway.

"Here and there. I have about three hundred people who have decided to follow my page and get fifty to a hundred comments per post so I'd say that's something. It's still pretty new and different."

"Yes, different that is a good way to put it." Sam was so over this guy. Who breaks up with their girlfriend and takes puking cats away from that entire experience?

Draining his second glass Gavin asked his first question, "So what do you say we order some food and get to know each other further?" As attractive as he was this wasn't a date she wanted to continue any further.

"Actually, I'm going to be honest with you. I'm not feeling the same connection I thought I would with you. It was a pleasure to meet you and I'm sure you are a great guy, but just not the guy for me." Running the words over and over in her mind she hesitated hoping she didn't upset him too badly. This was the worst part of a bad date and while she was never going to be good at it, Sam hoped it was getting better.

Gavin looked at her for a long moment and didn't say a word, Sam worried she just caused a huge issue and hoped Nick was still nearby watching at least a little. He wouldn't let this get out of hand, would he?

"Perhaps you're right. I enjoyed myself this evening and while you are a pretty girl we don't really have that connection or spark as some like to call it." Sam sighed with relief it hadn't ended as horribly as she thought it would. Thank God for small miracles. Gavin paid for their drinks and they said their goodbyes.

Sam made her way over to the bar as was usual for the first time she wasn't hiding. She'd take that as a small win. Nick's attention fell to her immediately, holding up a finger to let her know he would be right there.

She settled into her stool and relaxed, not having to sneak around after her dates was a nice feeling. She didn't feel great about it not panning out, but at least this one wasn't crazy. Lost in thought, she didn't see Nick approach and when he spoke, she jumped.

"Thought that one wasn't going to show up for a while. Did he redeem himself once he got here?" Nick smirked in her direction waiting for her to spill.

"Yes and no. He explained why he was late and given the fact that he showed up and apologized I wasn't as upset. If he would have never shown up, I would have been pissed. The only part that was a bit strange was his story." She rested her head in her hand and leaned her elbow on the bar to look up at Nick. Thankfully she didn't get all kinds of dolled up for this date. She opted for dressy casual. Her jeans were comfortable and her black tunic hugged her like a close friend. She wasn't showing much skin and it was perfect.

"What do you mean strange?" Why was Nick was always very interested in her love life? She decided to ask him instead of spill, at least just yet.

"Why are you so interested? You always ask and then you make fun of me the rest of the night."

"Would you rather I ignore you and just let you drink your sorrows away?" Nick had a smart mouth and it didn't bother her, it just made her want to push him further. Then she remembered they still hadn't discussed their clandestine alleyway kiss. *Clandestine? Great now I'm romanticizing something neither of us can talk about. What kind of person am I becoming? He probably doesn't even remember it. It's just something he does to women regularly and I didn't even make a blip on his radar. First, I wasn't dating and now I'm doing it nearly every free night. Hoping to find 'Mr. Right' when he probably doesn't even exist. Now I'm daydreaming about kisses in an alley thinking that they meant something they probably didn't mean.* With a sigh she laid her head down on her folded arms resting on top of the bar.

"Fine, he was perfect this morning. I met him at the Farmer's Market while trying to take some time for myself. I wasn't planning on having a date tonight. It just sort of happened." Everything she said was muffled by her arms because she refused to look up.

"Things sort of just happen to you a lot, don't they?" Nick's voice sounded much closer than before and it startled her. Sam glanced up from the safety of her arm wall and was met with Nicks face resting on top of his flattened hands resting on the bar. He wore his usual bar uniform of tight jeans and a black t-shirt, Sam wondered if he had anything else in his closet. Though if not she wouldn't be bothered because his clothes fit him so well she was pretty sure she knew what he looked like underneath them. With a smirk, Sam shook her head, but didn't raise it, nor did she hide her face back down inside the protection of her arms.

"Anyway, he asked me out and I agreed to meet him here. I'm starting to wonder why this is my 'safe bar'. Maybe I need a new one without a meddling bartender." Sam winked at him and continued when he smiled at her. "You saw that he was late, but he said he was taking a call about a gig he had been waiting to get. Turns out he is an Elvis impersonator from Vegas and is trying to figure out how to bring his act here. I'm not sure how that is working but I can guess as there isn't a huge market for them here. Unless Grandma wants to relive the glory days." Nick barked out a laugh startling Sam. Not that he hadn't ever laughed around her before he was always making fun of the situations she found herself in but this was different. He wasn't laughing at her but at her sense of humor.

"He didn't look anything like Elvis. How does he actually make money at that?" Nick questioned as he brought his round of laughter to a close but not without obvious difficulty.

"I have no idea, but that isn't the weird part of his story yet." She waited to gauge his reaction. Nicks eyebrows met his hairline.

"You're telling me that a guy who left Vegas for whatever reason and is continuing to pursue his life as a traveling Elvis isn't the weirdest part of his life?"

"Nope, that is just the tip of the crazy iceberg. Apparently, Vegas wasn't the first stop on his tour. He moved there from Utah. I guess he has a family there and things got rocky so he just up and drove off one night and didn't stop until got to Vegas."

"Wow, he's a real winner!" Nick was leaning back up now, as was she and the conversation, just flowed as it usually did. He really was a great listener and actively participated in the conversation not just grunting occasionally to let her know he was listening. Though, that wouldn't necessarily mean he heard her. Nick just made her feel like he cared enough to hear her side of whatever was going on, even though he wasn't directly involved. Sam mentally smacked herself again. *Why do I keep thinking like this? He isn't a knight in shining armor. He's a bartender hoping for a good tip. Talk to him or don't, that is fine. Do not glamorize it into something that isn't here.*

"Winner…yes. This one will make someone a fine catch one day. His past, paired with his job and his hobby that would be enough to seal the deal for anyone."

"Hobby? Did I miss something or did you leave part of this sordid tale out? I seem to be living vicariously through you, as I work so much I don't get to go out and have all the same fun you seem to have. How else am I going to get my daily dose of a normal dating life?" Nick had both hands on the bar and was leaning in obviously vested in what she would say next.

"That is what this is about? You want to know what horrible things happen to me so you can feel like you have lived some sort of life outside of pouring drinks and providing eye candy for the women who pass through?" Sam instantly regretted her choice of words but she had a habit of not controlling her verbal vomit when she was tired. All of these dates in their glory were taking their toll.

"What did you think I was doing? Researching for a book of what not to do?" Nick winked at her proving that he heard the last part, but for some reason chose not to comment, much to her relief. "Now what hobby did I miss?"

"You didn't miss anything but I'll warn you the prior two were just trivial compared to this one and it's what sealed his fate. If you can believe that the prior two could be topped." Sam knew she had him hooked when he bent that the elbow and leaned in close enough she could feel his breath across her face as he waited for her to reveal the juicy detail. "Puking cats." Just like the memes that tell you to post and say nothing, she left those two words to explain themselves.

Nick's nose curled and his brow wrinkled in confusion just as Sam knew it would, but she let it play out a little longer.

"Did he have cat puke on his shirt? How could puking cats have come up in conversation tonight? This is an indoor bar so I know you didn't see one in here." Nick was perplexed and Sam found it to be the most entertaining part of her evening.

"Oh no, none of the above." Again, she let it linger just a little longer.

"Did he sound like a puking cat when he laughed or took a drink? Oh, I know! He cleared his throat incessantly and therefore sounded like a puking cat." Nick was getting creative, but still didn't land on the right answer and Sam was enjoying herself. Instead of prolonging this any longer, Sam chose to put him out of his misery.

"No again. He is the creator of Puking Cats comic strip." She waited for him to show any sign of awareness but when he still looked confused, she breathed a sigh of relief. "You have no idea how happy I am that you don't know what that is. Granted he said he only has a few hundred followers but my opinion of you just jumped exponentially because you aren't one of them."

"I can only imagine what his inspiration is and what possessed him to publicize them to anyone outside of his head. Society has just taken a step down in my brain because people actually do follow him. Wait, did you actually think I was one of them?" Nick was good. She couldn't tell if he was actually offended or trying to bait her.

"Well one can never tell these days. You could be a sympathizer posing as a normal dude. It's better to play it safe and not assume." Sam winked at him letting him know she was playing even if he was still playing it close to the vest. With a wry look in his eye, he walked away without another word. Sam didn't stop him but leaned over to watch him begin to make a drink. Knowing what he was doing she watched him pour. She recognized most of the liquids he poured into the glass. Peach schnapps and vodka were the most obvious, but there was a dark syrup she couldn't make out then he added sour and Sprite followed by a quick stir.

As Nick made his way back to her, she made no effort to right her position on the bar. Eager to taste his latest concoction, Sam remained leaned over watching him approach. Nick placed the glass between her hands and she looked straight down to take in the drink with all of her senses.

Visually, it was a light pink color, she assumed because the clear liquids thinned out the mystery dark syrup. It was poured over ice so she knew better than to let it sit too long or it would contaminate the flavor once the melt began. Lifting it to her nose, Sam inhaled lightly to take in even more. The scent was light and fruity with very little of the alcohol's bitter scent coming off on the back end. Neither of these helped her identify the syrup that he used. She could ask but it was more fun for her now to try and guess. The worst that could happen was she was wrong. It wasn't as though she had any life-threatening allergies to be concerned with.

As she took her first sip, Sam closed her eyes in an attempt to block out her other senses to enhance the flavor. The fluid poured over her tongue and the flavors exploded in her mouth. The fruity taste she expected came first but was followed by a tangy flavor that was almost tart. She felt it in her jowls as it popped and tingled, working its magic through her mouth. Then the flavor settled and she caught hints of lemon and she assumed that was what got her mouth excited for that small moment of time. There was still something else there that she couldn't identify but she had identified part of it, so she felt like it wasn't a total loss.

"That is fantastic! I taste the peach and the lemon and not just the sprite, but what was the syrup you added? It was the only one I couldn't identify and there is a flavor I'm having trouble placing." She opened her eyes after she spoke since she was still trying to hang onto the senses as separately as she could. Her eyes took a second to focus but he waited until her eyes met his before he spoke. He held her gaze for a moment and Sam tried not to read anything into it.

"That was the lemon raspberry syrup. It has a stronger flavor than most of the mixes." Then a grin spread across his face like a storybook character and instantly it was contagious because Sam felt her own smile growing and she didn't know what it was for. "Are you ready for the name of this one?" Then she knew it had to be a good one.

"Hit me with it." Sam was ready for the worst.

"That my dear is what we like to call the Dirty Kitty." Nick spoke with a stuffy British accent. She could just envision him with a monocle and top hat but then when he said the last two words the image popped like a bubble floating through the air and pricked with a pin.

Sam's eyes were the size of saucers not just because that was the name of the drink but the double meaning. The look in his eye before he said it told Sam that he knew exactly what he was saying and how she would take it. While the name suited the moment, it was still slightly embarrassing to hear him say that out loud. Once again, she was thankful not to be a blusher. There were so many things with this man that a blush staining her cheeks would have outed her. Instead she did what she could to bury her reaction and move past it. Squaring her shoulders, she took another drink of the sweet and tart liquid to give herself a moment to not have to respond. Once again letting the drink float in her mouth for a short time she savored the flavors as they blended together.

"Well I'd say you chose a fitting drink once again." Sam glanced up at him and she noted a glint of something in his eye. She didn't know him that well but she would have been sure it was a hint of disappointment which he quickly wiped away with a blink and smiled. *What did he expect me to say? Surely, he didn't want me to react to that, did he?*

Quietly, he turned back to the other side of the bar. Sam knew he was hiding his face from her so she wouldn't see any other emotions cross his face. She just hoped he didn't stay upset long. She had a hard enough time keeping guys around let alone knowing how to make them feel better. The more she thought about it Sam realized that perhaps she wasn't cut out to do this and maybe that was why none of her dates were turning out. Reaching into her pocket, Sam pulled out her phone and opened up the apps screen and she promptly deleted her dating app from her screen. As soon as it was gone she felt a twist in her gut. "Did I just do the wrong thing?" she mumbled to herself.

"What did you say?" Nick's voice startled her because she was staring longingly at her phone screen she hadn't noticed him come back over. Sam picked up her drink and took a sip absentmindedly.

"Nothing, I just deleted my dating app, I don't think I'm made for all this." Sam admitted to him, as a confused look crossed her face. *Why did I say that? It was as though the words came out without my forcing them and I had no control at all over who they were spoken to.*

"Cut out for what? Dating? Seriously, you think there is a specific mold for people who are supposed to date and those who are supposed to be alone forever?" When Nick said it, Sam had to agree it sounded crazy. She just couldn't figure out what was wrong with her. Was she cursed? Was that an actual thing? Lost in thought she started to think of anyone she had pissed off to the point that they might want to curse her. Sam began counting people on her fingers, by the time she reached four Nick reached out and put his hand over hers.

"Stop, I don't know what you are counting, nor do I likely want to know given the look on your face. I want you to know one thing before I leave you to your thoughts and I'll probably regret saying it to you as soon as the words leave my mouth." That got Sam's attention and she didn't know if she wanted to hear it. Unfortunately, her mouth refused to work because she was scared that whatever might come out would run off Nick permanently.

"It's not you, not even a little bit. You are not the reason your dates are failing. It is completely and irrevocably those guy's fault. After spending these past few weeks with you," He didn't elaborate into their steamy kiss, but just kept it vague, "I can't figure out how you are attracting these creepers, but any guy would be lucky to have you and get to keep you." With that he turned and walked away without another word.

Chapter 8

The next few weeks went by with minimal incident, but that didn't mean she found her Prince Charming in the midst of the carnage. While she didn't have her dating app, she had her fair share of dates and fixups. Her last few dates still had their issues. One had a perpetual runny nose. Paul said, it was a condition he has suffered from since childhood. The problem was being in a bar, the napkins were merely tiny squares. While he did carry a handkerchief, it was saturated and Sam was repulsed every time he pulled it out to wipe away the newly gathered moisture. As expected that date ended without a kiss or scheduling another. Sam knew she couldn't sit through another date like that.

Then came Charlie, and his nervous sweats. Sam knew there were people who had medical conditions for overly active sweat glands and perhaps this made her superficial but she couldn't hang around a guy that needed to wear layers all year round to avoid soaking through. Charlie was one of these people and Sam didn't know how to handle it. While the smell was the least of her problems on this date. Poor Charlie spent the date with his arms locked beneath his armpits as though he were simulating a straight jacket. She could tell he was wearing at least three shirts and he still was soaking through his pits. The mere thought of it made Sam want to heave. Putting the guy out of his misery, she ended the date as quickly as she could.

Zane was attractive enough and Sam really thought he had a chance. At least until he got close enough for her to smell. His breath was thick with the smell of garlic as though he had eaten an entire clove for a snack before making the jaunt over to the bar. *Who does that? Garlic is the one thing people avoid when going on a first date and this guy clearly ate it in droves and had no qualms about it.*

That was the first red flag that he had less concern for her in a relationship. If he didn't consider her sense of smell before a date, what else would he forget to take into consideration later on down the road?

Sam didn't ever think her dating life would improve but she had a goal and was planning to see it through. Her mother had been the perfect parent for her. She never wanted for anything growing up. Sam had everything she ever needed and never felt as though she had been a burden for her mother. They had a great relationship and she was always comfortable talking to her, even through high school. Now her mother only asked for one thing, for Sam to find a man to settle down with and give her grandbabies before she died. After being such a wonderful mother, Sam didn't think she was asking too much of her now. Pressing on, she continued her adventure in dating. That is honestly what it was now, a new adventure every time, she accepted a new date.

Stanley was the sweetest guy, but unfortunately had a terrible skin condition that was reacting to the perfume she was wearing. Forcing him to spend the remainder of their date scratching as though he had fleas. Finally, he couldn't take it any longer and excused himself and never came back. That was a first for her to be left at the table, but in reality, it was for the best and she would have done the same if he hadn't first.

Ryder was different. Sam took her time and chatted via text with him for a few days prior to their date. After being in a slump for so long she needed a little bit to reset her mojo. Ryder was just what Sam thought she needed. He was witty and charming. Everything he said was just the right thing for the moment. He made her laugh and he made her think. After a little while she agreed to meet him for a date.

When he arrived at the bar he was all smiles and dressed in a Hugo Boss suit. She didn't know if that was an everyday thing for him or just him trying to impress her. She didn't dress down this time but he was by far out dressing her by a few thousand dollars. If she was honest, Sam was very impressed. He didn't carry himself on the phone in a way that said he was better than anyone else or had money. He was genuine in every conversation they had. That was the kind of person she wanted. Someone who could make her laugh and still be serious when needed.

As Ryder sat down he had a gorgeous smile that spread across his face. "You look beautiful Sam. I'm so glad we decided to do this. I've been dying to meet you for days. I feel like we know enough about each other that this should go like we are old friends hanging out." Sam's heart fluttered at his words and she settled in for an actual fun date. They ordered their drinks and just talked about anything and everything that came to mind. It was a perfect date in Sam's eyes. Ryder seemed to have no obvious issues and for once she was thankful to be on a date and actually was enjoying herself.

After about forty-five minutes of talking, Sam excused herself to go to the ladies room. For the first time she was actually planning to return. That though made the guilt hit instantly. How had every date recently, turned the bathroom into a place to go to escape and not just use the facilities? With that knowledge she made her trip quickly so Ryder didn't get any negative ideas.

Upon arriving back at the table, she noticed a tray of four shot glasses which contents was unknown, but two were already empty. Sitting back in her chair, Ryder smiled but his eyes were a little glassy where they hadn't been before she left. Gesturing at the glasses, "Having a mini party?"

Sam questioned while grabbing her wine glass and taking a drink.

"No, I just thought we could step up our night and enjoy some shots. I might have gotten started already, but I can just order more if need be." As Ryder finished speaking, Sam carefully reached up and wiped some spittle from her face. He didn't seem to realize he had begun spitting when he slurred his words. She silently hoped it was a random act and not a quirk that would continue.

"What are we drinking? I guess that plays a bigger factor as to whether we need more or not." Sam was willing to play along, there was no need to play it safe this late in the game.

"Tequila. My favorite shot and I try to drink as often as I can. I love it in mixed drinks too. The more the better in my opinion." He was licking his lips as though he was trying to get the last of the flavor off them so he didn't miss a single drop. Sam noticed the spray wasn't getting any better and mentally noted that him licking his lips was likely to support the issue rather than prevent it.

"Oh well, that one happens to be my downfall. My first tequila experience was in college and I had seventeen shots in a row. I thought I was dying the next day. While I found out I'm a very happy and friendly drunk, the next day was a bit a of a nightmare. That was the first time of many that I gave up drinking. So, while I will drink it in a margarita, shots are on my no-go list."

"Well, then that just means more for me." Quickly, Ryder threw back both shots without batting an eye. His cheeks were rosy and hot now from the amount of alcohol he had consumed. The shimmer in his eyes wasn't just a glimmer anymore, it was stark and obvious that this man was past tipsy and full on drunk. Sam had always made a point not to over drink on a first date and assumed others operated under the same thoughts. Apparently, Ryder didn't think that was a necessity seeing as he was three sheets to the wind.

"Wow you sure have a soft spot for that stuff. I personally drink but try not to over do it very often." Sam attempted to hint at his current state, but was shut down when he started back in spraying his way through it.

"I think we should all allow ourselves to enjoy our bodies no matter what form that is. If it be drinking or sexual, there should be no restrictions or penalty for making that choice." Ryder's statement should have been more of a turn on or attraction at least, but his constant spitting was getting beyond tolerable. Sam couldn't believe he had no idea he was covering her in the disgusting shower.

Unable to handle it any longer she snapped, "I'm not sure if you've noticed or not but I've spent the last few moments of our conversation wiping my face, arms and clothes because of your constant spitting. You seem to have a tick that while you drink you get careless in your speech. Slurs have become worse than holding a slobbering baby. You are a grown man and should be able to control your body better than a child. If you'll excuse me I'm going to have to end this date and take my leave of you before I need to go home and bathe properly in order to get your mess off of me. With that, Sam stood from the table and sauntered off to the bar.

Plopping down in her usual spot, Nick nods to tell her he sees her. Knowing he will be over soon, she reaches into her bag for tissue. To her surprise she has a wipe in her bag from her last shift and gratefully Sam begins to unfold and wipe down all of her exposed skin. As she finished Nick approached her side of the bar with a look of fascination.

"What are you looking at?" Sam started patting her face with her free hand worried she missed something she couldn't see.

"I'm sorry." Nick said with a shake of his head. "I got a bit lost in the sight of you wiping your chest off. Did your date throw a drink on you? Do I need to go after him and explain to him how not to treat a lady?"

"While I'm thankful for your chivalry, my date didn't do anything near that…obvious. It's nice to know you would have been there. I haven't had a drink spilled on me since college. That was, I'm sure, someone who thought I was stealing the attention of his frat brothers and therefore developed a deep-seated dislike of me. Not anything I actually did, just a perceived notion beyond my control." Sam stopped there realizing she hadn't thought of her college days in years but that memory popped into her mind at his suggestion. Laughing quietly to herself, she let it go.

"If you weren't cleaning off a spilled drink then why did you need to clean your chest so thoroughly after a date? Honestly, nothing comes to mind that would require that since you are acting so calm." Nick offered his hand to take the used wipe and threw it away.

"Well, I thought this one was different and I even hung out longer than I have for a while. I just didn't factor in the alcohol into the equation. He was the prefect dream of a date until he started drinking too much. Then he," Sam was about to continue and Nick interrupted her.

"Did he try something with you? Were you wiping off his slimy touch?" The look in his eye was unexpected. He was getting angry at the possible scenario and she hadn't even confirmed or denied it yet.

"No, he spit all over me!" She was so heated at this point because of his reaction, she couldn't control the exasperated tone. The look on Nick's face at her revelation was priceless. Sam couldn't tell if he was unsure of the truth of her statement or just couldn't fathom it. She opted to clarify this time before assuming. "He apparently has a bad habit when he starts to slur about not being able to control the saliva in his mouth. He either starts producing too much or he just has no power over it but I wore enough and just got fed up with the situation. I basically told him off and left the table. It was almost empowering if it weren't about spittle."

"I'm surprised you didn't go straight home to shower all that off. Do you always carry wipes in your purse? That seems very motherly of you. Is there part of your story you haven't shared with me?" Nick winked knowingly but proceeded to mix a drink using a bottle with liquid as black as night. Letting him continue it, Sam decided to answer him.

"No, I don't always carry them, but I had them in my pocket from my last flight and when I got to my car I realized they were there so I threw them in my purse and forgot they were there. This time I was pleasantly surprised to see something besides my usual tissues. Since most public bathrooms have gone to hand dryers and not towels, I try and keep something in my bag." As she finished explaining to him, Nick placed a drink in front of her that didn't let in much light. It was the darkest drink she had ever seen and she was worried he had mixed it with some form of tar.

"I'm only drinking this because you have lured me in with all your fantastic concoctions in the past. I honestly think this looks like you dug this up from the depths of Hell and I am likely to develop a demon complex after I drink it. Is there a tiny incubus in the bottom of this glass waiting to inhabit my body and give me unending orgasms? That is the only way I can fathom a demon possessing my body doesn't end badly for me." Sam looked up at Nick before she took a drink. Noticing his bewildered expression, she added, "Don't judge me!" With that, she took a gulp of the liquid, accepting her possible fate. Pleasantly surprised she didn't taste anything close to licorice. Nick should be glad because he probably would have needed a wipe next. She took a moment before speaking as she soaked up all the flavors of this demonic brew. Unexpectedly she tasted fruity undertones again. It seemed that Nick either had a thing for fruity drinks or assumed she did. *I should ask him to clarify that I'm not a stereotypical girl. While I like my fruity drinks it's not the only thing I want to drink.* Not that this wasn't good because it was and likely would be a drink she could let herself get drunk on if she wasn't careful.

Nick's watchful eye never left her face as she took in all the elements of his drink. She decided to go ahead and ask before she talked herself out of it, "Before I ask what you've named this Satanic potion and I run away to my room to enjoy the pleasures it is likely to give me in my sleep, what is it with you and fruity drinks? Is it you or is it me?"

"Neither. That isn't how my brain works. I have a knack for blending the flavors together that people wouldn't necessarily expect or attempt. While they might not all be unique ingredients, like the Blavod vodka in this one, they are all equally as thought out. In this case I paired the vodka with Southern Comfort. I wanted it to have a slight fruity tone with some spiced undertones, but not be the first thing you taste. You also seemed like you weren't an orange juice person. I can always tell the ones who prefer pineapple juice so I used that to balance everything out. Mixing drinks is like therapy for me. I can express so much more through a good cocktail than I can with words at times." Sam was taken back by his response. She'd never considered drinks in that way, but he always did have a way with drinks and they always did make her feel better, if nothing else they made her laugh.

"All jokes aside, what should I call this new form of therapy, that will likely get me beyond drunk if I don't set my limit to one?" Sam took another swallow of the blackened brew.

"Well, you weren't far off in your description, but on a different paranormal plane. This one is called 'Dragon's Spit'." The look in his eye was a cross between a leer and a sexy smolder. It sent fire through Sam's entire body. That made her wonder about that incubus one more time before finishing her drink and calling it a night.

Chapter 9:

That night Sam's dreams leaned toward the paranormal. She had never had so many sexually enhanced dream elements in her life. She was going to start calling Dragon's Spit something more appropriate, like Incubus Breath. That drink had her so worked up, or it was more likely Nick and his way with words and the way his eyes traveled over her body when she was wiping away the wayward saliva. If one could feel a pair of eyes on you, Nick's eyes would have been hot and lingering. Sam just wished he hadn't brushed their kiss under the rug then perhaps she would have had another experience to add to her imaginations.

Instead that night, she dreamed of demons pleasuring her beyond compare and they all shared the same face. Each with different emotions she had seen cross Nick's face in the bar. His sexy smirk was what the one pleasuring her with his mouth between her legs wore when he looked up at her. Another had one eyebrow raised in question as he approached her bare chest. As though he were asking for permission, but didn't wait for her to grant it before his mouth enveloped her aching nub, promptly making it's twin jealous. Not to worry because there was another Nick triplet there and waiting to take care of the neglect. She had never felt so cared for and wanted in her life. Just when the trio of Nicks had worked her almost to climax she startled awake. Instantly, Sam was left bereft of the thing she wanted the most.

Wiping a layer of sweat off her brow, Sam grumbled softly to herself. She had to get herself under control. All this dating nonsense had her worked up and tied up in knots. She hadn't had a good nights sleep in weeks. Either she couldn't fall asleep or like this she would wake up drenched in sweat all hot and bothered clearly unsatisfied.

She needed to do something soon or her next option would be mail order bride. In a moment of weakness, Sam pulled out her phone and proceeded to reload the dating app on her phone. Logging in and her phone was inundated with messages and heart notifications. "Wow! I take a few weeks off and the entire world blows up my phone."

Sam scrolled through looking for a diamond amongst the roughage. "Chef. Well maybe he could cook dinner if it panned out. Lord, only knows my cooking skills leave something to be desired." Sam kept scrolling opting for a better option than someone to provide sustenance on her days off. "Cabbie. Well I'd never have to pay for transportation. With my job I can fly anywhere and with a cab driver I could get around the city too." Shaking her head at her thought process, Sam moved on. There needs to be a deeper reason to date someone beyond basic problem solving. After a few minutes of speed scrolling she did a quick back swipe. "Well now, what do we have here? A doctor and he is gorgeous. Good job while being attractive, a girl could work with that." Then she clicked his profile to dig a little deeper, she didn't want to be so shallow that she merely dated a guy because he had a good job and was easy on the eyes. Even if those factors would add to her nighttime excursions.

Doctor, tall, dark and handsome was an understatement. He had that roguish look that spoke to her inner sex kitten. *I have an inner sex kitten? Wow, this guy must be powerful to uncover something I didn't even know I had.* Sam let her inner dialogue settle as she read through the doctor's profile. It seems he was a surgeon of some kind, but since Sam had little medical knowledge the title was the only part that was impressive. He must be very skilled with his hands to have a job like that. He seemed to like to do charity work overseas every few years. Did that mean he was compassionate and cared for others or that he just wanted everyone to know he could put on a show when needed? Sam knew that people with money had a tendency to flaunt what they had as a show of what they could do for others and to get a pat on the back. The right publicity for a charity event and their name would run through all the papers and tabloids.

Sam gave herself a mental slap, *you haven't even met the guy and you are already berating him.* Feeling ashamed of her constant inner ramblings, Sam sent him a message asking him to meet her at the bar tonight. If nothing else, giving this guy a chance should alleviate her of some of the guilt that was making itself at home on her psyche.

That night she opted to dress up a bit for her date. Since the guy was a doctor chances were he would be a bit more fashionable than a pair of jeans and a dress shirt. Deciding on a bandage style red number with a high neckline. She looked classy and sexy. Pairing that with a pair of black four-inch heels Sam felt she was the epitome of style and sex appeal.

Tania was working and for that Sam was grateful. She wasn't sure what to expect tonight as she hadn't taken a lot of time to get to know the good doctor beyond a profile search and the heart he gave her weeks ago. She wasn't even sure he would respond to her message with how spur of the moment it was. If this didn't pan out, in the future she would be more diligent in the take time method. Then again that could be her problem in the first place. She always spent extensive amounts of time in the getting to know period before agreeing to a date. They have plenty of time to give her false hope that the date will be promising. Only to be disappointed in the actual date and going home alone. Sam gave Tania a quick nod and the sweet waitress made her way over.

"Got another live one tonight?" Tania was starting to see the humor in Sam's dating life. Not that Sam could blame her, if she weren't directly involved she would find it amusing as well. Sadly, this was her life and she was living it, so finding the humor wasn't as easily done.

"I guess you could say that. I set up an online date again." Sam said with reluctance hanging her head slightly because it was still an embarrassing though to her.

"Online? I thought you gave that up weeks ago. What happened to making up your mind and sticking to it?" Tania was leaning against the table and practically sitting in the other bar height chair.

"Call it a moment of weakness after another restless night." Sam didn't lift her head unable to face the shame of her weakness.

"Restless? This has been happening for a while, I take it?" Tania was observant and wouldn't let a sleeping dog lie, not even if in this case it was obvious Sam didn't want to discuss it.

"Yes." Sam replied simply hoping her lack of details would tell her to drop it.

No such luck. "Too many dates and not enough overnights? At least some of these guys provide enough material for your spank bank, right?" Winking at her Tania wasn't shy about anything. This was her favorite topic. They had gone out a few weeks ago and tried to get Sam to take a guy home for the night, just to work out the kinks. Sam was so embarrassed because those were her exact words in front of the guy she wanted Sam to take home.

"Many of them have been attractive enough, but that hasn't exactly been my hinderance. Their individual issues out shine their physical features. Therefore, they are no longer eligible to be used for pleasure later." Sam purposely omitted the actual star of her fantasies since she didn't know if she could trust Tania to keep her mouth shut. If she knew that Sam had any interest in Nick, Sam wouldn't ever be able to come back to her favorite bar. Tania would march right over to the bar and lay it all out for Nick right then and there.

"I can see the problem. If this one doesn't pan out you need to let me take you out again on my next night off. We need to cause some trouble together." Tania wagged her eyebrows giving Sam the idea of what trouble she wanted to encounter and realized she needed to slow her train immediately.

"Well, let's hope I don't have to endure too many of these dates before I find Mr. Right." Sam glanced up and a debonair gentleman that looked a lot like her Dr. Date was headed straight for her. Giving Tania a subtle nod indicating the man approaching, she took the hint and wandered away.

Sam began to stand up, but her date waved her back down. "Hi, you look just as amazing as your picture suggested. I'm Travis, and it is a pleasure to meet you. I was surprised that you messaged and wanted to meet so soon. I wasn't going to pass up a chance to meet you so I cleared my schedule tonight." Travis was just as suave as his profile suggested. Sam found it very endearing but still didn't know him enough to decide if it is a front or not.

If nothing else, Sam was glad she opted to dress up. Travis spared no expense and was wearing a suit and tie. Though his tie was loosened and slightly askew and the top button was undone. She didn't know if that was work attire or just playing the part. Either way, paired with his five o'clock shadow, it had the added effect. She could get lost staring at this man and be happy to never leave.

"It's a pleasure to meet you Travis. I'm glad it worked out that we could get together tonight. I have to admit you are the highlight of my week so far." Sam realized she was being more upfront than normal, but perhaps it was for the best.

"Oh, trust me the pleasure is all mine. I'm in a very lucky position and I can't wait to see where the night goes," a glint passed through Travis' eyes and Sam wished she knew him better to understand what that meant. Either way it didn't give her any indication she should be alarmed. She was in a public place surrounded by people. Those who were working were friends or as close as they could get.

Travis placed his drink order and Sam decided to drive the conversation for a while. "So being a surgeon must be an exciting line of work. I can't imagine the dedication and schooling you had to endure to get to where you are today." Mentally patting herself on the back for making the question sound intelligent while still uplifting him for his accomplishments. In her life the amount of times she could say that could be counted on her fingers. She had a bad habit of saying the wrong thing at the least optimal moment.

"Oh, I'm not a surgeon." Travis replied simply. Sam looked at him in shock. She was sure that was what she had read on his profile. That would be hard to not see correctly as it would stand out to most women as a reason to accept a date. Travis shook his head and waved his hand toward her up and down as though he were tamping down or brushing away her anger in a placating gesture that just made the frustration boil under her skin. "I'm a surgical nurse in the pediatric field. My options are limited for space when listing profession and while I don't mind being a nurse it says something else about who I am to mention the surgical part. My profile isn't lying as it says I'm in the surgical field. Most women, like yourself, assume surgeon when they read it. It's ok. It's a common enough mistake I am willing to overlook it." The way he spoke to her didn't calm her simmering emotions. He had a way of speaking down to her and she hoped he realized what he was doing and planned to redeem himself in the near future or her previous attempt was going to be the best things she said or did all night.

"Well, I'm so sorry for my mistake. I'll attempt to read better in the future." Sam said through slightly gritted teeth and she attempted to get herself under control.

"I'm sure you're observant enough. Getting to know you will be an adventure of the heart." Travis' words were an improvement but still not reassuring Sam that this date would get better.

"What would you like to know about me seeing as I have learned a bit more about you in the last five minutes? I'm a flight attendant and I love the freedom my job gives me. I also learned how much I love to travel another aspect I get to explore this way." The look on Travis' face was unclear because Sam didn't know him that well. After a moment San realized it was almost an endearing look mixed with adoration. Sam was confused because they'd known each other for just a few minutes and as far as she could tell they were getting off on the wrong foot. Deciding to be the bigger person, Sam realized that likely she was the only one who took offense earlier when it wasn't intended. She wanted to give him a chance and so she let go of her anger hoping for a better outcome.

By the time they had finished their first drinks the night had improved. Travis was a wonderful conversationalist and while he loved his job, it wasn't the most impressive information she learned about him. Travis was a giver by nature. Growing up in a house that he never wanted for anything, Travis had gone to school with some kids who had to do more to get to where they were than he had. Something clicked inside him and he realized that he had to do more with what he had. So now he hosts galas and charity functions for underprivileged kids to be able to achieve their dreams. Learning this made Sam's wall crumble. She realized that she had misjudged Travis she was willing to let this date continue a little further.

They decided to order dinner which was huge for Sam because she rarely let her dates get to appetizers but she agreed to this because she felt bad for prejudging him just a few minutes into their date. Finding out how wrong she was made her feel a little guilty, allowing her to make this decision.

Their food had arrived and Tania winked at her, knowing that she was going out on a limb here. As they were just ordering their third round of drinks, something changed. Sam noticed Travis must be getting a bit tipsy and letting his guard down, not necessarily for the better.

Sam was nibbling a little on her salad and a bit of dressing slipped down her chin. Before she could reach it with her napkin, Travis beat her too it. Dabbing it with his napkin, Sam felt a little awkward as she didn't think their date had progressed into a relationship worthy of this behavior. Regardless she let it go and chalked it up to him being nice.

As Travis finished his third drink and was begging Tania to bring him another, Sam was noticing another red flag on his behavior. He had a tendency to pout when he asked for things. Not a big deal, but Sam wanted a guy who was manly enough to ask for what he wanted not beg for it like a child. Unfortunately, Tania was messing with him a bit and Sam learned it only got worse.

"I'm not sure you need another drink tonight, sir." Tania knew he only had had three drinks and he wasn't near cut off point, but Sam knew she loved to play with her customers and usually got bigger tips for it. She was notorious for walking away and telling them no. Then coming back later and asking if the changed their minds.

Sam never understood it but with her personality it worked so well for her.

"What? Pleease let me have one more." Travis whined at Tania and Sam sat there in utter shock. If this was how he acted when he didn't get his way after just a few drinks, she wasn't sure she wanted to know what a lot of drinks brought.

"Give me one good reason why you need another drink. If it is good enough then I'll let you have it." Tania played this game a little too well.

"I've been a good boy today. I think that I've earned it." Tania was in an interesting mood and Sam wasn't willing to listen any longer to Travis' whining. Instead she went back to her dinner.

After a while Tania left and they must have come to an agreement because she brought him another drink. "You're awfully quiet now, missy. Cat's got your tongue?" Travis was being very playful and under the right circumstances this could be fun, but Sam didn't find it fun at the moment. Instead of answering she just shook her head and continued eating. Travis waited a moment then continued. "Oh well if the cat got your tongue, can I have your nose?" Then without hesitation or warning, he reached across the table and attempted to remove her nose as one would a child at a birthday party. Sam leaned back in utter shock.

"What are you doing?" Sam pulled back far enough to be out of reach of him and wasn't sure what else to say. This was peculiar behavior to say the least. Who acts like this on a date, let alone a first date?

"Oh, did Sammy whammy get a boo boo? Do you need a kissy whissy to make it better?" Travis started puckering and making kissy noises as he leaned closer. Sam's eyes were wide with shock. What was happening? This pediatric nurse was taking his work home with him and Sam wondered if perhaps he had actually escaped from a different ward of the hospital and not the surgical wing. Instead of answering the question asked, she grabbed her purse and excused herself to the bathroom.

Sam felt juvenile herself, as she hid out in the ladies room, but what else was she supposed to do. She never ran straight home for fear of these guys following her. Leaning against the wall, she was thankful that this bar sported a sitting area, off the bathroom area, for longer waits on busy nights.

After what felt like an eternity in the bathroom, the door opened and Tania walked in with a sassy look on her face.

"Have you taken up bathroom sitting as a new job? You've been in here forever. I walked by your table a few times and you weren't there. I figured since your date hadn't left yet you must be in here. Have you figured out the escape plan yet?"

"Not exactly, the window in here is a bit high and a tad small. I'd say if I succeeded in climbing the counter to reach it I would either get stuck halfway through it or fall off the counter and crack my head open. How did you know I needed an escape besides my lengthy stay in the bathroom?" Sam didn't frequent the bathroom on her date nights but there was always the chance that she was having a stomach issue and that was the cause of her new residence choice.

"Well, I wouldn't have even bothered coming in to check on you since you are a grown woman and can field these problems by yourself. The thing that made me take an early break to sneak in and find you was your date put a pacifier on you plate. I noticed it when I walked back the last time and I knew it hadn't been there the previous rounds I'd made." Sam looked at Tania with an incredulous expression. This guy was the epitome of insane. Not only did his childlike behavior increase the more he drank, he actually pushed the issue into his dating life. He probably has some crazy fetish too, that involved dressing up his partners before sex to resemble a younger generation. Sam shuddered at the thought of him during a sexual encounter and made her decision.

"I'm a coward and I'm not going back out there. We have two options, wait him out and see how long before he takes the hint or you could go tell him I received a call in the bathroom and have a family emergency. I'm just hoping he isn't actually insane and escaped his padded cell somewhere and we have bigger problems to deal with." Sam looked at Tania with pleading eyes and internally cringed because she remembered Travis' begging for a drink.

"I'll go get rid of him for you, girl. I'd hate to think of you hiding in the bathroom all night, but that means you owe me a night out and tomorrow is my next night off. I know you don't have to work so don't even try to get out of it." Sam rolled her eyes, not that she wasn't looking forward to a night out with Tania, but because her goal will be just to get both of them laid. Sam just wanted to get through this without having to see her psycho date again. She'd agree to run away to Mexico, if that was what Tania suggested.

"Deal, just tell me when to be ready and where to meet you and it's a date." Sam would take anything at this point over her current situation.

Tania made her way back to the door then turned back to Sam, "Like I'd make my date meet me anywhere. I'm going to pick up my girl, as is proper." Tania wagged her eyebrow at Sam, making a giggle burst out of her. The alcohol she had consumed was working but she had been so distracted by Travis' actions that she hadn't let herself feel the effects. Not being able to form words through her laughter, Sam just waved Tania out the door.

"I'll be back in a bit to let you know the coast is clear." Tania disappeared out the door, letting it swing shut behind her. Feeling a bit more relaxed now that her evening was sorted out, Sam let herself sit on the sofa. Slipping her heels off she tucked her legs up underneath her and got comfortable. She had no idea how long it would take Travis to leave and she wasn't going to stand on precedence all night while waiting.

Not moving was taking its toll. That combined with the stress of the evening and the drinks she had consumed Sam felt her eyes getting heavy. Not having anything else to do she tried to fight it for a while, but ultimately gave up. It was a slow night and the bathroom wasn't the hotspot this evening so, no one had come into the bathroom and Tania hadn't made her way back in yet.

She felt something brush across her cheek lightly. In her sleepy haze she didn't know what it was but brushed it away with the back of her hand. She lived alone and had no pets so wasn't concerned with anyone needing her attention. Then Sam was startled by a slight snickering sound. Afraid to open her eyes, Sam thought, *who is in my house?* Not having a reason to hear a voice in her sleep, Sam's eyes flew open and it took her a moment to focus on what she was seeing. Soon it all flooded back, her above average horrible date, her hiding in the bathroom, Tania running off said date and apparently, she dosed off while waiting for her to return. Internally cringing she was even more surprised by the deep blue eyes staring at her. They looked like the deepest part of the ocean as seen from above. Sam was always thrilled when looking out of the airplane. Seeing the water below and being able to see where the depths were greater than a section before.The problem was she was in the ladies room and these eyes were attached to a stubble covered masculine face that she knew immediately.

"What are you doing in here?" Sam questioned, while trying to get her bearings. It wasn't every day she fell asleep in a public restroom.

"Tania got busy and your date wasn't ready to leave when he heard you had to leave. Apparently, he wasn't too upset and continued drinking until I had to cut him off. Finally, he left, but that was after a couple hours. Tania hasn't had a minute to herself to come and let you know. Looks like you found something to do with your time though. Has anyone ever told you that you are adorable when you sleep?" Nick was standing in the women's bathroom and he didn't feel the need to address that, but he told her how cute she was while she was asleep? How long did he stare at her before waking her up?

"I've been in here for over two hours? How did no one notice the sleeping girl in the bathroom?" She muttered to herself, deciding not to dignify his question with an answer.

"Actually, someone just came out of here and told me someone was in here sleeping and since I didn't have anyone else I could send back to check, I just had a customer come and make sure the bathroom was empty besides you and I came myself. You can imagine my surprise when I saw it was you sleeping. Then I went out and checked with Tania to see what happened as to why you were in here before I woke you, but hung an out of order sign on the door so you wouldn't be disturbed before I got back and I knew I could run back in here without needing to check again." Nick had a look on his face that said he was proud of his subterfuge and actually she was thankful he gave her that privacy with minimal embarrassment. While she would have preferred Tania find her, this was equally acceptable.

"Thank you! I don't frequently take naps in places like this, but as a flight attendant, I've learned I can fall asleep anywhere if the conditions are right. This sofa is quite comfortable and seeing as I was stuck in here and didn't have much to do, I suppose my body opted for the next best thing. That and I had enough to drink and hadn't let it burn past the relaxed point." Sam shifted her feet slowly and slipped her feet back into her shoes. From the corner of her eye she noticed Nick's eyes never left her as she accomplished this. He watched her legs emerge from beneath her. She was thankful, that even though the dress was a bit restrictive, it hadn't ridden up too far, but still more of her leg was exposed that would normally be. Nick noticed and took in every inch of exposed skin as though it were a lifeline and it he could feast on just the image.

When she had finished adjusting her shoes to a comfortable place, she shifted and started to lower the hemline of her dress. In a moment of empowerment, she looked up and met Nick's eyes while she accomplished the task. The heat in his eyes radiated from him as though if he left it too long unattended his entire body would incinerate from exposure. Sam scooted to the edge of the sofa in an effort to get up and she had barely made it to her feet when Nick gripped her hip firmly and pulled her towards him and pressed her body against his own. She hadn't forgotten what it felt like to be pressed against him though she didn't mind it either. All of her nerve endings were firing and she felt every delicious inch of him. They didn't move and he didn't release his hold. Nick never once broke eye contact with her and Sam could feel her breath catching as she didn't know what he was going to do. His eyes which were dark normally were nearly black with his desire. She knew he wanted her but it seemed he was fighting an internal battle. She didn't know if she could make the move and stop him from doubting or fighting with himself.

Without another thought, Sam laced her hands around his neck and in a fluid motion she rose to her tiptoes and pressed her lips to his. Sparks ignited once again as though they were happy to be in this position again. Their bodies acted as old friends even though they had only met once. This was entirely out of sorts for her but instead of fighting her instincts Sam let her body control the situation. After a few moments Nick took control and guided her back to the sofa that she had just woken from. Pressing her back into the cushions he locked his fingers of his right hand into her hair and his left hand stayed on her hip to keep her locked into him. She wasn't going to complain. Everything about Nick drew her in and all she wanted was for him to have his wicked way with her.

"Nick." Sam moaned between kisses as he continued down her neck. Caressing every inch of her with his hands, his tongue made a meal out of all the exposed skin on her body. Then his hand that was locked on her hip began traveling down her body and between her legs. She moaned his name again as he pushed her dress up and his fingers ran over her soaked panties. Pressing up with her hips she pushed against his fingers to create a delicious friction.

"Please!" She begged as he ran his finger down the edge of the soaked cloth. Sam wanted more than anything to have him tear them away. A moment later she got her wish as the fabric tore away she knew she would be left with a scraps but it would be worth it. She sighed in pleasure as his fingers sunk deep into her slit and his thumb put the right amount of pressure on her nub. She screamed out when his pumping fingers curled and hit the soft and sensitive spot that most couldn't find. She knew Nick would be more than skilled at seeking and finding her intimate areas that would bring her to the most amazing climaxes. Quicker than she had ever known, Nick brought her screams back and she gasped in pleasure as light exploded behind her eyes. That was the fastest she had ever reached climax in her life.

Moments later he was pressing his thick rod to her entrance and her eyes flew open hoping to catch a glimpse but their clothes were in the way. As he pressed inside of her she cried out at the fullness. He inched in slowly to adjust her to his size and he started moaning her name the farther he reached. "Sam... Sam... Sam!"

When he was fully seated, he shouted her name again "SAM!" Only his voice was different this time. Not quite as husky as the previous times had been and much more *feminine*. Sam knew something was wrong and this time her eyes flew open in surprise and with immediate disappointment.

Tania was standing above her in the bathroom.

Chapter 10

"What are you doing sleeping in the bathroom?" Tania had taken a step back in disgust after Sam had finally awoken from the best dream she had ever had in her life.

"I got tired of waiting and I don't play games on my phone. I must have dozed off waiting for a green light." Sam wiped her face in an attempt to wake up and realized she had drooled just a little during her nap.

"Girl! I got slammed and couldn't break away. I'm so sorry. I assumed you had snuck out long ago. Your date finished his meal and was out in thirty minutes. When I went to the bar, Nick asked about you and that was when I knew you must have still been in here." Sam glanced at the clock on her phone while Tania was talking and realized she had been huddled in the restroom lobby for two and a half hours. She should have guessed by how deep she was into her dream and that Tania's words had barely made their way in. Then her brain honed in on one thing that Tania said.

"Wait, Nick asked about me? Why did he do that?" she perked up a bit at the thought that Nick wondered about her. Perhaps she had made a bigger impression than she originally thought.

"He just noticed you in the front house earlier in the night. You have made a habit of visiting the bar after your dates to get away. He assumed you liked this one and you guys left together. I informed him otherwise and then I remembered I was supposed to come here and finish my rescue. This is why I'm not a white knight. There are men much better skilled at this and I'll gladly leave you to them." Tania was a character. She always had a thought and a fun anecdote for any moment. Even now, she was making light of Sam sleeping in the bathroom lounge and taking the blame on herself. Sam had found herself a great friend through all of this. Tania even worked as much as Sam and equally loved her job. They were two peas in a pod. Even though Sam was off work more days in a row and Tania was forced to take a day off every week or two, they still had the same work dedication and would move mountains if work needed something from them.

The girls spent another couple minutes laughing about the the evening they'd had, then Tania spoke up again.

"Let's get out of this nasty bathroom. I can't believe you'd want to spend another second in here. I'll buy you a drink at the bar, before you head home. It's the least I can do after the night you've had and part of it being my doing."

Sam followed Tania over to the bar happy to be rid of her most recent date from Hell. This one was close to the topping the worst list. *Why are all the best ones the most creepy in the end?* Sam's thoughts were kept to herself though, since she really didn't want an answer to that question.

Catching Nick's eye, she sat down at the bar. Tania flagged Nick over quickly. "Take care of our girl here. She has had a rough one and has spent the last couple hours in the ladies room because of Yours Truly." Tania pointed at herself to help make her point a little clearer. "I've got anything she has on my tab tonight. It's the least I can do for what I made her endure." With that she flitted off to check on her tables and left Sam in the capable hands of Nick.

"That sounds like another great story, but do you need anything before you start. Two hours in the bathroom is quite a long time to go without." Nick was always very considerate of what she needed and he actually listened. Unfortunately, Sam's body began to hum again after her dream, earlier. Now, being so close to the star of said dream was almost too much to handle. Tania didn't mention it so perhaps she wasn't a sleep talker after all and there was nothing to be concerned about.

"I'd love a bottle of water just to clear my parched mouth. I feel like I ate a bag of cotton balls after my time in there." Like magic, a bottle of water and a cold glass appeared on the bar. Nick flashed her one of his signature smirks and she knew that she was helpless to his wiles and there was going to be no use trying to use her legs in the foreseen future. *This bar top could be comfortable. Perhaps after the floor is mopped for the night it could become a suitable bed.* As Sam pondered her sleeping arrangements to come since she wouldn't be able to walk out of the bar to go home in her current state, she sipped her cold water grateful for the hydration to her lacking system.

"This must have been a doozy for you to have spent so long in the bathroom and for Tania to be buying your drinks. I'm not gonna lie. This guy is dying to hear what happened like an old maid getting ready to play bridge with the town gossips. This one is bound to make my day." Nick was practically bouncing with unspent energy and she hadn't ever seen him like this before. Sam wasn't sure that it was a good look on him. Other than the fact that he looked years younger when he was this excited about something.

"Well there's not much to tell. My date showed up and I thought I had hit the jackpot on this one. I should have known that wasn't the case and just went home. They always were too good to be true." Sam sipped her water and then continued since Nick was patiently waiting for the good stuff to come out. She opted to downplay it a little longer. "He kept up his side of the conversation which is always a bonus. I hate one-sided dates. Since it had been going so well, we ordered some food. That is usually the sign of a good date, right?" She asked this question not really expecting an answer but Nick nodded his head in agreement. She had him on the line and it was time to set the hook and reel him in the rest of the way. "WRONG! My date of choice for the evening gets a little wonky with alcohol consumption and not just chatty or handsy. He gets down right certifiable." She paused for effect and made him ask.

"What did he do? I didn't hear any complaints from nearby customers?" Nick was leaning against the bar and so close her words could have been a whisper and he would have heard each and every one. She had him right where she wanted him and could smell his cologne. It was warm like sandalwood but with an undertone she couldn't quite identify. Either way she would have crawled into him just to take it in and memorize it. Shaking her head slightly to regain her thoughts that had strayed farther than intended, Sam continued.

"It was subtle at first a word here a phrase there, but he had a tone that set me off. I didn't understand in the beginning what was happening. When our food came out he offered to cut my meat and that was beyond odd. I turned him down but then his tones turned into references and he was speaking mostly in baby talk and had abandoned adult speech patterns. I was at a loss and didn't know what to do. Finally, I excused myself to the ladies room to regroup and Tania followed me. She advised that I should stay put until she gave me the okay. Apparently, she only followed me because this wonderful perfection of a date, had laid a pacifier on my plate." Nick was frozen. Sam didn't know if he was still digesting the entire story or what she should be preparing herself for. Slowly after an extended silence, Nick's face began to animate once more. A slow smile spread across his face but still he didn't move or say anything. So in order to avoid prolonging this uncomfortable silence Sam continued.

"I didn't know what else to do. I was so appalled by his behavior and antics. I had never heard of anyone like this. I could only imagine the sorts of fetishes he could be into. All I could see was me dressed up in a dolly outfit painted with Raggedy Ann makeup and sat in a chair forced to have a tea party." At this point Sam knew she was rambling but Nick still refused to speak or add in anything to let her in on what he was thinking. He just stood there with a Joker -like grin plastered across his face.

Finally, after what felt like an eternity and many words spoken by Sam just to fill the silence, Nick moved. He began mixing and Sam knew then what was coming. He still had yet to speak, but she knew a drink would be in her hands shortly. Nick did his best communicating through his drinks. It was becoming a novelty between them and one that Sam was starting to look forward to. The drink names no longer made her angry or frustrated with him. She knew it was his way of expressing his thoughts in that situation. When words failed him, he always had his drinks to fall back on.

A beautifully colored shot was placed in front of her moments later. She had stopped watching him mix drinks because she found it more fun to try and taste the concoction and figure out what secrets it contained. This one was a bit surprising because before he slid it the final distance to be within reach for Sam to drink it he whipped out a lighter and set the drink on fire. She was pleasantly surprised because she had never ordered a flaming drink before so this would be a first on so many levels. Usually, Nick didn't give her shots either. She had received cocktails before now.

Nick slid it over to her and indicated that she should blow out the flame. Doing as instructed, she blew on her drink as though it were her birthday. Picking up the glass she threw it back like a pro. She didn't frequent the shots scene but it was old hat whenever the urge called on her. This time the flavors were heavy on the sweet and fruit juice for sure. It reminded her of a beach cocktail and she could imagine it sporting a itty bitty tropical umbrella if treated to one at a resort. She twirled the glass of the now empty drink and let her imagination wander to sunny days and warm sand. She could almost hear the waves as they hit the shore. It was one of her most favorite vacations when she was afforded the time off or a few days layover on a coastal destination. Sam was always known to pack a polka dot bikini just for such occasions. As her mind drifted to the gulls squawking over head, a throat cleared. Sam was brought back quickly to the present and a small frown tugged at the corners of her mouth. Wishing she could sip her drink once more for one last taste, she cleared the negative thoughts from her mind. Who was she to be upset to be stuck in the reality that was her life? No one else had the luxury to magically change her situation. Why should she?

"Okay, I'm stumped. Besides the fact that this drink takes me to a tropical island, I'm lost as to the ingredients."

"That description is very apt. It is equal mixture of orange, cranberry and pineapple juices. Then rum to top it off. As you can see it needed a flame to finish it off with a little bit of flare."

"No wonder I couldn't isolate the individual flavors, it was sensory overload for me. So what is the name of this beachtastic delicacy, that will likely be very apropos?" Sam was intentionally building this up knowing she would be pleased with whatever he had come up with. She wasn't disappointed.

"Oh Baby! Oh Baby!" Nick was very proud of himself and it showed through every fiber of his being.

"Well, *Baby* I'm happy to announce you succeeded in ridding me of my flaming drink virginity. I'm pleased to have been able to have shared this experience with you." Sam rested her head on one hand folded on her fingers as her elbow rested on the bar top. Only she realized what she had said a moment later, but it was too late to take back her choice of words so instead she owned it, and kept her confident façade in place.

"Oh, to have divested you of such a thing is unheard of at your age, you should have had so many more experiences than just one little shot." He placed his hand over his chest in mock surprise. Sam had to work to hold in her giggles. "I would be happy to plunder any other lingering innocence from you in any way necessary." His undertone wasn't missed and a chill ran up Sam's spine and back down into areas that she had been trying to tame since emerging from the restroom. She shifted in her seat to apply some friction where she needed it in an area that was now on fire from Nick's mere words. To think he could set her aflame with a few carefully chosen words, what could he do if he just touched her again. Something he hadn't slipped up and done since their shared kiss in the alley that had turned her world upside down. Deciding to keep her situation under wraps she tried to remain in control.

"You talk as though you are a man experienced with such talents. How would someone know you were trust worthy?" She didn't know if those were the words she was really thinking but it was better than telling him how she was feeling.

"I guess that is the allure to someone across the table from me. She would need to know if the dark mystery of the situation was enough to warrant going out on the edge and taking a risk." Now Nick was speaking in some sort of code. She didn't know if he was talking to her, about her or just using this as a 'women in general' situation. Instead of giving away her naivety, Sam took a large swallow of her water and smiled flirtatiously and excused herself for the evening.

*****

The next morning Sam was still confused about the previous night's escapades. Between her fiasco of a date and the strange interaction with Nick, she was out of sorts. Needless to say, she had some more dreams that eluded to her own personal state of insanity.

After wallowing in bed longer than necessary, Sam needed to get up and around. She only had one more day in her string of days off and needed to get started on her routine of prepping for being away from home for a few days.

After Sam was able to get her first cup of coffee poured, her phone started blaring on the counter. She was so startled by the sound she spilled a couple splashes of her coffee onto the floor and her pajama pants. After setting the mug onto the counter and calming from her minor reaction to the heat, she reached for the offending device.

"Hello?" she spat angrily into the receiver without checking the caller ID.

"Good morning to you, too." Sam realized it was Tania and felt bad for her reaction instantly. Tania's words were direct and Sam's reaction to answering the phone was obviously unwarranted. She was just mad because now she would have to pretreat her pants to avoid permanently ruining them. That also meant she would have to do laundry before leaving town.

"I'm sorry Tania, I had a rough night and the phone startled me. I was scalded with coffee and didn't even check to see who it was." Sam truly felt bad and wished she had checked before answering to reign in her anger.

"It's all good, chica. I was just calling to see if I could convince you to let me take you out. Nick didn't charge me for anything but a water last night and after what I put you through I owe you more than that. I even asked for tonight off because I know you are probably back to work shortly." Tania was practically pleading with her. Sam hated it when she did that because it was hard to tell her no. So instead she just hesitated to make Tania think she was actually considering her options.

"Well, I do have a lot of things to get ready before I fly out tomorrow. I would hate to forget something because I was distracted by planning to go out tonight." Sam was very good at hedging Tania because she was a helper by nature. She knew exactly what Tania would do but that just played into her plans.

"Oh, I wouldn't think of it. Why don't I come and help you get your things ready and if we get done early we can plan to go out tonight. It will be a reward for accomplishing everything ahead of schedule. With both of us working on it surely, we will finish faster than if you were to do it on your own. It would be nice to have some girl time to catch up." Tania knew what she was doing and Sam realized she had just played into her hand. Sam thought she had the upper hand, but in reality, Tania had set her up perfectly.

"If that is how you want to spend your day off, I'm not going to deny you something that means that much to you. What kind of friend would that make me? I'm just now sitting down to grab a bite and drink what is left of my coffee. Then I'm going to take a shower and get down to brass tacks. So you can come over whenever you are ready." Sam would use Tania's generosity as long as it lasted. She might even find some ridiculous chores to make her do just to see how far Tania's charity lasted.

*****

The day moved a lot faster with Tania's help, even though it felt like they spent more time laughing and gossiping, instead of actually accomplishing much. Though little by little, it came together and Tania flopped down on the couch to take a break. "Whew! Do you do this every week by yourself?"

"If I didn't my house would be a wreck every week when I came home and I'd have to take two days working on tidying up my life after a long shift at work. If I do it on the front of the shift, I'm a little more motivated on the back side of my time off." Sam wasn't much of a cleaner but her mother always kept a tidy house and it was ingrained deep in her psyche.

"I don't know how you do it. I would just give up and live in filth. It's just me at home, like you, and I just don't care much these days. I'm rarely there and so besides keeping up on the laundry, it is nearly impossible for me to make a mess without taking a few days off in a row and that is just unheard of these days." Tania was a workaholic and Sam knew that it was something they had in common.

"Did you get the bathroom done while I was in the kitchen?" Sam had used Tania through and through today, but after taking a nap in the bathroom for two hours last night it was the least she could do to pay her back. She could only imagine what any passerby would have thought about seeing her lying passed out in that restroom sitting area.

"Yes, but I don't know why it needed to be cleaned. I think you only use it once in a blue moon. It's like even though you are here so many days in a row you don't actually touch down anywhere long enough to make an impression." Sam knew her propensity for a clean house extended to the bathroom. If she left any streaks in the bowl after an extended stay in there, she always swirled the brush around to avoid any staining. So, cleaning her bathroom involved nothing more than a wipe down with some Clorox wipes and it would be more than clean.

"Well, you were right both of us working together meant we got done faster. Only problem is I can't stay out super late I have an early flight. What do you want to do tonight? I'm not sure with my early schedule I'll be much fun." Sam knew Tania like to get her drink on when she went out so she didn't want to be a buzz kill.

"Nope, I just want to go dancing. If we drink we drink, but I have to work tomorrow too. Can't we just have a night out that we both get to do something fun before working tomorrow. Goodness sakes, your dates haven't been exactly fun of late. I feel like dating life for you is more like a second job than entertainment. You should get to have more excitement on your days off that don't result in your own personal pain or chagrin." Tania was right. Sam knew she wanted to enjoy her time off for once so she and Tania agreed to go dancing just for them. No sights set on fixing up Sam or Tania getting someone to take her home. They were out just to enjoy each other no matter what it took.

*****

Heels were an everyday part of Sam's life, but also one of her personal vises. She went shoe shopping more often than necessary on her layovers. She always made extra room in her luggage for at least one extra pair in case she got a sudden urge or found a pair she couldn't live without.

Getting ready to go dancing with Tania was a lesson in decision making. A dress that twirled just right was easy, but shoes…now that was another story all together. Did she opt for something high and showed off the length of her legs? Perhaps a red shoe that makes a bold statement would be better. She could choose a subtle black with a red sole to show her fun side. This was always a decision she dreaded to make and saved it for last. Seeing as she was nearly unable to make these choices on a work day, let alone out for a fun night on the town when she had less stipulations to hold her back, at this rate she wouldn't be able to choose before morning.

Tania threw the door open to Sam's bedroom showing her impatience. "Girl, you need to hurry up or the dance floor will be so crowded we won't have a choice but to sit at a table all night. Where is the fun in going dancing and getting stuck on the sidelines?"

Sam stopped what she was doing to acknowledge Tania, but then Tania actually took in Sam's situation. Sitting in the middle of the room, Sam was sitting surrounded by at least fifty pairs of heels. It was as though they had been drawn to her like a magnet and she was the strongest force in the room. Not an inch left to move, Sam was trapped by her hoard of shoes and obviously in distress. Grabbing the closest pair of shoes, she held them up in Tania's direction. "How am I supposed to go out tonight I can't even figure out what pair of shoes to wear. I'm a mess and this is the first time in forever that I've gone out just for me without the intention of possibly meeting someone. Which of these shoes screams women empowerment?" With a frustrated humph Sam threw the shoes back into the ever growing mass that was around her.

Reaching into the center of the pile to take Sam's hand, Tania pulled her from the midst of the possessive shoes. They were obviously wreaking havoc on Sam's ever present sense of doubt. It was up to Tania to sooth this situation. "Do you trust me?"

It was a simple statement that took Sam a moment to answer. She didn't not trust her, but never actually considered whether or not she would throw herself from the top of a ladder in hopes that Tania would catch her. This gave her pause and then Sam chided herself because she was doubting her friend. Tania had never given her a reason to distrust her. Squaring her shoulders back Sam gave Tania a hug.

"Of course, I trust you. Why would you ever ask that question?" Sam owned her response and didn't see the next thing coming.

With a heaty shove, Tania pushed Sam from the room and locked herself inside Sam's bedroom.

"What are you doing? That is my room and I still need shoes to go out in." Sam was banging on the door, but Tania didn't respond or even grunt in her direction. The only sounds Sam could hear were scuffs and shuffles nothing giving away any information as to Tania's bedroom activities.

Fifteen minutes later, the bedroom door lock clicked open. Sam had resorted to leaning her back against the door and waiting out Tania's plan. When the door latch clicked, Sam sprang into action. Her flowing dress only came down just above the knee so it didn't inhibit her movements at all. Before Tania had the door open an inch, Sam pummeled it open the rest of the way and caught Tania off guard knocking her to the floor.

"What did you do?" Sam started speaking fast and in a panic scouring her room to figure out what Tania did while locked away. Then she screamed because the pile of shoes was just gone. "What did you do with my shoes? Do you realize how much money I spent on those shoes?" They were like little babies for her. She didn't have pets or actual children so she spent her extra money on shoes.

"Don't worry they aren't far, check your closet." Tania sounded like she was talking through an intervention and that worried Sam more than anything. She didn't want a shoe-vention. She just wanted her shoes back. So she rushed over to the closet and tore open the door. Letting lose another blood curdling scream, Sam was less than happy about what she found. Instead of her giant shoe collection that sometimes was spilling out to her feet when she opened the door, she found maybe fifteen pairs of shoes in its place and that included her tennis shoes and house shoes. Turning her anger on her dear friend who just moments ago she had decided to trust explicitly. Sam was quickly regretting that decision.

"WHERE ARE MY SHOES?" Sam screamed at her not even trying to reign in her temper. Tania had taken her trust and stomped on it without remorse. She threw Sam from her own room and had taken away the one thing that was always there to make Sam's bad moods go away.

With her hands in the air, Sam didn't know if Tania was trying to calm her down or protect herself if Sam decided to throw punches. "Calm down! I didn't steal them or destroy them. I've only hidden them from you to make the choice an easier one for you." Immediately Sam started visually searching her room for where they might have been stashed. "Don't even try to find them. I promise you won't. It is a place even you won't think to look. Just know I'll come back in about two weeks and swap them out for a new batch to rotate in new styles and make going out with you less of a time consuming process in the future." Then Tania started laughing almost to herself. "So you can't go unfriending me anytime soon because you won't have any idea where your precious collection is without me." Taking in this new information, Sam found herself laughing right along with Tania. The situation was actually pretty funny after she thought about it and let go of her anger.

With that settled and before she had a handle on her own giggles, she turned back to the closet to survey her options. She was left with her peep-toe black ones with mesh screening around the ankle and the toe, almost a Mary Jane style without the buckles. These had a sexy four-inch heel that made Sam feel like she could own any room just by walking in with the confidence she knew she had seeping out of her pores. She also had a beautiful pair with a slightly lower heel but made her feel like a gladiator. They were laced up back and forth like tennis shoes from the opening behind the toes all the way up her ankle. They gave a whole new meaning to strappy heels. Tania had taken away her colored shoes and left her only black. This simplified the process that much more and for that Sam was grateful. Looking past her casual shoes although Tania did leave her a pair of ballerina flats and her everyday tennis shoes as she had seen before. Sam wanted sexy shoes for their dancing extravaganza that night. She wanted to make a statement walking into the room. Her shoes would be necessary for setting the mood. Her dress was silver and hugged her curves the way she knew drew attention to all the right places. Since she was dancing she loved the flare at the base of the skirt giving her legs the freedom to move here and there in anyway necessary. She could even Salsa dance, but she would need some spankies for that to be modest enough.

Then after looking at each pair Tania had been kind enough to leave out for her, she found the perfect pair. Towards the back almost hidden in the darkness of the shadows created by her clothes, she saw her pair of black glittered stilettoes. They were simple but eye catching and the three-and-a-half-inch heel was perfect for dancing in without being too short. The last thing she wanted was to be caught wearing a kitten heel to go dancing. They weren't just a solid black though. As the light hit them they would ombre to silver as the glitter offset them. She hadn't worn these shoes in a long time and had forgotten about them. They would be the best shoes for dancing and the lighting in the room would surely make them the highlight of her outfit. Sam reached out and procured the dazzling shoes and showed them to Tania. When her eyes reached

Tania's face she saw her friend was wearing a knowing grin.

"I knew you were going to choose those. I was going through your mass of shoes and by the looks of them they didn't see the light outside that closet of yours very often. I also realized the effect the light had on them would be perfect tonight. Now let's hope I don't trip too much tonight while watching your shoes change colors." Sam stifled another set of giggles not wanting to get out of control again after just getting them back in line from before.

*****

The club was hopping by the time the girls arrived. They were both decked out and ready to be exhausted from a night of dancing. Since the night was just about them, there was no stress or worry of who they were impressing. They could just be themselves and let loose. Without any warning, Tania grabbed Sam's arm and drug her to the dance floor. They didn't need a drink to have fun. The rhythm was thumping and Sam could feel it in her bones. Closing her eyes, she let the music carry her to another place. Song after song played and Tania stayed on the floor with Sam. They were a bit sweaty from excursion and soon they were both desperate for something to quench their thirst.

"I'm going to need some water or I'm likely to pass out soon." Tania leaned into Sam's ear and screamed to get over the music. With the volume of the beats Sam wasn't bothered by Tania's words they actually sounded closer to a whisper.

"Let's head to the bar." They linked arms and strolled to the bar. No thoughts or cares of those around them, they just wanted time together. While leaning against the bar, it took a few moments for the bartender to come over. It was a busy night and the bar was crowded with people. The girls barely breeched the mass of customers in order to be seen. The bartender nodded at them to let them know he would be over shortly.

The girls turned their backs to the bar to watch the dance floor. Taking in the sights and sounds around them. It was a bit quieter away from the thick of it and they could speak to each other without shouting.

"Man, I've missed this. I really need to do this more. I feel like its been ages since I've just been able to let loose like this." Tania's eyes were closed and she was still swaying to the beat enjoying the moment as she spoke.

"I agree. We should plan this more often. At least a couple times a month. That would require you to take more time off work though." Sam looked pointedly at Tania and watched her as the words sunk in. Slowly, one eye cracked open followed by the other. Tania looked at Sam like she had grown a second head.

"How about we start with once a month and then we can build on that. I don't know that I can say with one hundred percent certainty that I will take off two days a month just so we can go dancing. As much as I love it and think the idea bears merit, I can't be sure once the moment wears off and we are away from this atmosphere I won't revert back to my old ways even if you are here to hold me accountable." Tania was a realist at heart, while she knew what she thought would be the ideal moment and idea, she would always fall back to reality very quickly. This was something Sam envied about her friend. She wasn't even the slightest bit like that. If she had been perhaps she would have given up after the first couple dating catastrophes. Instead she kept meeting new guys and being further disappointed by each one. No one had even come close to meeting her standards and dreams of the perfect man. With the exception of perhaps one particular bartender who wasn't even in the running.

"What can I get you fine ladies this evening?" a rough baritone voice came from behind them. They each turned abruptly and almost swayed into each other. To the causal observer one might think they had already been drinking, but this was just Tania and Sam. They were a little woozy still from their need to hydrate and having danced like they were in a Richard Simmons exercise video. Giggling with their heads still together they replied simultaneously.

"Water!"

The bartender was stocky but still tall probably around six foot tall. He was broad shouldered and looked like the weight bench was his best friend. He looked like he could take on a Mack Truck and the winner would be questionable. The girls took their time perusing his ripped form as he reached into the cooler and procured two ice cold bottles of water. He handed them to the girls and Sam reached for hers first and turned the bottle to its side. Rolling the cold plastic around her neck and bust line without thinking. She was only concerned with cooling her sweat pebbled skin. With a sign of contentment, she realized she had garnered an audience. Tania had paid for the drinks but Mr. Tall and Bulky hadn't moved on and all the men around the bar within a six to eight-foot radius had turned and began staring at Sam. Looking over at Tania, her friend gave her a wide smile.

"I can't take you anywhere." This elicited another round of giggles between the girls and broke the awkward silence surrounding her. For a bar, that area got pretty quiet for a long stretch of time. Cracking the lid, Sam gulped down half the water before coming up for air. With a deep inhale, she signed her contentment at the refreshingly cold liquid. It was just what she needed to gain her second wind.

"Let's hit the dance floor and dance until we drop. I can't imagine going home and not just hitting the pillow. I'm just glad I set my alarm before we got here so I wouldn't forget later. Even without drinking, exhaustion has a way of controlling my brain even more so." Sam pulled Tania this time as the girls drank the rest of their water down on the way. The music taking over them before they made it to the floor and they were once again lost.

"Dancing is so primal and exotic, don't you think?" A deep voice breathed into Sam's ear after she had been caught up for a while in the music. She had let time get away from her again, but her phone was set to go off in her bra at midnight so she knew she wouldn't miss her self-imposed curfew. Startling from her own little world she twirled around to find a stunning man behind her. He was dressed a step above the typical jeans and t-shirt sometimes paired with an open button up usually seen worn by the men around these places. Unfortunately, Sam had been fooled by appearances before, but that was still where her eyes took her before her mind and heart caught up.

This perfect specimen of the male species was by far the most down to earth she could have dreamed up. He had a slightly shaggy cut, but it was done in a way that he still had control over it. So he didn't look like a sheepdog gone wrong. His clothes, while they weren't overdone, seemed to have been thought out. He wore jeans that looked like they were tailored to him in a darker denim that gave them a dressy feel. While he wasn't as filled out as the bartender she noticed earlier, he leaned more to a basketball player physic. His shirt, while it wasn't stretched over him like a second skin, was still fitted to show off his sinewy chest. Letting Sam know there was something there that would be perfect to rest her hands on and grip while dancing or in the throes of something more passionate. He layered that with a soft leather jacket in a tan color one just doesn't see very often. On this olive-skinned man, it was spot on and suited him to a tee.

"I'm sorry, do I know you?" Sam knew she didn't know this mystery man, but she wasn't sure what to say to him. She wasn't here to meet anyone and wasn't expecting to be approached. She had spent the evening captivated by the trance of the music. She hadn't even noticed the other patrons beyond her attempts to not collide with anyone.

"No but I've been admiring you all night. You have a grace on the dance floor that is all your own. You don't need anyone to dictate to you what is right or proper. You feel the music in a way I've never seen anyone before. I couldn't stop myself any longer. I had to speak to you and hear the voice that accompanied the presence you have made for yourself on this floor. My name is Derek, what is yours?" Impressed by his way with words and his assertiveness, she decided to play along.

"Sam" she held her hand out to Derek. "It's nice to meet you."

"The pleasure is all mine. Let me buy you a drink?" He nodded his head towards the bar and she held up a finger to him.

"Wait right here. I'm going to let my friend know where I am." Derek nodded and motioned that he would stay put.

After a quick search of the area, Sam found Tania a few feet away grinding on another guy but still lost in herself. Sam wondered if the guy realized he was merely a prop and not actually getting anywhere with her friend. Smirking to herself, Sam made her way over to Tania's side.

"I'm gonna grab a quick drink with something tall and mysterious. I'll be at the bar if you need me. Sam shouted in Tania's ear. Instead of halting her movements Tania just gave her a thumbs up and a slight nod. Sam didn't know if she should be insulted or pleased that her friend trusted her enough to wander off with a strange man. She shrugged, at least she wasn't leaving the building with him. That would have been just plain stupid.

As she fought the wave of the dancers, she noticed Derek had indeed stayed right where she left him. Luckily they were slightly at the edge of the dance floor when they met because otherwise he would have been mauled by dancers in the heat of the moment. Some weren't as watchful as Sam in their movements and would plow over anything and anyone in their path.

"Ok, that's settled. Let's get a drink." Sam said when she reached her mystery man.

Derek offered his arm and she walked with him to the bar. "What would you like?" he asked her when they reached the front of the line.

"Actually, I'd love a water first to quench this thirst from dancing. I probably am a mess. Dancing makes me work up quite the sweat." Sam instantly regretted bringing attention to her appearance as she hadn't been to the restroom at all to check to see if she had makeup running from sweating profusely.

As though Derek had read her mind, he caught her chin rather presumptuously, "The glow in your cheeks alone is enough to set my blood to boil."

Stunned, Sam didn't know how to respond to that. Thankfully, the rugged bartender chose that moment to make his appearance. "Need refreshment so soon?" Sam just nodded. He placed two bottles of water and the beer that Derek ordered in front of them. Sam pointed questioning at the extra bottle. "That one is free of charge. Figured you'd want a cold one to drink and I'm happy to fund the show you put on earlier. I sure don't get the pleasure of watching those very often." Sam smirked at him, not even embarrassed by his words. She still remembered Tania's words and owned the attention. She would probably not see any of these people often enough to matter anyway.

Turning her attention back to Derek, they started chatting. It was nothing deep or enlightening but still it was nice to have a conversation with a man that didn't end in turmoil for her. They hung out for about thirty minutes when a rather angry looking woman approached Derek.

"What are you doing here?" he asked her proving that he knew who she was.

She didn't say anything, just lifted her beer bottle and just poured it over Derek's head. Sam jumped back to avoid getting hit with any of the offending liquid. Then the girl stormed off, but then without warning a couple of men approached.

"Mr. Franklin, you're under arrest!" Sam stood there in shock. It took her a moment to recover from what was happening, but then the officer turned his attention to her. "Please don't go anywhere I will need to ask you some questions." Sam ruffled at the statement and complained.

"What? Why? I don't know anything about this guy. He just bought me a drink." She was fuming as she pulled out her phone and realized she was due to head home in a few minutes.

"I'm sorry ma'am, this is protocol and I need to speak with you before I let you leave. You were the last known person in contact with Mr. Franklin and therefore we need your statement." The officers handcuffed Derek and guided him through the club. Sam dutifully stood still, but wasn't in the least bit happy about it. Tania made her way over after noticing the excitement and stopped in front of Sam.

"What's going on?" Tania asked when she got to the bar and a water appeared for each of them. Sam glanced behind them and the bartender was standing there with an apologetic look.

"On the house again, this is a bad situation you didn't ask for." Sam smiled at him for understanding and explained to Tania.

"I have no idea. I was standing here talking to Derek and a girl came up and doused him in beer. The next thing I knew I was being detained for questioning while he was being arrested." Sam just wanted to go home and hoped that the police would hurry up.

As if on cue, the aforementioned officer made his way back to Sam. "Can we step outside so we can talk without having to yell at each other?" He was nice enough but looked like he had been undercover on this assignment. He wasn't too tall but still came eye level to Sam. Nodding she grabbed her water and she and Tania followed him outside.

"Like I said I don't know how much I can help, but if it gets me out of here quickly I'll answer any questions you might have." Sam leaned against the building for support as she was now feeling the exhaustion from dancing all night.

"Thank you for your cooperation, ma'am. I'm Officer O'Malley. Can I have your name for the statement?" he was trying to play nice it seemed so Sam would just answer what she could, as honestly as she could.

"My name is Samantha Martin." Not trying to be evasive, but she decided she would just answer what he asked and nothing more, in hopes to speed things along.

"Ms. Martin, how long have you known Mr. Franklin?"

"Long enough that I didn't know his last name was Franklin. He bought me water and we've been chatting for the past half hour." Sam knew she was being catty but this was ridiculous.

"Ok, I understand ma'am. Have you ever seen Mr. Franklin in any other capacity before tonight?" Sam thought this line of questioning was pointless, but she just answered anyway.

"No."

"Well, it seems you were just in the wrong place at the wrong time then. Thank you again for your help. If you think of anything that might be pertinent to our investigation please give us a call." He produced a business card and handed it to Sam.

"Forgive me, but I don't know how I could find this useful. Not having ever met 'Mr. Franklin' before thirty minutes ago. What did he even do? It seems he just pissed off an ex-girlfriend to me." Sam was tired and ready to go home, but she thought she'd try and find out what was going on.

"I'm not supposed to say anything about an ongoing investigation, but it seems Mr. Franklin got into an argument with his roommate and took things a little too far. It appears he knocked him unconscious, lit him on fire and pushed him down the apartment staircase." The fact that Officer O'Malley spoke so matter-of-factly, didn't help Sam's brain grasp the words any better.

Sam looked at Tania to be sure she heard the same thing as Sam. Judging by the stunned look she was wearing, it was likely that they were both living the same nightmare.

Chapter 11

Work the following week went by without a hitch. She kept reliving the highlight reel from the other night at the dance club. It was beyond her to think someone would be so crazy as to act like nothing was wrong or had happened after something so traumatic. What kind of crazy person had she attracted that he thought he would be able to pull that off?

After that night and working her long shift, Sam was more than ready to be home in her cozy apartment. With winter coming in just a few short months, she was going to need to consider purchasing a few items for her apartment. She always like to buy a new blanket or two so she had something that hadn't been washed a thousand times and was the softest it could be. Sam was always a sucker for something fluffy to snuggle into on a cold winter night. A shopping trip would be in order very soon. Not to mention, the different states she traveled to for work would be a seasonal change sooner than her Midwest home. Denver was a common hub for them and she had been snowed in a time or two. It would be a wise decision to purchase some cozy socks and sweaters to throw into her bag, in case of emergency. ICE was her favorite form of shopping. Not necessarily something she needed right now but there was a chance she would need it in the future. Therefore, she wasn't needlessly spending money and she still got to shop for things that she might never use at home. This was another reason she loved her job. It fueled her love of shopping without causing her conscience any unnecessary grief for shopping without purpose.

Wrapping up her final shift before her mandatory time off, Sam planned a shopping trip for this week. Maybe she could convince Tania to come with her before work, one day. Then maybe she could wrangle an answer out of her on where she hid Sam's shoes. Not that Sam was even a little concerned since she knew Tania was going to alternate them, but it would be fun to try and get her to slip up and give up the information on accident. If shopping didn't work then there was always their next dance night and Sam could get her drunk.

*****

Night had fallen by the time Sam got to her car after work. It wasn't unheard of but it wasn't her favorite time to be getting to her car. Normally a pilot or group of attendants would walk each other to cars. They all parked in the same area of the lot so it was safer. Turns out this wasn't in the cards for Sam that night. She took a call from her mother when the flight ended. Since her mother hadn't checked in for a bit, the call lasted longer than usual. Sam didn't want to hold everyone up so she waved them on. Sam knew she wasn't the only one who was tired from working long shifts. Commonly everyone thought they had an easy job, but dealing with people on a daily basis could take its toll. Passengers weren't always nice and most were cranky for one reason or another. They could be stressed, tired or even a fear of flying could make the nicest person, the most hateful of all. It was their job to calm any and everyone down, no matter the reason for the upset. That required a lot of thinking and planning to handle whatever might come to pass.

Sam knew everyone had a rough time this round and they were all ready to be on their way.

"Mom, I just landed and I'd really like to get home before the sun comes up. I can't figure out why you are up now anyway. Aren't you tired?" Sam was exhausted and talking to her mother was doing nothing but make it worse.

"Well if you would ever call me I wouldn't have to stay up late to talk to you when you can't avoid me. Now, the only

174

way I'm hanging up is if you agree to dinner with me this week, twice. You pick which days you are willing to free up for your dear old mother. I haven't seen you since I fixed you up with Christopher. That sweet boy is still heartbroken that you never called him back. You really should be nicer to these boys you date." Her mother trailed on and Sam regretted answering the phone. She loved spending time with her mother, but after she set up the date with Christopher that had been an utter disappointment, Sam was a bit gun-shy around her mother for fear of getting fixed up again. Even just talking to her mother about her love life was frustrating. She thought it was Sam being too picky. Not thinking her mother would quite understand the epic disaster her romantic life was becoming, since Sam decided to marathon date to find love now. Sam had already second guessed herself too many times to look back now.

"Fine, let me get some sleep and check what I have going on this week and I'll text you tomorrow and let you know when to expect me. I want to be wined and dined though, so break out all the stops and fix all my favorites. Who knows when I'll be able to clear my schedule like this again." Sam laid it on thick, but perhaps she could get some amazing home cooking out of it if nothing else. Her mother agreed and allowed Sam to end the call.

Making her way through the parking lot, Sam was grateful for how well lit the airport kept the areas. They spent countless dollars on crews to make sure lightbulbs were changed regularly to avoid dark spots. Shadows were always a cause for alarm for women like her when walking alone to a vehicle. Sam made it to hers without incident and for that she was pleased. Not that she expected anything to happen, but she had watched enough movies to have a vivid imagination.

Warding off the night chill on that late summer evening, Sam turned on her heater. She wasn't sure if it was so much the cold or partially due to the fear that was building just under her skin from the late night walk through the parking lot. She made it a few miles away from the airport and the car jolted to the right jarring the steering wheel with it. It took quick reflexes for Sam to maintain control and guide the car to the shoulder.

Shutting off the engine and turning on her emergency lights, Sam glanced behind her to check for oncoming traffic. It was late enough that the roads were quiet. Cautiously, she exited the vehicle and walked around the front into the bright beam of the headlights. As she approached the passenger side her heart dropped. While Sam was a teenager, her father made sure he taught her how to change a flat, it hadn't ever been an issue. Before now, he had always been there for her when the problem arose. In this case, on the side of the road on a nearly deserted highway, she was in a pickle. Fortunately, this is why she paid extra on her insurance for roadside assistance. If she was already paying for someone to come here in case of an emergency, why bother trying to do it herself? Even though this would result in her getting home later, still it was worth not having to do it herself and potentially do it wrong and have to call someone in the end anyway.

Climbing back into the driver's seat, Sam reached for her insurance card to locate the contact information on the back. Sam dialed the toll-free number and let it ring. She was almost ready to hang up after the call rang a few times.

"Safety First Insurance, Stanley speaking. How can I be of assistance?" the voice on the other end of the phone was a bit nasally and higher pitched than Sam expected and her phone volume was set a bit high, forcing her to pull the phone way for a moment before responding.

"Yes, my name is Samantha Martin, I have a flat tire and I need you to send me some help." Sam gingerly placed the phone on her ear, better prepared for his response this time.

"I'd be happy to help you with that. Let me pull up your policy information." Sam heard a few clicking of the keys as he typed into the computer seeking the information he needed in order to dispatch the correct team. "You said flat tire?" he was still typing as he queried further.

"Yes, I'm on the side of the road on Highway sixty-four." Sam didn't know how much information he needed and she was alone in the car. That made her ramble more than normal.

"Actually, if you have your GPS on your phone activated, I can use your phone number to locate you in your car. That was an added feature your plan allowed for and you seem to have chosen that upgrade." Stanley was speaking very directly and without much emotion as he tapped away on his keyboard. If Sam didn't know any better, she would have assumed she was speaking with a computer or robot instead of a human man.

"Oh good, my GPS is on and I'm so glad that was an option because I have no idea what the last mile marker was that I passed. I was dead set on getting home I was in my own little world." Sam noticed nights like this she almost drove mindlessly. It was a miracle she had the wherewithal to get the car to the side of the road safely.

"Okay, I have your order processed your tow truck will be there in thirty to forty-five minutes. Is there anything else I can do to further assist you?" Stanley was matter-of-fact and to the point didn't leave room for error by filling the silences with mindless chit chat.

"No I think that will be all. What do I do if the truck doesn't make it or ends up lost?" It was the only fear Sam was currently holding on to that she would be stranded out here until someone happened upon her when traffic started to build again.

"I'll give you a ticket number for you to reference if you need to call back in. Any of our customer service technicians can help you as I will key in the notes of our conversation. When you are ready I'll give you the number." Stanley paused waiting for Sam to get a pen and paper. When she told him she was ready, he rattled off the number and she wrote it down and they ended the call.

Sitting in the car in the dark, Sam watched the night sky. Stars filled the darkness with little spots of light. She never took the time to just observe nature anymore. When she was a girl she used to love to watch clouds shapes go by and catch lightening bugs in the summer. Now she was doing good to slow down long enough to sleep. She was always on the go for this, that, or another thing. Her priorities had definitely taken a turn in a different direction over the years.

Lost in her thoughts, she didn't hear the tow truck approach and was startled by the rapping of knuckles on her passenger window. The darkness was an inconvenient cover and made her uneasy. She couldn't make out the face of the person on the other side of the glass or even the size. Unlike in the city, where the driver would have been backlit and she would have been able to make out a basic idea of what they looked like. Here she couldn't even tell if the driver was male or female.

Unsure of what exactly she should do, she lowered the passenger window less than an inch to make speaking easier between them. The voice that came back was a tenor sounding voice. Not as high pitched as Stanley, but not a deep timbre of a mountain man or the bartender from the dance club. This voice wasn't unpleasant or frightening. That was a start.

"Sorry for startling you. I hate these calls after dark because I always end up frightening someone. I got a call from Safety First that you needed a tire changed. They didn't say if you had one or not so I brought the rig just in case." The driver was pleasant enough and set Sam at ease with his words.

"I think there is a spare. It was a stipulation my dad made when I picked out my first car that all cars I owned needed a spare, no matter what. Just don't ask me where it is because that is why I called you. While he taught me all the stuff, it was a few years ago and I've never had to put those skills to the test. I'm sure in a pinch I could force myself to remember the steps, but if the emergency can be handled by someone else, why not let a professional tackle it. Let me hop out and pop the truck. Then you can get to work." Sam did as she said and made her way to the side of the road out of the impact range if a wayward car were to hit either vehicle now parked on the side of the road.

"My name is Levi by the way." The driver mentioned, as he rummaged through the trunk to see if the spare was located in there or beneath the car. Sam let him do what he wanted because she wasn't in any position to be the smartest person at the moment.

"Levi, its nice to meet you I'm Sam but you probably already knew that since you are billing me for your time. I'm still sorry for having to bring you out so late and pull you away from your family." Sam didn't know if he had a family at home but her mother raised her to be polite in any situation and this one was just as important as any other. The darkness made it difficult for Sam to get a good look at his features, but it didn't stop her from trying. She had nothing better to do anyway.

It seemed he had blonde hair and a square jaw. He wasn't necessarily well built in muscle but he wasn't lanky either. She was pleased to see that someone of his build was so into cars. Then she chastised herself for stereotyping his profession. His hair was a bit rumpled as though she had woken him up. Which made sense since she was getting home so late and he likely would still have to get up for work tomorrow. She instantly found herself feeling guilty for this call even more. Perhaps she should have tried to attempt to fix the tire herself so as not to disturb someone this late.

"No worries. I was just at home tonight hanging out. No one to steal me from, that is why they put me on call most nights. I prefer it anyway. I get a bonus on each call and when I get calls I get to go in late anyway. So it's a win-win for me. Even better when I get to help a pretty damsel in distress, like you." Levi was a real ladies man if he could slip in a line like that so smoothly. Sam laughed at his change in tone.

They talked while Levi changed the tire. He really was a sweet guy. He worked hard and didn't always leave himself much time for play. She found that rather endearing. As he lowered the car back to the ground and released the handle from the jack to pack it up, Sam moved a little closer. Knowing he would be finished soon, she didn't feel the need to stay so far away.

"Well, there you go. All buttoned up and you are ready to go. I'll just slip this tire into your trunk so you can get it fixed or replaced." With that he wheeled it to the rear of the car and Sam followed him in case anything needed to be rearranged.

"Thank you so much, Levi. You really did rescue me tonight and I appreciate it more than you know." Sam was entirely grateful and wanted him to know that. While her insurance company was paying the bill, it was still important for her to mention it.

"It was my pleasure, but I wanted to ask you something before I leave. I don't usually do this, but after talking to you this evening I feel like we sort of clicked. Would you be willing to go out with me some time?" Levi was shifting his weight back and forth, proving how nervous he really was and Sam thought it was cute. Since she didn't have any plans the following night she thought why not take him up on the offer. That would, if nothing else, delay her mother by one day.

"If you aren't on call tomorrow night, why don't we meet at Joe's Bar at say, eight? Then we can grab a drink and see where it goes." Sam was pleased with how this had worked out in her favor.

"That sounds great. I'm not on call, since they don't ever put me on back to back if I've had to take a call. This works out perfectly." With that they went their separate ways and Sam was able to make her way home and into her bed after a very long week.

Chapter 12

Sam allowed herself to sleep in for the first time in weeks. She had had the week from Hell and her previous night was just the icing on the cake. She had no set plans for her first day off until that night. Everything that needed to be done would happen over the next few days, there was no concern there.

Snagging her phone when she woke up, she quickly texted her mother.

I have plans tonight. How about tomorrow night and Thursday this week? I expect the works and to be pampered.

She knew she was being demanding but her mother would come through as always and Sam wouldn't leave her house hungry or unsatisfied unless something catastrophic happened. Now she would be free to handle the rest of her day, in peace.

In a moment of inspiration, she fired off a text to Tania.

Hey lady! Want to go shopping sometime this week. I need to stock up on nonessentials since the weather is going to turn in the next couple months. You know how it is here, hot one day snow the next.

Realizing it was nearly lunchtime, she decided to skip her morning coffee and breakfast and decided to go to the diner for lunch. Then she could restock groceries before the week got away from her and she ate out every day, all day. She really needed to get her eating habits in check. She ate out so often, it was almost second nature. She needed to fall back to old habits and then perhaps would start eating healthier. She used to cook all the time before taking this job. Now it was her last thought because she wasn't home so much she just ate out more.

Her phone chirped as she was headed out the door and she saw a text from Tania.

Can't today because I work tonight but let's get an early go at it tomorrow and we will have plenty of time before my shift starts. I can't wait! I love to cool weather shop.

Sam smiled to herself. She'd forgotten what it was like to have a friend she could call on with a moment's notice or to plan things with for fun. Tania was that perfect friend. They just clicked from day one and the remainder of their short time together was history because it felt like they'd known each other for years.

I'll be in there later tonight. I'll see you there.

Sam had barely hit send before her phone went off again in her hands.

Got another one? Is this one going to be worth it or another bust?

Sam laughed because she always loved how straightforward Tania was to her. There was never a question of what Tania was thinking because she always voiced her opinion very loudly.

Honestly, who knows. Had a flat last night and this one came from the repair shop to fix it. It was late and quiet on the road. We chatted and he seems nice.

Sam got to her car and saw the spare and realized she needed to drop off the flat to the shop to repair. She could pick it up later or the next day. Making a quick detour before lunch, she did just that.

*****

The day went by fast and before she knew it, she needed to get ready for her date. Since Levi was a mechanic, she opted for jeans and a three-quarter sleeved Henley style shirt. Nothing too fancy, but still looked nice.

The bar was quiet when she arrived, but it wasn't the weekend. Just a few patrons here and there made it easy to select a high-top table in the center of the room. Trying to make a direct line of sight to the door, Levi should have no trouble finding her.

Tania made her way over to Sam's table with a knowing look. "So you're trying out a new type this time?"

"What do you mean new type. I don't have a type as it is." Sam wasn't sure what Tania was talking about she was out on a date just like any other. The success rate wasn't better or less since she didn't know much about Levi. Then again, she hadn't known much about any of her dates as of late.

"'He's just nice.' I believe were your words this afternoon. I just wanted to check on you beforehand to find out how much I needed to watch you guys. It's slow, but you are always my priority, even when we are swamped." Tania was proving to be a great guard dog and worried if a guy ever crossed her.

"I'll be fine. It's a quiet night and you are in and out. I'll take a vodka cranberry though when you get a chance." Sam wasn't in the mood to drink heavily, but she did want something to ease her nerves that were slowly building before Levi made his appearance. She hoped he wouldn't stand her up.

The longer she waited the more worried she grew. It was only five after when he strolled through the door. He smiled when he saw her and in the light of the bar she saw he had a strong smile that showed his confidence. His features were more pronounced than she had considered as well.

"Sorry I'm late. I didn't get out of the shop on time and that set me back the rest of the night. I'm a punctual person by nature and this is just one of my pet peeves when work messes with my time schedule." He winked at her when he sat down, but she didn't know if he was flirting or joking. Opting not to ask, she waved Tania over so he could get a drink.

"Well good evening there. What can I get you to drink?" Tania was a well-trained waitress and had been doing it for years. She told Sam she had many opportunities to get a regular nine to five job, but turned them down. She said she made more money in tips than she could ever dream from an hourly or salary wage. Levi placed his order for a large domestic whatever was on the tap. Sam appreciated that he knew there was a difference and wasn't too snooty to order a domestic anyway.

As they waited for his drink to arrive, he whipped out his phone and Sam thought he took a picture. It was odd, but she didn't say anything. He still wasn't carrying a conversation, just playing on his phone. Sam hesitated, but overlooked it figuring since he is usually on call, it could be work related.

"So you said work ran long, was it a busier day than normal or was it just like any old day?" She didn't know what she was asking but was trying at mutual conversation.

"No today was killer. So many cars were brought in and we had at least a dozen tow jobs. They were all brought in and put on the list too. The next few days will be like that and thankfully, they didn't promise any rush jobs or it would have been mandatory overtime for everyone. Those days are the worst." Levi answered her, but never once looked up from his phone. After another minute or two, her phone vibrated. While normally she would have thought it rude to check it, Levi had set precedent and so she pulled it out and checked the alert. Much to her surprise it was a friend request from Levi. She glanced up at him, but he still didn't look at her or say anything. She accepted his request without a word and set her phone on the table to let it play out.

Tania brought his beer back at that moment. She glanced at Sam and she just shrugged at Tania. Levi's behavior was odd but it was still within society norms to act just the way he was. It just wasn't so much dating norm. Tania placed his beer in front of him he thanked her - or more like, thanked his phone for the beer. Tania rolled her eyes and moved on.

Little to no conversation wasn't Sam's idea of a great date. She was about to say something else when her phone vibrated again. Deciding it wasn't worth mentioning as she would normally apologize for answer a message while on a date she chose to play Levi's game. Grabbing her phone, she saw it was another alert. Clicking on it, she saw Levi had made a post and tagged her in it. Curiosity got the better of her and she checked it. Much to her surprise, it wasn't just a status update.

His relationship status now read "in relationship" with her picture below it and it was tagged "my woman" below it. Again, no acknowledgement from Levi visually, but he stayed locked into his phone. She couldn't believe what she was seeing, so again, stooping to his level, she screenshot the status and texted it to Tania.

WHAT IS THIS??? He doesn't speak but then takes a picture of me and changes his relationship status. I'm a crazy magnet, aren't I?

Tania was helping another table, but Sam knew she kept her phone stashed in her apron. So she just needed to wait until Tania could get away from the customers to check it. Choosing to not say a word to Levi about the status update. She moved on to try and get him talking again.

"So what do you do for fun when you're not working or saving damsels in distress?"

"Not much, I like video games and music. I could live on Netflix, if the world would just stop spinning and I didn't have to go to work." This was a red flag and a half. This man would literally veg out in front of the television or on his computer or phone for the rest of his life, if he didn't have to work. Tania chose that moment to reply. Since Levi was still not making eye contact with her even though she was 'his woman', it made it easier not to feel guilty for checking the message.

Wow he's a winner. You should shut that down real fast and back away. Don't creep away…run! Should I warn Nick you will be headed his way shortly?

Sam snickered at Tania's question. She knew that Sam was worried about guys following her home and since the best way to combat that was to hang out, that is what she did. Most guys didn't want to linger in this hole in the wall any longer than necessary.

Yes, tell him if I don't make it over in thirty minutes or less to send out a search party.

They hadn't moved onto talking about the oddities between her and Nick's non-relationship, but she knew Nick had rescued her once and would likely do it again if need be.

"Well, I hate to be rude, but seeing as that isn't an issue tonight, I'm going to be honest. You haven't looked at me past walking in and sitting down. You haven't looked up from your phone since then. I would like to say I'm flattered for you status update, but let's be real…. that is insane. You can't go out with a girl you just met, not even pay attention to her and then openly claim her on social media.

You won't get very far with any girl acting like this." She had gained his attention with this start, so she pressed her luck and continued. "Let me offer you some advice, in the future leave the phone in the car. If there is an emergency, they will find someone else to call." With that she stood up and started to walk away, but then turned and added, "Oh and even though I accepted your friend request, I will promptly be deleting and blocking you. So, you might need to find another woman to claim or take down that post before too many people see it. That might be hard to explain come tomorrow when you're at work."

With a sense of empowerment by standing up for herself, Sam flipped her hair back over her shoulder and strolled with confidence over to the bar to spend the remainder of her evening. Before she made it, Tania caught up with her.

"Wow that was the sexiest thing I've ever seen in my life. Who are you and what have you done with my friend?" Tania pulled Sam into a side hug to show her support.

It was really the most amazing feeling to not just let the guy do as he pleased, no matter how it made her feel. She was a person, first and foremost, and if her date couldn't treat her as such in such a short meeting then they didn't deserve her. No longer would she feel bad for them and feel like she needed to fear her inner thoughts. If a guy wasn't for her then that was how things were. Nothing dictated who she was destined to date or fall in love with. If she didn't click with a guy, who was to tell her that she was being hard on them or rude by telling them that? The reality of the situation was like a weight had been lifted off of her. One that she had born for years and years. Her mother had always told her she should choose what was best for her, but as she got older her mother's tune had changed. That she was somehow expiring and that her options were limited. The fish in the sea must have been becoming extinct and that Sam should make her decision quickly and with less criteria. Therefore, turning down someone from that ever shrinking pool was something to feel bad for.

Squaring her shoulders as she reached the bar, *Never again! I will date who I want and not call back anyone I deem unfit. It is my decision who I will and won't love. I won't settle for anything less than what I deem perfect.* Sam's words were almost an anthem that she would now be living by. Tania looked at her confused. "Oh, did I say that out loud?" Tania nodded and the girls burst into a fit of laughter.

Nick was waiting for them when they approached the bar with humor in his eyes, "What was that? Did you girls just have an 'I am woman hear me roar' moment?"

"You're just jealous because without us your life would be boring." Tania threw back at him and Nick barked out a loud bellowing laugh that startled the girls. While he was always good-natured Sam had never heard him this lost in the moment. She could tell that he really did enjoy their company, she just didn't know why.

"If you say so Tania but you might want to go check table seven. Those guys look like they are ready to eat you alive if they don't get another round." Tania turned and saw the table Nick was referring to and rolled her eyes before heading off in that direction.

"As for you, Princess, you seem to have had an enlightening night." Nick took his towel and started wiping the bar top meticulously, more out of habit than for the actual need to clean.

Sam hesitated at the use of his pet name for her. She almost didn't say anything but then again, she had just announced her freedom to make decisions about her life, only because they needed to be said. So, she pushed past her insecurities and blurted out her thoughts again.

"You haven't called me that for weeks." Sam started to second guess herself, but decided to push her luck, "not since you kissed me in the alley." She may have been brave enough to say it but that is where her courage ended because her eyes didn't lift from watching the movement of his towel as it swiped in circles over the wood. She watched it slow to a crawl and then stopped as her words sunk in.

Nick didn't respond right away and he also didn't move. Sam didn't know what was going through his head but as she let her eyes travel up to his face she noticed his smile had fallen away.

When she thought he wouldn't say anything, he surprised her, "I shouldn't have done that. You didn't ask for my help that night, but the way that guy was acting was just shy of the bat shit crazy line. I heard what he was saying and I knew you were too nice to stand up for yourself. I didn't know how he would react but I knew that if I were there I could at least protect you from the worst of it." Nick's voice wasn't as strong as it usually was. She knew he had thought about this before and had gotten really good at berating himself. She had to do something.

"Out of anyone who could have done anything in that situation, you didn't do anything wrong that night. Had you crossed a line, I would have stopped you. Instead you stopped yourself." Sam was obviously in a sharing mood and she needed to reign herself in before she revealed anything that needed to remain hidden. She just needed to free him of the guilt he was inflicted with.

Like a light had been switched on his face transformed into the smile she was used to. Nick didn't say another word on the topic. He was now back to the happy-go-lucky guy she had known from day one.

"So what did the latest guy do to squeeze your trigger? You seemed to have a moment of enlightenment on the way over here. It was nice to see you empowered for a moment." He smiled at her slightly allowing Sam to get a glimpse of the man she was seriously crushing on. Her dreams hadn't diminished at all in their time apart, but she did notice she had better control over situations in the dreams.

Since the bathroom incident, Sam's dreams became more vivid and the leading male never faltered. Nick was always there for her while she slept.

"He ignored me the entire date." Sam stated without any clarification.

"Ignored you?" Nick asked with disbelief. "How could anyone ignore you on a date?"

"His phone was much more interesting or so it seemed. Then he had the audacity to claim me on social media." Sam waved her phone back and forth in the direction of Nick and then made an overstated gesture of clicking buttons on her phone as she deleted and blocked Levi's contact information, not only from her phone but from Facebook as well.

"Wow, that is a bold move. What kind of a loser is so lost in a virtual world to not notice *you* in front of him." Nick's words weren't lost on her. He had a tone of awe mixed in there that gave her an idea that his words weren't just spoken.

"Yeah, well I got tired of it and something snapped. I just couldn't take it anymore. I realized I was worth something more. So, I decided to stand my ground and end things now."

"Sounds like you played that card at just the right time, Princess. I was worried you wouldn't be able to do it. You surprised me." While he was speaking, she missed that he had made a drink for her. Without any flourish or another word, he placed a glass in front of her.

Sam had reached a level of trust with Nick that she just picked up the highball glass and took a generous drink. Lately, Nick had been mixing her more fruity flavors. This drink was a bit different. While there were fruity undertones, they weren't necessarily sweet. This one had darker notes too, almost like the sugar was toned down somehow. Then a secondary flavor hit, showing that he had offset the saccharine flavors with something tart. If she had to guess, Sam knew something about Nick and he had a preference for lime. When the flavor of the alcohol hit her, she knew it had to be gin. The dry earthy notes gave it away in a heartbeat. While it wasn't her favorite drink Nick had made her, it wasn't all bad. Gin just wasn't her favorite and it made its presence known. Making a face as she swallowed she replaced the glass.

"This isn't the worst drink you could have served me, at least you left the Jägermeister out of it. That result wouldn't have been pretty." She was smiling, but she had always hated Jäger. That black licorice flavor was just too much.

"Not a fan of gin. Okay, I'll make a note of that for the future. I thought this would have enough cherry and apple to cover the gin. Not completely but enough to get it down. That is my favorite drink to mix it in."

"What is the magical name that made you mix it for me tonight?" Sam knew this was going to connect somehow but didn't know her drink names well enough to put them together.

"Oh, this little thing?" Nick gestured to the drink with nonchalance. "This is called the Status Quo. Something with a little class but a slight twist." He held his faux arrogance, but it didn't last Sam watched as his features broke and she smirked at him causing him to burst into laughter. It wasn't that Nick wasn't classy, it was just that he was so much more than that.

"How does your brain work that you remember all these off-the-wall drinks without having to reference a book or your phone or something?" Sam was genuinely curious and hadn't thought about it until now that he seemed to have a card catalog of drinks just sitting in his head to be accessed on a moment's notice.

"Oh, I have a eidetic memory. Something that was a cause for much grief as a child, but now as an adult, has become more of a novelty. I've found new uses for making it worth my while to use it. I used to gamble but that lost its appeal and can lead to legal issues. So, a few years ago, I took up bartending. If the crowd gets boring, I can just change bars or styles and it becomes fresh again. I'm a bartender by choice and I can move anywhere and always have a job." Sam was shocked, he never gave anything away about this before. Not that she thought she should have known for sure something was up, but deep down it seemed like there should have been some kind of clue that she should have noticed.

"That is kind of like my job. I love to travel and see new things. If there is a place I've never been, I can volunteer for a run. There is enough downtime between most runs I can spread my schedule out and still feel a little touristy. The fact that I'm not there for long makes each trip feel new. I can go see something new with each trip. It leaves me feeling free even though I still have to work my regular shifts. I'm never trapped in one place for very long I can always head out and feel free." Sam had realized after college that she was more of a free spirit and didn't like to be forced to stay in one place for very long. Unfortunately, her mother was here and loved to have Sam over for dinner. It used to be weekly, but ever since Sam took on the task of finding a husband, that had occupied all of her free time. *Wow, when I think of it like that I sound like a woman on the prowl. Maybe I am or does that just make me desperate?* Realizing that line of thinking went against her new personal anthem, she shoved those to the back of her mind for now in hopes of finding a reason to disbelieve them in the future before they resurfaced.

"How is it that we've not talked about what you do for a living in all of our conversations? I know because I would have remembered. We have a lot in common that I wouldn't have ever considered. I think we might have been gypsies in another life." Nick winked at her like he always did and it made her stomach flip. She was having a harder time controlling her emotions around him. A small glint in his eye was enough to send her over the edge.

"If that were our life, we might never have met." A hint of sadness crept into her tone and she tried to clear her through and hoped he didn't notice.

"Wouldn't that have been fun though - all the different possibilities and the randomness of our actions to then have possibly crossed paths? Gypsies lived a different life and met so many people in different walks of life. They were the most feared or loved people and they never knew what to expect as a reaction from people in the towns they passed through. The ability to stay on the outskirts and mingle amongst their own people and still meet different ones from a different group." Nick looked like he was lost in a dream as he described it.

"Looks like you have considered this as an option before? Would you actually do that today? Living the nomad lifestyle these days is so much different. There are so many more dangers out there and the possibility of human trafficking is an ever-present concern. That is why I like that my travels still keep me reigned in a bit and not just roaming the wilds of life."

"Don't get me wrong, I know human trafficking is a concern. I won't discount that but don't you think we can't let our lives be dictated by society's public scares? If everyone wanted to shut down those criminals, the world would never go anywhere or do anything. It would revert back to the times where traveling was unheard of." Nick paused for a moment. Sam thought it looked like he was gathering his thoughts. "How did our conversation drift from out freestyle lives to politics? I never talk about that, it is my least favorite subject." Sam stifled a laugh. She didn't know how they made that drastic switch either, but it might have had something to with her trying to reign in her N.E.R.S. -Natural Emotional Response System. Nick had this uncanny way of knocking it off balance.

"I'm not entirely sure, but it was probably my fault." Sam considered telling Nick about her N.E.R.S. problem, but second-guessed herself as usual. While she had decided to take control of her romantic life, she didn't want to commandeer Nick's without his consent. Up until this conversation they hadn't even talked about their alleyway kiss. Even then, Nick shut down that topic all on his own. She didn't want to reopen it. Sam decided she would wait until he took that step on his own and made the choice himself.

"Let's take equal blame. We obviously got there mutually through choice of topic." Nick went back to meticulously cleaning the wooden bar. Sam decided it was time to call it a night. Since she had already voiced that his drink choice for the night wasn't her favorite, she opted to leave it unfinished.

Chapter 13

They say time heals all wounds, but Sam thought there was never enough time to heal the pain of being through so many dreadful dates. Her time was split between work and her dating life and she did this first for her mother and secondly for herself. She wanted more than anything to find the love of her life, make her mother proud and then move on to the next chapter of her life. At this point while she had decided to take control of her relationship, it wasn't going to be easy and the constant imbalance of her love life was taking its toll. She hadn't been in a healthy relationship in years and Sam wasn't a one-night stand kind of girl.

Although, if her dream world didn't get a clue, she was going to have to start. She spent her night dreaming of the perfect man who gave off mixed signals that confused her. Sam didn't even know where to start on decoding. She wondered if there was still such a thing as a decoder ring from back in the day that her mother spoke of so fondly. She didn't know what they decoded but it had to be a start. She needed a leg up in order to figure out this guy that was so stuck in her mind that her waking life was becoming confusing.

Rolling over in bed, Sam remembered that she and Tania were going shopping today. A glimmer of excitement rolled through her at the thought of some girl talk and much needed Sam time. *Maybe I should spring for a couple's massage and we could get some extra relaxation. God only knows, I owe Tania for all the times she has come to my rescue.* Making a mental note, she thought about the best place to surprise Tania with the news.

*****

Exiting the third store and countless shopping bags later, the girls decided they needed a coffee run.

"This was a great idea. Why haven't we done this sooner?" Tania kicked her feet up on the chair next to her as they sat in the coffee shop relaxing from their shopping extravaganza so far.

"Because if we shopped for fall and winter items in the summer, our options would be vastly limited. This way we get the cream of the crop and that is what we deserve for all our hard work and long hours we put in on a regular basis." Sam sipped her coffee and soaked up all the day had given them. While they had been shopping all morning, she wasn't tired. They had laughed and talked so much it had taken the effort out of the task at hand. She found housewares to create a comfortable vibe in her apartment and also sweaters to bring on the cool weather in style.

"I'm so glad we met." Tania declared after a few minutes of silent reverie between them. "You and I are so similar and I think we are good for each other. For all the things we have in common, we have twenty things that are so different it is a wonder we get along."

"It just works." Sam agreed. "You and I are true friends at heart. It is as if we have known each other forever and in reality, it has only been a few months. I don't know what I would do without you." This was the conversation turn she had hoped for without knowing this is what would be said. "On that note, I have a surprise for when we finish our coffee. As a thank you for saving my bacon more times than you ever were required, including the very first time that sealed our friendship into what it is right now, I booked us a massage to end our day of shopping. That will make you either love or hate work tonight but I did it anyway."

"If I hate it, then are you going to at least be there to give me some entertainment to my otherwise drab and repetitive evening?" Tania pouted, but was obviously covering up her excitement. Who didn't love a good massage? Even if working afterwards wasn't anyone's idea of a good day.

"You know I have to go to my Mother's for dinner tonight. I've been neglecting my daughterly duties and I'm trying to redeem myself." Sam said leaning on the table of the coffee shop. It wasn't too cold yet so they were sitting outside at one of the metal tables with glass tops. The chairs weren't the most comfortable but they were able to absorb a little extra vitamin D before the weather made its gloomy seasonal turn.

"Whatever, don't try and lie to me. I know you are only going because your mother will resume her daily phone calls if you didn't agree to her demands." They dissolved into a fit of giggles and couldn't drink their coffee for a few minutes for fear of blow back or nostril reappearance.

When they had settled a little, Sam spoke, "It's not that I don't love my mother. She is really great, you'd probably love her. I just don't know how to tell her that my love life is a complete wreck. She just wants me to settle down and have babies like any other daughter who loved their mother would. Maybe I'm just not cut out to be the ideal daughter." Sam reflected with a hint of self doubt. This was in direct contradiction to her new anthem and she hated herself for voicing the concern. Then again if she couldn't show her personal misgivings to her friend then who could she open up to. She always believed friendships should be transparent, without fear of ridicule.

"You are the best daughter any mother could ask for. Who cares if you haven't exactly had a textbook romantic relationship. Seriously, if there were a textbook, who would have written it? You tell me someone who had the most perfect beginning to end romantic story." Tania looked at her pointedly as though she expected her to answer.

"Romeo and Juliet" Sam said flatly without question.

"Seriously? They had to die to be together. Who wants to have to constantly battle one's family in order to be told countless times that you can't be with the one you love. Only to decide that death is the only answer. Try again, put some effort into it this time." Tania was apparently enjoying this and Sam didn't want to ruin her fun so she chose to play along.

"Rhett and Scarlet" Sam decided on they were the perfect example of a happy ending in her mind.

"Oh please! Scarlett, was a two-time widow by the age of sixteen. When she met Rhett, she hated him. It took time and perseverance and even though he didn't want to be, Rhett was tied to Scarlett from day one. So not the perfect relationship everyone automatically associates to them because they have a happy ending. Relationships are up and down at the best of times." Tania just looked at Sam, expecting her to continue and now the game was on, to stump Tania versus actually accomplishing an end goal of proving Tania's point.

"Elizabeth and Darcy." Sam threw out just to see what Tania did with it.

"Aside from the fact that they are fiction, as with the previous two and I'm noticing a common thread, I'll analyze anyway. So taking their inevitable happy ending out of the picture. Darcy wasn't attracted to Elizabeth from the beginning and while her intelligence intrigued him, he wasn't sold on the idea of how opinionated she was. What finally won him over was the fact that despite her family's downfalls she was herself, and never let another's opinion of herself change that. He was a complete pompous ass and Elizabeth hated him for it. Though, as we all know, sometimes our emotions manifest themselves in frustration and anger initially. Deeply seated feelings can grow to stronger ones and while we all have our downfalls and differences, there is an underlying attraction that blossoms into romance. They couldn't write the manual either or the world would be a very hateful one in hopes of a budding love somewhere in the depths of stronger emotions." Tania seemed to have put a lot of thought into these people and so Sam decided to throw her a curve ball. Sticking with her fictional theme, Sam blurted out her next answer.

"Fred and Wilma!"

"Oh my God! Really, this is where your mind goes when you want to talk love and romance?" Tania hesitated but Sam didn't give her any indications that she was messing with her, forcing Tania to continue with her rant. "Fine, I'll explain why a sixties cartoon couldn't write a textbook on romance. Fred was chaos embodied. Poor Wilma, while she obviously loved him, she was subjected to deal with a second child. He had a temper from another world too. He could do no wrong and when he did, it wasn't his fault. A man that can't take ownership of his mistakes is no man in my book. Even Barney knew he was usually going to get into trouble by hanging out with Fred and hesitated. Unfortunately, Barney didn't have a strong enough backbone to stand up to Fred. In the end, Wilma would always be the perfect wife and so much like June Cleaver, they could have been sisters if they lived in the same era. Honestly, Wilma could write the textbook on why a good marriage takes work. Oh, you should read her book. It would be better than reading a textbook on the perfect relationship." Sam couldn't stand it at this point she sputtered out a snicker and had to cover her mouth to avoid literally spitting on Tania. Tania's face grew in recognition.

"Are you just messing with me?" Tania hit Sam with a glare that didn't have any effect.

"Not at first, but the longer your explanation, the more time I had to come up with options that were just plain funny. I get it, no relationship is the same and will likely take work. You can't seriously be saying I'm being too picky. At least I hope you aren't, that is." Sam finished off her coffee and started gathering her bags as Tania continued.

"NO, I'm not saying that at all. Yes, relationships are going to be good and bad but I want you to know that your mother can't be mad at you because you haven't found your Prince Charming yet. He is out there somewhere. Who knows, you might have met him already." Sam wasn't sure but she thought she saw a glint in Tania's eye that hinted at a knowing look. Sam was just about to call her out on it when Tania bounced up from her chair.

"Right now, you and I have an appointment that I don't intend on missing."

Chapter 14

Arriving at her mother's house, Sam trudged to the door. Her talk with Tania helped, but still left her feeling torn. On one hand she wanted to talk to her mom about all the dates she had been on, hoping her mother would understand. On the other hand, she realized that it would only lead to a worse conversation. Dragging her feet she was still trying to plan her course of action, when the front door swung open revealing her mother standing in the doorway.

"Are you planning on staying out there all night? I have dinner ready and it's getting cold." Sam took in her mother's appearance. Even though her mother was in her late fifties, she was still gorgeous. She stayed fairly trim over the years and with minimal exercise only to stay healthy, she was well within her ideal weight. Sam got her curves from her dad's side of the family but it was something she cherished rather than hated because it was one of the few appearances she got from him. With a smile, her mother shoved her into the house none too gently.

"Hey, I am still capable of walking. Watch it with all that pushing. I was just taking my time coming inside. Is that a crime?" Sam balked at her mother's bit of brutality.

"It is when I know you are avoiding me. Now get into the kitchen and let's eat before your jambalaya gets any colder. I for one prefer my dinner to be on the warm side." Sam followed her mother into the kitchen and enjoyed the smells of dinner. It was, as promised, one of her favorites. She loved the spices as they mingled together. It was never an issue of heat but a blending of flavors that lit up her taste buds in a way that made her remember each bite individually, tasting different flavors with each mouthful.

This time it was no different. Her mother quickly served up two large bowls and placed them on the table along with two large glasses of sweet tea. While her mother wasn't against drinking, she never served any alcohol with meals.

The first bite brought back fond memories of their family around this very table. Sharing stories and tidbits of their day was one of Sam's favorite times with her parents. It was something she cherished and missed on a daily basis. Which was why she felt so guilty about dodging her mother these past few months. There was a time when it didn't matter what, it was, easy to share everything with her mother or father, when he was alive.

"Now that I have you placated with food, do you care to tell me what you've been up to lately? I feel like it's been forever since I last saw you, let alone talked to you on the phone lately has been disjointed at best." Her mother sounded hurt and that killed Sam. That was never her intention when it came to creating distance. She just didn't know how to talk to her mother about this. For the first time in her life it wasn't her mother she wanted to run to first.

"I've been working and had some longer calls. When I get home, I'm beat and barely get out to buy groceries." The lies sounded cold in her ears and the more she spoke the harder it was to pull them out. Sam hated lying to her mother. The look in her mother's eye was more telling. It was obvious she either needed to come clean or lie better.

Then before she could think better of it her mouth flew open. "I met a guy." It started out small but the look on her mom's face was very telling. Her eyebrows shot up and a smile drew across her face slowly. Sam instantly regretted the words. *What am I doing. I can't do this to her. If she figures it out, she will be crushed. The only thing this woman wants in the world is happiness, family and GRANDKIDS! I'm just digging a hole I will never get out of.* Before she could backpaddle her mother started in.

"Really? Who is he? What's he like? He must be a real catch if he's kept you wrapped up like this for months and you haven't shared anything about him with me until now." Not knowing what else to do at the moment she did the only name she could think of.

"His name is Nick. He works at a bar I like to go to sometimes." Mentally smacking herself there was nothing else she could do now, but own it and make it sound as believable as possible. "He's absolutely the nicest guy ever. He was there for me after my date with Christopher didn't go as planned. It just took off from there and we've been inseparable."

"My little Sammy has finally found a guy worthy of her, I'm so happy." Her mother leaned around the table and put her arms around her daughter. That hug was the worst hug she had ever received from her mother. It had nothing to do with her mother's love and everything to do with the guilt festering in Sam's stomach. What would happen when her mother asked to meet Nick?

*****

That night in an effort to rid herself of the guilt that was sitting in her stomach like rotten milk, Sam reloaded the accursed dating app that she was determined to steer clear. She had to do something to fill this hole she had created where the not so fictitious Nick was filling in the gap. Just as she feared, her mother, asked to meet Nick as she was leaving for the night.

Figuring they had been dating now for months, it shouldn't be an issue to bring him to family dinner night. Sam played dumb and said she would ask and see if he was available. Warning her mother that Nick, since he was a bartender would probably already have his schedule locked in stone. The chances were slim he would be available.

Now she needed to find a fill in and fast. The last thing she wanted to do was lie to her mother further, but she couldn't very will just ask Nick, to come home and meet her mother under the elaborate ruse she concocted.

Scrolling through looking for anyone she could use to fill in. She secretly hoped she could find a guy already named, Nick. That would save the issue of names being wrong or her date forgetting to respond when called upon. The next best things was finding someone who could at least talk the talk if asked about his job.

After what felt like hundreds of pages later, Sam stumbled up on a guy who resembled Nick even if just slightly. He was taller than her and had his rugged complexion. Well, Sam could see Nick if she squinted hard enough, at least. This would have to do. Crossing her fingers, she hoped he would be available tomorrow for a dry run and again the following night for an impromptu dinner with her mother, if all went well.

It didn't take long and her phone alerted her to a response. He must have been up late just like her and already on his phone.

Hello, I'm Bradley and I'd love to meet up tomorrow night for drinks. I've been scrolling over your profile a few times and saw you were inactive. I had wished I could have messaged you first. Glad you found me instead.

Thankfully he had taken the hint. There were at least thirty emails in the apps inbox waiting to be read. Sam didn't want to weed through people who hadn't figured out she was offline and suspended her profile. While she hadn't taken the time to remove it completely, Sam had hoped it would deter people from messaging her. Somehow, she believed people actually read the little things like that.

Perhaps those men weren't detail people. Looks like Bradley had something going for him.

She whipped out a quick message giving him the details on where to meet her and then she decided the thing she needed most was a very hot shower. While she might have indulged and had a wonderful massage with Tania today, the stresses of life had taken their toll. So, she needed to unwind. As she went into the bathroom, she changed her mind. Heading to the cabinet she pulled out a bath bomb and started to run the water into the tub. Such luxuries were reserved for the worst of times. If there were ever such a time, this was it.

*****

Lying in the hot water watching the colors swirl around, the scents of lavender and vanilla waft through the room. Sam, with her eyes closed, does all she can to not relive every second of dinner with her mother. Would she ever be back on point with her mom that she could talk to her like she did not so very long ago?

The water splashed with her subtle movements, the air around her nipped at her exposed skin. Sinking lower into the water to avoid the chill, Sam contemplated dunking her head under the water to block out her remaining senses for a short time. Not intending to harm herself, but to bring some clarity to her over stimulated world. That was what she truly wanted, clarity to see through to the end of her problems and work out a solution without resorting to trial and error.

*****

The following day went quickly enough, Sam had few things to do on her list but they were all fairly time consuming. First on her list was renewing her driver's license. No one ever liked to do this and it usually involved long lines and terrible photographs. If she was lucky and got in line early enough it would be a manageable portion of her day. This was how Sam always approached this particular task and unfortunately it never worked out that way. This year she was once again hopeful and once again let down, only slightly differently than usual.

Standing in line as usual wasn't any big deal, until the lady in line behind her piped up, "Don't I know you from somewhere?" Sam turned not realizing one hundred percent that the question was directed at her, but as soon as she saw the lady's face, she cringed. There staring back at her was none other than the angry ex from the dance club. Sam would never forget the face of the woman who nearly doused her in beer in an effort to nail the jerk-wad Sam was talking to. Deciding to take the high road in this one, Sam acknowledged her the only way she could.

"Yes and no. While we haven't been formally introduced, I owe you a huge thank you. You saved me from a potentially horrible decision."

"That's right! You, were the poor girl Derek was hitting on the other night. I didn't get any of that nasty beer on you did I?" Sam shook her head but didn't speak. "Good! It wasn't mine, I just grabbed it off an abandoned table as I passed by. I'm not even sure it was all that cold when I threw it." The girl shuddered as if reliving the moment and Sam laughed remembering the look on Derek's face.

"That was a crazy night for sure. I wasn't even looking to meet anyone he just happened along." Sam confessed, but didn't know why she was still talking to this strange girl.

"That sounds like Derek. I honestly think he goes hunting for the girl who looks the least bit interested and tries to get his hooks in them. It's like his own version of a conquest game. Sure, he could wait for a girl to fall all over herself trying to get to him but where is the fun in that. He is all about the chase."

"Well from the way I last saw him, I don't think he will be having any conquest issues in the future. I think he will make a very lovely conquest for someone else while he is locked up. I think orange will look quite lovely with his complexion." The girls both laughed at Sam's prediction and soon the clerk called Sam's number.

"Number twenty-two. Now serving number twenty-two."

"Oh, that's me. It was nice to see you again and clear the air. I'm glad the anger was all focused on Derek and we have no hard feelings between us." Sam never got that girl's name but it was nice to feel vindicated and have more information about that disaster of a night.

Making her way to the window, Sam was pleased to note they hadn't changed any of the information requirements. For some reason the DMV loved to switch it up without notifying the tax-payers and Sam was caught unaware last time and had to make a drive to her mom's house to locate her birth certificate. That was something she hadn't needed since she moved out and wasn't even sure her mom knew right where it was at.

"My name is Nicole and I"ll be happy to assist you today." Nicole seemed anything but happy and Sam didn't blame her. That was a job she didn't wish upon anyone. The idea of helping perpetually angry people through hard situations wasn't something anyone aspires to in life.

"I'm here to get my license renewed today. I have all the required paperwork and here is my existing card." Sam produced all the information she mentioned and set it on the table. What she didn't expect was Nicole wasn't particularly friendly and very sarcastic.

"Well, it's funny you should say that. I would be happy to assist you but that isn't my job today." Sam was shocked. Wasn't it people's jobs who were in customer service to take care of the customer? Nicole wasn't taking care of her, she was shutting her down because she didn't want to work? Great, Sam found the one agent who wasn't going to go the extra mile and just work through each ticket and get through her day.

"What do you mean that isn't your job? You're in the DMV, it is your job to help me get what I need taken care of and today, that is my driver's license." Sam wasn't in the mood to take her crap and was fully prepared to throw it at her. That was until Nicole threw out her final verbal punch.

"No that is what those three windows are for. The ticket you pulled was for car registrations. My sole purpose today is to provide tags and plates for vehicles. Do you have a vehicle you need to register, ma'am?" Sam was stunned to silence. Glancing up at the service window, she saw her mistake. The three windows Nicole pointed to on the left were indeed marked *Drivers Licenses*. The three on the right including Nicole's window were clearly marked *Vehicle Registration*. There were separate tickets to pull to keep the lines in check. Sam had pulled from the wrong wheel.

Glancing over at the other line, now well into the morning, she was likely to be here a while. It was twice as long as the registration line and she would now be bringing up the rear. With a scowl in the direction of Nicole, who was now beaming at Sam's error, she removed herself from the window and trudged over to the alternate wheel and tore out a new number.

Chapter 15

Sitting in her usual hightop at Joe's Bar, Sam spun a glass of white wine between her fingers across the table. Nerves had taken over the moment she crossed the threshold and she still didn't know what she would do. This was outside of her dating plan and she hadn't told a soul what was happening.

Bradley was due to arrive in five minutes and she needed all the time she could get to put her head on straight. It was more of an opportunity to lay all her lies out on the table so she didn't get anything confused.

Sooner than anticipated a man approached her table, "Sam?" he questioned and she nodded. "I'm Bradley, sorry I'm a bit early it has become an annoying habit but hey, at least I'm not late." He laughed to himself but it came out a bit faster and higher pitched than his voice suggested. Sam wondered if he was nervous too. The thought calmed her slightly perhaps humanizing the situation more and making him seem more down to earth than just another hyped-up date.

"Bradley, it's a pleasure to meet you. Please sit down and let's get you a drink. Sounds like you could use one." She hoped her words didn't upset him she just wanted him, to realize that she understood what was happening. These were still essentially blind dates and nerves were high. Sometimes we all need something to bring us down to level the playing field.

"That sounds great." Bradley said with a sigh of relief. Her words obviously having the desired effect.

"So what do you do, Brad?" She shortened his name to something less professional sounding and hoped he didn't mind. Before he answered, Sam noticed the tops of his ears tinged just a little pink, she hoped she didn't embarrass him.

"Bradley, please." His tone hinted that she might have offended him but he didn't elaborate. "I'm a computer tech. I work for a team that handles IT for approximately twelve micro companies."

"That is really awesome. I'm almost useless with the inner workings of my computer. If anything goes wrong, I panic and call a few friends for help. They are usually more knowledgeable than I am and save me from having to go into debt finding repairs for my idiocy." Sam laughed to show she was joking and not actually berating herself, but Bradley didn't crack a smile. She was worried, so she continued, "What is a micro company? I don't believe I've heard the term before."

"It's not a commonly used term. We just use it to simplify the explanation. Basically, there are multiple companies that aren't large enough to hire a major IT firm to work on their systems. So they hire a team like ours that is large but spreads its resources between many smaller companies. It balances out the cost for them and they don't have to worry about calling the Geek Squad with their sensitive information. They also can guarantee to be at the top of our list for any issue because we can just assign them a team member who is always at their disposal." Bradley's response was very meticulous with very little emotion. Sam actually thought halfway through that Bradley might be a robot disguised as a humanoid. She held back her snicker at that, but only barely.

"So how do you keep everyone busy if certain companies have individual handlers, for lack of a better word? I would think not every one had a major issue all the time." Sam was genuinely interested in this topic but before she could continue and get an answer, Bradley blurted out something Sam never expected to hear in her entire life.

"I can't do this. This isn't working. I thought I could but this is too much." Being vague as he spoke, Bradley looked at her intently and leaned in to show the importance of what he was about to say. "I'm in love with someone else. It's not your fault. You didn't know and I can't control it. I thought I could but the power is too much. My ex-girlfriend, Molly, she is amazing and beautiful and all around just the sweetest thing, we broke up not too long ago. That isn't the issue though. The problem is she is a witch." Sam stared at him while he rambled on and wasn't sure she heard him correctly, but before she could ask Bradley clarified, "Yes I said a witch, and I don't mean a nice way to say she is a bitch. She isn't. I love her and could never think something so awful about her." Sam was thankful for his clarification but she was still growing more and more confused by the second.

"She is a witch, and she cast a spell on me. I only know because she told me the night she broke up with me. She felt bad because there was nothing she could do to reverse it and she had fallen out of love with me. The love potion was quite clever and when she cast it, she thought I was her one true love. I just didn't know it at the time. So a few months after meeting me she got me to agree to a date. She cooked for me, and it was the best meal I'd ever eaten, but then she poured my wine and said it was a special vintage just for me. Little did I know she had mixed the potion and laced my wine. Well, in order to tie the potion to her, and only her, she had to mix it with some of her menstrual blood. It was the one thing that was uniquely hers and no one would be able to use against me." This story was getting more and more odd by the passing moment. This was worse than the alien looking for a wife and Sam didn't have a clue how to respond.

"Well, you don't have to say anything. I thought this date would be my way out and I could overlook the drawing desire to Molly but I was wrong. I can't ever see past her stunning face and that is unfair to you. So instead of drawing this out any further than necessary I'm going to end this now." With that, Bradley got up and walked out of the bar. Sam sat there stunned to silence and frozen with confusion. She had no idea what had just taken place. The only thing she knew for sure was her last chance at a saving grace to not disappoint her mother just left the building. *What am I going to do now?* Sam thought to herself, as she dropped her face into her arms on the table top. Willing herself not to cry, Sam kept her face covered for fear she would fail at that task too.

Taking deep breaths, Sam slowly regained control over her emotions. A short time later she felt someone touch her shoulder gently. Through her clothes she couldn't tell who it was and the pressure was so light she just assumed it was Tania. Steeling herself she sucked in a breath preparing to tell her best friend of the mess she had brought on herself. As she glanced up, Sam's eyes widened when the deep pools that stared back at here were not those of Tania, her new best friend.

"Are you alright? It was hard not to notice the commotion over here and I waited as long as I could to give you your space." Nick's kind expression eased the heartbreak just a little. Not that it was the rejection from Bradley that stung her but that of the grave she had dug and her hopes and dreams of redemption walked out the door.

"I'll be fine I wasn't expecting much out of that one. The reaction was more of shock from what he said." Sam assumed Nick heard it all and didn't clarify.

"Yeah, I'd say that one was the worst one yet." He started to move her back and forth on the chair looking behind her, around her side, then her other side and back to her front.

"What are you doing?" Sam chuckled at his antics, but was baffled as to his motive besides humor.

"Looking for the magnet on you that is attracting these freaks. There has to be something because no one in the history of dating has ever had this many. You are a wonder of nature that is for sure." He said the last part with a slight touch of awe. Sam didn't know if he was still being playful or if his mood had changed.

"Well, I can assure you if there is a magnet on me anywhere, it will take a surgery to remove it. I've been over every inch of my body and haven't found anything that would be causing this mess." Sam's shoulders slumped in defeat and she leaned back against the table for physical support. She just wished it had provided a little emotional support but it was her mess, no one could help her clean it up.

"I might not be able to take it away but I know just what you need. First, we have to get you over to my office and I'll take care of everything." Nick hooked her arm by the elbow and half drug half carried her back over to the bar.

Flopping onto a stool, "Okay, I'm here, now what?" Sam said with a petulant tone not unlike a spoiled teenager.

"Sit back and relax and let me take care of this." She watched him get out his ingredients and it looked like this would be a perfect blend of comfort food and alcohol. What better way to get out of a funk? Nick scooped ice cream into the blender and Sam's mouth watered. That was her favorite snack when in a bad mood. She had a quart of rocky road sitting in her freezer just for such moments. There also was never a need for a bowl since she was the only one who ever consumed it. "Sad ice cream doesn't get bowls" her mother always said. No sense in reliving the pain while washing the dishes.

Nick added strawberries and what looked like vodka but she wasn't sure. Then he poured in some sort of cream that she didn't recognize and was now anxious to figure it out. She almost asked but at that moment, Nick dropped in a scoop of ice, and pressed the button on the blender came to life causing a noise that drowned out her words. He didn't even turn to look at her because the sound never reached his ears.

It didn't take long for the mixture to smooth out for that Sam was thankful because she hated the sound of crunching ice. Blenders always amplified it and made it that much worse. Nick raised the pitcher and poured it into a waiting margarita glass that he had pulled from the cooler. Pressing a freshly sliced strawberry to the side of the glass, he presented it to her with grandeur only Nick could pull off. She still laughed at his silly display, "I think this is the prettiest drink you've served me yet. Let's change things up a bit. I usually taste before I ask questions but I have one first this time. What was the cream you poured in there? I tried to ask but I wasn't faster than the blender."

"Should I tell you? I really enjoy your faces that you make when you try and figure it out on your own. It also tells me more honestly if you like it because you are dissecting every taste with your tongue before you open your eyes and you've already spelled everything else out on your face. I've learned a lot from this little game we play." Nick was leaning on the bar as usual and his chest was flexed between his arms as he crossed them in front. Sam was a bit distracted but she focused enough to hear her words.

"So you're saying you know so much, prove it." Sam challenged him and expected him to falter. Instead his eye seemed to light at the twist in the night.

"Let's see you admitted you didn't care for gin or Jägermeister. That is too easy to make you believe me. You love anything with vodka or rum, doesn't matter the flavors, of either. You don't like citrus flavors as I've pointed out in the past, but you love sweet juices for your mixers. While you tolerate your dry alcohols, you prefer them on the lighter side and with more bursts of flavor. For you, it's about the experience and not the intoxication. Your high is living in the moment and not over indulging. You could drink half a drink and get more out of it than a person who drinks three and walks out tipsy or drunk." Nick stopped and just stared at her gauging her reaction. She knew she was stunned and it showed on her face, because his smile creeped in slowly and sure of himself. Those hypnotic blue eyes seemed to darken under her inspection of them. She was lost in the moment. No one in her life knew her like that. Not just the details, but the reasons behind them. While his explanation was wrapped around her drinking habits, there was more there and she caught it. She noticed that he saw her above it all. It wasn't about whether or not she like rum over gin. He spoke of her experience and how she saw life, not just her drinks.

Without another question, she gave him what he wanted and knew that it was for him and not her. Showing him how she felt about the moment, giving him what she knew would make him happy worked both ways and she was filled with more emotion in this drink than ever before. It wasn't just flavors this time, it was the thought put into each drink just for her. Created with every ounce of care and passion for his work, as for what he knew she was going through.

Every flavor washed over her and she knew it was the perfect drink for her. The emotions of the past couple days were gone and she wasn't concerned for the lies she told her mother anymore. It was just her and Nick and that was all that mattered. Everything blended perfectly in that situation the flavors, their personalities, their thoughts. None of other times they had been together had been this perfect.

Opening her eyes, she looked at Nick. His eyes were on fire, blazing with the unspoken words between them. Sam knew it was about more than a drink. It was about the breath shared between them and the knowledge that there was more they had both not shared over the past few months. It was then, and only then, that Sam knew what she needed to do.

"I need a favor." Simple and direct but it was the foot she needed to throw in the door to get to what she ultimately wanted.

"Favor, as in between friends or something else." Nick left the room for her to chicken out but she didn't take the bait, though she did volley it back to him.

"That depends on you. I screwed something up and you are the only one who can save me. Since you make such a stunning knight in shining armor, as we have proven in times past, I figured I would give you a crack at it."

Nick considered his next statement and Sam held her breath. If he said no, she was back to square one and the only alternative was to tell her mother the truth and likely disappoint her.

"Fine. I'll do whatever you need me to do. I'm not even going to wait for you to explain before I agree because I think you've had enough bad lately. I'll see if I can brighten your end game." Nick's words bolstered her courage and the next words were spoken so fast, she nearly didn't get them out.

"Oh you have no idea how wonderful it is to hear you say that. So last night I was at dinner with my mother and in order to keep her from asking about my love life, which she loves to do, I told her I was seeing someone. Since there is only one guy who I talk to frequently that doesn't drive me completely insane, for some reason my mouth opened and your name flew out. No thought process, just open mouth and out came words. I didn't mean to tell her anything else but then she asked questions and it was easier to tell her about the real Nick than to make things up. You are now perfectly ok to say no to this, but she invited 'Nick' over for dinner tomorrow night. I'm sure you are working and I told her that but she was adamant that I ask anyway. Now I'm rambling so I'm just going to shut up before I stick my foot in my mouth further."

When she looked up at Nick's face, she wasn't sure what to expect. What she saw was certainly not anywhere close to expected. He wore the biggest grin she had ever seen and promptly began to bark out the loudest laugh ever. People started to look at them and Tania who was swamped in the dining area was even glancing over a look of bewilderment on her face.

"So your mother invited me over to dinner, sight unseen, all because you said we were dating and had been for a while?" Nick parroted back to her, while trying to reign in his laughter.

"Pretty much." Sam replied hesitantly, not sure where Nick would take this.

Rubbing his scruff on his strong chin, Nick brought his emotional outbreak under control. "Well, I guess it is good that I already have tomorrow off work. I originally took off to help someone move and they got it all done today. So I'm free as a bird and at your disposal m'lady. Before you lock this in, maybe I should tell you what it was you just finished off in that glass." Sam slowly lowered the glass she had just polished off to the counter.

"Should I be concerned, because now you have me worried?"

"Oh, probably not. That was just a little something I concocted called 'Love Potion Number Nine'. There is nothing to fear, unless you are feeling a little woozy or an exceptional urge to wrap your arms around me." Nick was joking but that was how she felt around him all the time. All he had to do was encourage her a little and she would be all over him and not even bat an eye.

He handed her his phone and she programmed her number in and texted herself so she would have his information as well. With that they parted ways for the evening with a promise to pick her up tomorrow at six-thirty.

Chapter 16

"What do you mean Nick is having dinner with you and your mom." Tania practically screeched into the phone.

Sam had rehashed her evening to Tania later that night after her shift. She had called promptly and Sam was already in bed so it was with great effort to wake up and regale the tale.

"He's getting me out of a jam. Mom is expecting me to have a boyfriend tomorrow night and my last chance bailed on me, very loudly I might add, and you may have heard it too." Sam knew very well most of the restaurant heard it and knew how crazy her date was.

"Yeah, that was a very screwed up date, for sure. Are you going to tell me why your mom believes that you have a boyfriend or how you got Nick to agree to that?"

"Not a chance, you will just have to wait for the cliff notes version after dinner sometime, when I feel like sharing. Until then I would like to get back to my bed and dreamland that is filled with very hot guys and they want to do wild and crazy things with me." Sam was only half serious and Tania was already laughing.

*****

The moment of truth, Nick would be picking up Sam in fifteen minutes. Since her mother expected this to be a meet the parent's opportunity, Sam felt like she needed to make an effort to dress up. She wore a flirty blouse with black and white flowers embroidered into it. She almost hadn't bought it because it looked a little older style on the hanger, but the sales lady convinced her to just try it on. As soon as she did she fell in love with it. Realizing it was asymmetrical made it better too, because it hung long enough to wear over some nice leggings. Paired with a pair of calf high black boots with golden buckles up the sides, Sam felt perfectly dressed up for the evening without feeling like she went over the top. She fashioned her hair up in a French twist with curls falling off the back. Letting it look like it had been that way all day but in reality, it took her over an hour to get the right amount to spill out.

Just as she had finished putting the final touches on her makeup, a firm knock sounded at the door. The once calm and collected Sam that had gotten lost in the preparation step, was now fighting giant boulder sized knots in her stomach. *How did so many of those fit inside me?* She absentmindedly wondered, but promptly attempted to put them all out of her mind and made for the front door.

Grasping the handle, it took all her power to pull the door open and not just leave him on the other side. Once revealed, she was instantly at ease. The man on the other side of the door was the most handsome person she had ever seen. Dressed in a pair of black slacks, Nick had even gone so far as to don a tie for the event. Nothing too crazy and it wasn't tightened all the way into a noose around his neck. It laid loose and the top button on his black shirt was open. He didn't shave, to her delight, because she had lots of ideas of what that scruff would feel like on other parts of her body. He did have his leather jacket on, which she hadn't seen since the first day they met when he ran into work after she had already arrived.

"Are you going to invite me in or just stare at me all night with that lustful look? Nick's words jolted Sam from her thoughts and she took a step back to let him in.

"I'm sorry, I was getting nervous and almost didn't open the door. When I saw you, I was instantly grateful that you took this seriously. You look wonderful, by the way." Sam watched as Nick's eyes ran over her in an appreciative way.

"You look beautiful." His words were so soft she almost didn't hear them. Smiling she turned to grab her purse and keys.

"I'll just lock up so we can go. Then we won't be late. Do you want to take my car?" Sam avoided the statement in an effort to stay focused.

"Let's just take mine, it's already running and warm. It's a bit chilly tonight, I think the weather is getting ready to turn for the season." Sam hadn't been outside since the darkness fell and was thankful he mentioned it.

"In that case, I'll just run back and grab a sweater."

*****

The drive to her Mother's was almost awkward. She didn't know how to talk to Nick outside of the bar. They had never been alone let alone away from Joe's. So, silence descended besides the occasional directions from his GPS that he insisted on using so she wouldn't have to worry about forgetting to warn him about an upcoming turn.

When they pulled into her driveway, Sam reached for the handle. Before she could pull away, Nick reached for her other hand. Not saying a word, he gave a tug and pulled her towards him and his lips met hers in a gentle kiss. She was stunned since she hadn't seen it coming. After a second her lips began to respond and she returned his kiss. It wasn't anything that lasted too long and he broke the kiss a second later.

"What was that for?" Sam asked as her hand fluttered to her still tingling lips. She could still feel the ghost of his lips on hers and didn't look up at him yet.

He tipped her chin to look at him, "Because you needed to calm down. I am here because I want to be. I could have told you no anytime and I didn't. Also, if we're supposed to

222

have been dating for months your mother, will see through this awkward façade before we set foot in the door. I'm sure she is just as intuitive as you are." With that he opened his door and ran to the other side and opened Sam's. He reached down to help her out of the car.

"I'm honestly surprised that you don't have a motorcycle." Sam blurted as they walked up to the door.

"Actually, I do and I would have brought it, but it was a bit cold and I figured my car made a better mom impression than riding up with her baby girl on the back of a death machine." Nick sent her a knowing look and Sam considered his words.

"You're probably right." Before Sam could say more the door flew open again. There stood her mother, in all her glory, beaming at them both. Sam had never seen her mother this happy. Instantly she regretted the entire situation and wanted to run. Unfortunately, it was too late for that and hoped Nick was one hell of an actor to pull this ruse off.

"You're here!" her mother crooned and Sam cringed. "Come in, come in, so we can be introduced properly." Her mother had dressed for the occasion too and Sam thought she looked a little too much like June Cleaver. Her mother always loved the style and only broke out the dresses on special occasions. Sam just hoped, her mother didn't have any crazy ideas for this dinner.

She shooed them both inside and closed and bolted the door. *Is she expecting him to run away and thinks that will stop him?* Sam wondered absently as she hung her sweater on the back of the sofa informally, earning a scowl from her mother. Quickly she relocated it to the coat hook beside the stairs. Taking Nick's coat, she repeated the motion. This had her mother beaming again.

"Nick this is my mother, Barbara. Mom, this is Nick Porter." Sam was thankful they had exchanged last names via text before falling asleep last night. It was a last-minute thought on Nick's part and for that she was grateful. It wasn't anything that had crossed her mind since it had never come up in conversation, but since they were supposedly dating, it was information they should have already known.

"Mrs. Martin, I'm so glad to finally meet you." Nick laid it on thick but her mother just lapped it up.

"Oh Nick, please call me Barbara or Mom. I don't go by Mrs. Anything, after so many years I almost don't even respond to it anymore."

"Whatever makes you happy, Barbara. Now I hear we are having something that Sam considers to be the best cooked meal I'll ever eat. I don't doubt her in the least as she wouldn't lie to me about food." Nick offered his arm to Sam's mother and she led him toward the kitchen.

"Yes, we are having shepard's pie and it is an old family recipe. You won't have had anything like in your life." Barbara was in her element and Sam knew it.

"Don't try and get the recipe though, because she hasn't told a soul and I won't even know until the book gets passed to me through her will. I just hope there isn't a fire before then because it will all be lost." Sam added sarcastically because she knew her mother had backed up all the files years ago for that reason and put them in a safety deposit box. The women in their family were serious when it came to food.

"I can't wait to taste it. Sam has told me so many wonderful things about your cooking I feel like I've been robbed by her not inviting me along before." Nick's words made Sam want to lash out and stop him. Her mother would scold her later for her lack of awareness.

"You are welcome over here anytime without an invitation, or even without my daughter, if she is going to be so selfish of the people she cares about." Barbara was obviously taken with Nick and Sam didn't know if that was a good thing or a bad thing.

*****

Dinner went off without a hitch. Actor wasn't the word Sam would use for Nick's skills. He was born for this role. It was like he wasn't even trying. He spouted things about Sam she didn't realize he knew. Little things, like how she always preferred to eat her food separately rather than eating each dish as one. So, shepherd's pie was a challenge for her because while it was the most amazing food she'd ever consumed and it was the top of her like list, it was also all mixed together and she was forced to overcome her issues and just eat it.

"How did you know that about my eating habits?" Sam finally asked as they drove home.

"You ate a meal or two at the bar and I'm observant when it comes to you." Nick replied and never took his eyes off the road.

"What do you mean 'when it comes to me'?" Sam's brain caught on those words and not so much the rest of what he said.

"I notice you whenever you come into the bar and not just when you appear at my bar. You are the only voice I can hear over the crowd and I can't help but seek you out. When you didn't come back from the bathroom after one of your dates, I sent Tania to look for you because I couldn't leave the bar or I would have been there myself. I was worried and I couldn't find you." Nick confessed all of this without hesitation, as though he had been holding back long enough and now it was time to release.

Sam remembered that Tania mentioned that Nick asked about her, but after the dream she had been having, didn't think it was a good idea to question anyone.

"I think of you more often than I probably should," Nick continued. "You're on my mind from the moment I wake up until the time I go to bed. I miss you when you are at work and not coming in for a few days. I am jealous when your dates get to spend any time with you and I'm angry when they upset you. That time I came to your rescue was because I couldn't control myself in that moment. He was talking about marrying you and I didn't want anyone to take you away from me."

In a second of bravery Sam piped up, "I don't want that either. I think of you all the time and if I'm honest probably compare all my dates to your standard. While you frustrated me in the beginning with your snarky comments and dry humor, eventually it grew on me and I started to look forward to it. I appreciated that you were you all along and not trying to be fake for me or change anything so I wouldn't notice your flaws. We all have flaws and that can't be changed. We are better for them. Without them we are just machines and robots, all trying to be the same person. I can't get you out of my head and after that kiss I was ruined for anyone else. I've dreamed of you and that kiss every night since. Which is probably why I'm doomed to have the worst dating life in history because none of them are you." Before Sam had even finished speaking Nick had pulled over and she didn't realize until she was done that they were at her apartment.

Nick reached for her and without another word, sealed his lips to hers. His lips didn't need more words to convey what he was feeling. He poured it all into that kiss and Sam did everything she could to let him know everything through hers as well. She felt his tongue run across the seam of her lips and she opened for him. They battled in a broken rhythm for a bit as their kiss went out of control. Their emotions were untamed and it flowed through their connection. When Sam tried to move closer, the console got in the way. The kiss was broken and they both laughed.

"We are acting like a couple of teenagers. I have a perfectly good apartment up there we can do this in without any obstructions," Sam finally stated.

"Do you mean that? Not one obstruction?" Nick questioned with a gleam in his eye.

"More than you know. I've been waiting for this moment for months now. If you only knew the imagination I've had to put up with because I thought you weren't interested after you stonewalled me after that kiss," Sam admitted and for the first time in her life she felt her cheeks heat and she was thankful it was dark and he couldn't see it.

*****

They couldn't get into the apartment fast enough and Sam practically dragged Nick down the hall and into her bedroom. Thankfully, she hadn't been home much since she had been off work, so the bedroom was still better than clean, the bed was even made. She had never thought tonight would become this in a million years.

Standing in the bedroom, Sam didn't wait for Nick to take the lead. She needed to know if her imagination had embellished any of Nick's features. She reached for his tie and pulled the knot loose. She didn't tear it away from his neck. She just left it laying on his shoulders. She dove straight for his buttons and fumbled with them one by one, until Nick took over to finished for her. He never once removed her hands from his body. This was their moment to share all over again. It was a theme with him and she was starting to love it.

Reaching the last button, Nick let go and let Sam unwrap the present before her. Still touching his skin, she peeled the shirt away. Her breath caught as his taut abs came into view and just as she had imagined, he wasn't bulky, but a better version in her eyes. She could feel him and not just what he had added by working out too much. He was fit and trim of course, but she could feel all his dips and soft places and enjoy them under her fingertips.

"I think you are overdressed, Samantha." Sam's eyes shot up and were wider than ever.

"That is the first time you've ever used my actual name. I was starting to think you'd forgotten it completely." Sam was frozen in shock and couldn't move.

Nick took that opportunity to divest her of her buttons and slip the blouse from her shoulders. "I've never forgotten a word about you, Samantha." He used her name again to reinforce it. "Even if it were possible for me to forget something, I would never forget anything about you. It is all valuable and important information to me." Nick proceeded to unclasp her bra and even up the wardrobe situation.

When they were both standing there topless, Nick leaned in connecting their skin to each other and everything seemed to click into place. Then, and only then, was Sam pulled from her shock.

"I never knew I meant that much to you," Sam admitted shyly.

"You mean so much more." With that Nick proceeded to show her just a fraction of her worth.

He kissed her neck and down to each of her nipples. It was just as she had pictured it and she almost lost the ability to stand. This man had such a way with his mouth that she had no way of resisting him.

Without releasing her breast, he slipped one hand beneath her butt and lifted her into his arms. Nick carried her over to the bed where he slipped off her pants along with her panties and smiled. No words were needed to translate the look in his eye. His adoration of her shone through so clearly, she could feel how much he cared for her and was more than pleased to be the recipient.

As their eyes stayed locked his head disappeared between her legs. She jumped when his lips descended onto her inner thigh. She was all too aware of his scruff and signed as it scratched a path up to her most delicate places. Without warning his tongue snaked out and tasted her lower lips. It was the best feeling she had ever experienced and it had been too long since someone had spent this time with her. Nick was the only one she had wanted for some time now and would have likely sabotaged anyone else who tried.

He made quick work of lapping up her juices and suddenly his tongue was replaced by a long finger pressed inside of her. Sam gasped and then moaned as that finger curled deliciously into her most sensitive spot. When his lips sealed over her bud, his speed increased bringing her quickly to her first climax. As she screamed out her pleasure, Nick groaned with satisfaction, as he lapped up all she gave him. When she settled, he looked over her and smiled.

"That was the most beautiful thing to watch. I want to watch it again." As he began to lower his head back down, Sam stopped him with a tug of his hair. He moaned his enjoyment of her reaction.

"No, I need you." Sam felt herself blush again and knew the room's lighting exposed her embarrassment but didn't care, she looked him right in the eye and pleaded.

"You have never once blushed around me since I've known you." Nick ran his hand over her cheek and cupped her jaw. Leaning forward he kissed her and she let out a mewl of enjoyment. One of his hands made it to her breast and caressed the side and his fingers pinched slightly on the nipple. Her entire body arched into his and she begged again.

"Please, Nick, I need you now!" She didn't know if it was her tone or if he was just as ready as she was but he didn't waste another moment.

Their bodies separated and he stood from the bed, the bulge in his pants was tight and she could only imagine he was in pain from the strain. He deftly unfastened his pants and shucked them and his underwear to the floor. Sam made a mental note to take things slower in the future to see if he wore boxers or briefs and enjoy the view.

Nick was back on her in less than a minute showing his urgency. He lined himself up and plunged inside. His girth was more than she expected but she was more than ready after Nick's ministrations. Her body accepted every glorious inch of him. She arched as he sank further and further and with one last groan of pleasure from Nick, he was fully seated. He waited a moment for her to adjust, as any gentleman would. Unfortunately, Sam didn't want a gentleman at that moment.

"Nick, you need to move NOW!" She yelled her demand and Nick was ready to comply. Taking control of the situation again, Nick thrust out and back in, increasing speed. Sam hadn't felt such pleasure in her life. No one had ever made her feel this way. The sound of Nick's grunts and groans said he wasn't going to last long either. They were both primed and ready to go. With one last thrust, she screamed and it seemed to go on forever. Sam feared she would pass out from lack of oxygen before she was able to enjoy it all. Then when Sam thought she couldn't take any more her body relented and Nick spilled his release. They were both spent and just rested for what felt like the rest of eternity.

*****

The next morning, Sam did something she hadn't done in years. She rolled over and curled into a warm body lying next to her in bed. Opening her eyes and seeing Nick watching her sleep made Sam smile. She took a moment to relive the previous night's activities. After their first round, they relived it another four times and Sam was blissfully sore this morning.

"Good morning, Samantha," the use of her name made Sam smile again.

"Good morning, Nicholas," Sam returned the favor of using his full name that she had learned the previous night during dinner, causing Nick to laugh. She was laying on his chest and it sounded like a rumble that she felt through to her bones.

"You're the only person besides my mother who has ever called me that. Strangely though, I like it, don't ever stop." Nick held her close and kissed the top of her head.

That wouldn't do at all. Sam leaned forward pressing lightly on his chest to not cause any grief and kissed him soundly on the lips. The kiss grew heated and Nick broke them apart.

"You had better stop or that will start something you might not want to finish."

"Who said I don't want to finish?" With a sultry look, she climbed on top of him. Sam was more than ready to finish anything Nick ever wanted her to, all he ever had to do was ask.

THE END

Thank you, Readers!

You as my reader, are why I do what I do. Without you, I'd be useless and find less enjoyment in what I do. I love to write and share my crazy thoughts and ideas with you.

As a way to show my gratitude for you reading my book, I thought I should give you something fun that you can use again and again. If you read on, you can enjoy the same drinks that Sam was gifted by Nick after each date, along with a few bonus recipes as well.

Read on and I hope you enjoy a small piece of book reality.

Follow me on social media and on Amazon for updates on future released books. You can even join my fan group the links are all below.

Leave a review at the end of this book. This helps me know if I need to improve or keep doing what I'm doing.

Email me:

bookinfo@erinthorntonauthor.com

Website:

www.erinthorntonauthor.com

Author Page:

www.facebook.com/authorErinThornton

Fan Group:

https://www.facebook.com/groups/5078175395577875

Chuck Norris – Christopher

-Enough Lemonade to fill a pint glass

-2 Shots Jägermeister

-2 Shots Cherry Sourz

-2 Shots DOM Benedictine

Add 2 shots of Cherry Sourz, 2 shots of DOM Benedictine and 2 shots of Jägermeister to a pint glass. Stir and top up glass with lemonade.

Cocky Carrot – Marcus

- 1 ½ oz Vodka
- 1 ½ oz Orange Liqueur
- 1 oz Carrot Juice
- 1 oz energy drink of your choice

Combine ingredients in a cocktail shaker and stir. Strain over ice into a Collins glass. Garnish with an orange wheel and serve.

Blue Bruise – Kyle (*Wiggle Wiggle Wiggle*)

- 1 1/5 Gin
- 1 Tbsp Lemon Juice
- 1 Tbsp Lime Juice
- Lemonade/Sprite
- 1 splash of Blue Curacao Liqueur

Pour the gin, lemon juice and lime juice into a cocktail shaker half-filled with ice cubes. Shake well and strain over ice cubes in a cocktail glass. Fill with Sprite/Lemonade, add Curacao, and serve.

The Bitter Frenchman - Philippe

- 1 oz London Dry-style Gin
- ½ oz Campari
- ½ oz Simple Syrup
- ½ oz Lemon Juice
- Dry Champagne (or other dry sparkling wine)

Put the first four ingredients (gin, Campari, simple syrup and lemon juice) in a shaker, and shake with ice until chilled. Strain into a Champagne flute, and top with Champagne.

Fountain of Youth – Richard

- 1 ½ oz Vodka
- ¾ oz St. Germain
- ¾ oz Fresh Lemon Juice
- 2 springs Fresh Mint Leaves
- 2 oz Mionetto Prosecco

In shaker add, Vodka, St. Germain, Lemon Juice and the leaves from 1 mint sprig. Add ice and shake vigorously. Strain to a highball glass over crushed ice. Top with Prosecco. Garnish with remaining mint sprig and an orange wheel.

Fuzzy Balls – Benjamin

- 1 part Absolute Citron Vodka
- 1 part Bacardi Limon Rum
- 1 part Peach Schnapps
- Fill with 7-up/Sprite

Mix alcoholic ingredients one part each into shot glass. Then top up with 7-up/Sprite.

Retribution* - Gregory

- 1oz Cinnamon Schnapps
- 1oz Tequilla
- 1oz Jägermeister
- 1oz Rumplemintz

Mix together with crushed ice in a glass and garnish with mint leaves.

*bonus drink not listed in storyline, but Gregory needed his drink story told. Due to the ingredients including Jägermeister, Sam is NOT condoning the mixing of this drink for her own consumption.

Fantasy* - Cooper

- 4 shots Milk
- 1 shot Crème de Menthe
- 1/5 shot Amarula Cream

Half fill a cocktail shaker with ice and pour in all ingredients. Shake well and strain into a cocktail glass.

*bonus drink not in the storyline, but some guys are jealous.

Poison* - Eli

- ½ shot Vodka
- ½ shot Orange Liqueur
- ½ shot Bitter Lemon Soda

Mix vodka and orange liqueur in a highball glass. Fill with bitter lemon, and serve.

*bonus drink not in the storyline because Eli needed to share his Poison.

Death by Chocolate – Kevin

-    1 cup crushed ice
-    2 scoops chocolate ice cream
-    1 oz chocolate syrup
-    1 oz coffee liqueur
-    1 oz dark crème de cacao liqueur
-    1 oz vodka

Pour all ingredients into a blender. Blend until smooth. Pour into a stemmed glass such as a hurricane glass. Top with whipped cream and garnish with a maraschino cherry.

*bonus drink not in storyline, but Kevin thought it would help his research.

Alien Nipple – Shelton

- ½ oz Butterscotch Schnapps
- ¼ oz Bailey's Irish Cream
- ¼ oz Midori Melo Liqueur

Add Butterscotch first, layer Irish Cream, and pour in Melon Liqueur.

Dirty Kitty – Gavin

- 1 ½ oz Sprite
- ½ oz Peach Schnapps
- 1 oz Lemono Raspberry Syrup
- 1 oz Sour
- ½ oz Vodka
- Lemonade and Sprite

Ice one tall glass. In shaker, pour Raspberry, vodka, peach schnapps, sour and fill with lemonade and sprite shake and pour into glass. Garnish with slice of lemon and a raspberry.

Nervous Breakdown* – Charlie

- 1 ½ oz vodka
- ½ oz Chambord
- Spalsh of cranberry juice
- Club soda or sparkling water

Combine vodka, Chambord and cranberry in tall glass filled with ice. Top with soda and garnish with an orange slice.

*bonus drink not in storyline because Charlie almost had a panic attack about not being included.

Tropical Itch – Stanley

- 1 ½ oz Bourbon Whiskey
- 1 ½ oz Bicardi 151 Proof Rum
- 1 oz Orange Juice
- 1 oz Passion Fruit Juice
- 1 oz Sweet and Sour mix

Build in order in a highball glass and garnish with ¼ pineapple wheel, a cherry and a cocktail umbrella connecting the cherry to pineapple.

*bonus drink not in the storyline but everyone needs a little allergy relief.

Dragon Spit – Ryder

- 2 parts Blavod (black vodka)
- 1 part Southern Comfort
- Orange/Pineapple Juice

Pour orange or pineapple juice into a half pint glass. Add two measures of Blavod and one measure of Southern Comfort (or any whiskey). Mix well. This cocktail should turn a murkey green color. Tastes a lot better than it sounds!

Oh Baby! Oh Baby! – Dr. Travis

- 1 part Orange Juice
- 1 part Cranberry Juice
- 1 part Pineapple Juice
- Fill with Bacardi 151 Proof Rum

Fill 2/3 of shot glass with all three juices. Carefully top with rum. Light it on fire, blow it out, take the shot.

Flaming Asshole – Derek

- ½ oz Grenadine
- ½ oz Green Crème de Menthe
- ½ oz Crème de Bananes
- ½ oz Overproof Rum

Layer in this order Grenadine, Crème de Menthe, Banana Liqueur, White Rum. Ignite rum before serving. Serve with a straw.

*bonus drink not included in the storyline, but even an asshole like Derek gets to share.

Status Quo – Levi

- 3 oz Gin
- 1 1/5 oz Cherry Heering
- Apple Juice
- Splash of Tonic Water

Mix everything together top glass with Apple Juice and a splash of Tonic Water add some crushed ice and olives. Serve in a highball glass no garnish.

Love Potion #9 – Bradley

- 1 oz Strawberry, Vanilla or Clear Vodka
- ½ oz Crème de Cacao
- ½ cup fresh or frozen Strawberries
- Scoop of Vanilla Ice Cream
- ½ cup Ice

Pour ingredients into blender, mix until smooth, pour ingredients into chilled margarita glass. Garnish with strawberry.

The White Knight – NICK!!!!!

- ¾ oz Scotch Whiskey
- ¾ oz Coffee Liqueur
- ¾ oz Drambuie Liqueur
- ¾ oz Milk
- ¾ oz Single Cream/Half & Half

Shake all the ingredients with ice and fine strain into a chilled glass. Garnish with a dusting of grated Nutmeg.

*Bonus drink not included in the storyline, but we all want a little bit of Nick to have of our very own.

Letter to Readers

Dear Loyal Readers,

Thank you for taking the time to read Disaster In Love. I know you are probably anxious to find out what I'm writing now and without any actual teasers you are likely cursing me right about now. I understand, but so I'm writing as quickly as I can. A new books will be released before you know it. Not to mention, I can't silence the voices in my head for too long. They are already screaming to have their stories told and released so all of you wonderful readers can get lost in their worlds.

That said, in the meantime, I would you please go and leave me a review on Amazon and/or Goodreads? What you don't realize is this helps, not only other readers, but me as well. I get to know what you loved and what you hated of each story and this helps me grow as a writer. I'm never going to have everything completely figured out. There will always be something I can improve upon. You can assist me by telling me all these things in a review.

I'm not asking you to write a book or anything crazy or untrue. I want an honest opinion of your reading experience. This can be as simple as "I loved it" or a complex review detailing the synopsis as you see it. No review is unworthy as long as it comes from your heart and is the truth you won't upset me.

Reviewing is what helps other readers decide if something is for them or worth it for them to try. Everyone has a different viewpoint and yours might influence someone along the way.

Thank you again and I hope you will follow me on social media and on my Amazon author page. Links are included in the front of the book for you to find easily. You will be first to hear about new releases and possible beta/ARC opportunities. I love to share my books with everyone and can't wait to hear your opinions!

Acknowledgements

I want to shout out and say THANK YOU to my awesome editing team. While I might just be a lowly author I know you as readers don't want to read a subpar product. Therefore, I have recruited a fantastic team to help me with my eversion to commas! Cause let's be real I, Hate, Commas, and, Commas, Hate, Me!

I want to thank my Beta Readers for always being there to support me in my new visions no matter what.

Thank you to my family most of all. This book has been a work in progress for a bit. When I first started writing it I spent a lot of time on it trying to release it quickly. Then it got shelved for another project. Now that it is finished I have had to put some serious hours into getting words on paper. Without the support of my family, I wouldn't be able to write as quickly as I do.

About the Author

Erin Thornton for the past 13 years has been a mom first. Now with six kids, she felt like she'd lost her own identity. She no longer had a first name and was always someone's mom or her husband's wife. It became very discouraging.

Erin has been telling stories since she was a kid. Her mom always told her to write her stories down, but she just rolled her eyes and moved on. As an adult, instead of reading a book for a bedtime story or on a long drive she would tell a made-up story to her kids. Keeping them sometimes captivated for hours. Some of them were amazing works of fiction and fantasy. Others were awful, and her kids still remember their insanity to this day. She wasn't afraid to take the stories to their most abstract point just to get a laugh from her kids.

Instead of letting her identity crisis overtake her, last summer Erin decided to write a novel. A story that was for her, not for her kids.

With her days spent on 100 acres with chickens and kids that act like the chickens most days, Erin writes whenever she can get a spare moment. Between musical practices, sports, and just plain mom life to distract her she tries to get in her words for the day with Disney Princess movies in the background or while her youngest naps.

All jokes aside, Erin Thornton is a true writer at heart. This won't be the last book she writes. The stories in her head are always screaming to get out. The only way to free her mind is to put them on paper.